Charlotte Mary Yonge

Henrietta's Wish; or, Domineering

A Tale

Charlotte Mary Yonge

Henrietta's Wish; or, Domineering
A Tale

ISBN/EAN: 9783337079550

Printed in Europe, USA, Canada, Australia, Japan

Cover: Foto ©Andreas Hilbeck / pixelio.de

More available books at **www.hansebooks.com**

OR,

DOMINEERING.

𝔄 𝔗𝔞𝔩𝔢.

BY

CHARLOTTE M. YONGE,

'AUTHOR OF "THE HEIR OF REDCLYFFE," "THE TWO GUARDIANS," ETC.

"The lesson of sweet peace I read,
Rather in all to be resigned than blest."
Christian Year.

𝔖𝔦𝔵𝔱𝔥 𝔈𝔡𝔦𝔱𝔦𝔬𝔫.

LONDON :

J. MASTERS AND CO., 78, NEW BOND STREET.

MDCCCLXXXV.

LONDON :
PRINTED BY J. MASTERS AND CO.,
ALBION BUILDINGS, BARTHOLOMEW CLOSE.

HENRIETTA'S WISH;

OR, DOMINEERING.

CHAPTER I.

ON the afternoon of a warm day in the end of July, an open carriage was waiting in front of the painted, toy-looking building which served as the railway station of Teignmouth. The fine bay horses stood patiently enduring the attacks of hosts of winged foes, too well-behaved to express their annoyance otherwise than by twitchings of their sleek shining skins, but duly grateful to the coachman, who roused himself now and then to whisk off some more pertinacious tormentor with the end of his whip.

Less patient was the sole occupant of the carriage, a maiden of about sixteen years of age, whose shady dark grey eyes, parted lips, and flushed complexion, were all full of the utmost eagerness, as every two or three minutes she looked up from the book which she held in her hand to examine the clock over the station door, compare it with her watch, and study the countenances of the bystanders to see whether they expressed any anxiety respecting the non-arrival of the train. All however seemed quite at their ease, and after a time the arrival of the railway omnibus

and two or three other carriages, convinced her that the
rest of the world only now began to consider it to be due.
At last the ringing of a bell quickened everybody into a
sudden state of activity, and assured her that the much-
desired moment was come. The cloud of smoke was seen,
the panting of the engine was heard, the train displayed its
length before the station, men ran along tapping the doors
of the carriages, and shouting a word which bore some
distant resemblance to "Teignmouth," and at the same moment various travellers emerged from the different vehicles.

Her eye eagerly sought out one of these arrivals, who on
his side, after a hasty greeting to the servant, who met him
on the platform, hurried to the carriage, and sprang into it.
The two faces, exactly alike in form, complexion, and features, were for one moment pressed together, then with-
drawn, in the consciousness of the publicity of the scene,
but the hands remained locked together, and earnest was
the tone of the "Well, Fred!" "Well, Henrietta!" which
formed the greeting of the twin brother and sister.

"And was not mamma well enough to come?" asked
Frederick, as the carriage turned away from the station.

"She was afraid of the heat. She had some business
letters to write yesterday, which teased her, and she has not
recovered from them yet; but she has been very well, on
the whole, this summer. But what of your school affairs,
Fred? How did the examination go off?"

"I am fourth, and Alex Langford fifth. Every one says
the prize will lie between us next year."

"Surely," said Henrietta, "you must be able to beat him
then, if you are before him now."

"Don't make too sure, Henrietta," said Frederick, shaking his head, "Langford is a hard-working fellow, very exact
and accurate; I should not have been before him now if it
had not been for my verses."

" I know Beatrice is very proud of Alexander," said Henrietta, "she would make a great deal of his success."

"Why of his more than of that of any other cousin?" said Frederick with some dissatisfaction.

"O you know he is the only one of the Knight Sutton cousins whom she patronises; all the others she calls cubs and bears and Osbaldistones. And indeed, Uncle Geoffrey says he thinks it was in great part owing to her that Alex is different from the rest. At least he began to think him worth cultivating from the time he found him and Busy Bee perched up together in an apple-tree, she telling him the story of Alexander the Great. And how she always talks about Alex when she is here."

" Is she at Knight Sutton?"

" Yes; Aunt Geoffrey would not come here, because she did not wish to be far from London, because old Lady Susan has not been well. And only think, Fred, Queen Bee says there is a very nice house to be let close to the village, and they went to look at it with grandpapa, and he kept on saying how well it would do for us."

" O, if we could but get mamma there!" said Fred. " What does she say?"

" She knows the house, and says it is a very pleasant one," said Henrietta; "but that is not an inch—no, not the hundredth part of an inch—towards going there!"

" It would surely be a good thing for her if she could but be brought to believe so," said Frederick. "All her attachments are there—her own home; my father's home."

" There is nothing but the sea to be attached to, here," said Henrietta. "Nobody can take root without some local interest, and as to acquaintance, the people are always changing."

" And there is nothing to do," added Fred; "nothing possible but boating and riding, which are not worth the misery which they cause her, as Uncle Geoffrey says. It is very, very—"

"Aggravating," said Henrietta, supplying one of the numerous stock of family slang words.

"Yes, aggravating," said he with a smile, "to be placed under the necessity of being absurd, or of annoying her!"

"Annoying! O, Fred, you do not know a quarter of what she goes through when she thinks you are in any danger. It could not be worse if you were on the field of battle! And it is very strange, for she is not at all a timid person for herself. In the boat, that time when the wind rose, I am sure Aunt Geoffrey was more afraid than she was, and I have seen it again and again that she is not easily frightened."

"No: and I do not think she is afraid for you."

"Not as she is for you, Fred; but then boys are so much more precious than girls, and besides they love to endanger themselves so much, that I think that is reasonable."

"Uncle Geoffrey thinks there is something nervous and morbid in it," said Fred: "he thinks that it is the remains of the horror of the sudden shock—"

"What? Our father's accident?" asked Henrietta. "I never knew rightly about that. I only knew it was when we were but a week old."

"No one saw it happen," said Fred; "he went out riding, his horse came home without him, and he was lying by the side of the road."

"Did they bring him home?" asked Henrietta, in the same low thrilling tone in which her brother spoke.

"Yes, but he never recovered his senses: he just said 'Mary,' once or twice, and only lived to the middle of the night!"

"Terrible!" said Henrietta, with a shudder. "O! how did mamma ever recover it?—at least, I do not think she has recovered it now,—but I meant live, or be even as well as she is."

"She was fearfully ill for long after," said Fred, "and Uncle Geoffrey thinks that these anxieties for me are an effect of the shock. He says they are not at all like her usual character. I am sure it is not to be wondered at."

"O no, no," said Henrietta. "What a mystery it has always seemed to us about papa! She sometimes mentioning him in talking about her childish days and Knight Sutton, but if we tried to ask any more, grandmamma stopping us directly, till we learned to believe we ought never to utter his name. I do believe, though, that mamma herself would have found it a comfort to talk to us about him, if poor dear grandmamma had not always cut her short, for fear it should be too much for her."

"But had you not always an impression of something dreadful about his death?"

"O yes, yes; I do not know how we acquired it, but that I am sure we had, and it made us shrink from asking any questions, or even from talking to each other about it. All I knew I heard from Beatrice. Did Uncle Geoffrey tell you this?"

"Yes, he told me when he was here last Easter, and I was asking him to speak to mamma about my fishing, and saying how horrid it was to be kept back from everything. First he laughed, and said it was the penalty of being an only son, and then he entered upon this history, to show me how it is."

"But it is very odd that she should have let you learn to ride, which one would have thought she would have dreaded most of all."

"That was because she thought it right, he says. Poor mamma, she said to him, 'Geoffrey, if you think it right that Fred should begin to ride, never mind my folly.' He says he thinks it cost her as much resolution to say that as it might to be martyred. And the same about going to school."

"Yes, yes; exactly," said Henrietta, "if she thinks it right, bear it she will, cost her what it may! O there is nobody like mamma. Busy Bee says so, and she knows, living in London and seeing so many people as she does."

"I never saw any one so like a queen," said Fred. "No, nor any one so beautiful, though she is so pale and thin. People say you are like her in her young days, Henrietta; and to be sure, you have a decent face of your own, but you will never be as beautiful as mamma, not if you live to be a hundred."

"You are afraid to compliment my face, because it is so like your own, Master Fred," retorted his sister; "but one comfort is, that I shall grow more like her by living to a hundred, whereas you will lose all the little likeness you have, and grow a grim old Black-beard! But I was going to say, Fred, that, though I think there is a great deal of truth in what Uncle Geoffrey said, yet I do believe that poor grandmamma made it worse. You know she had always been in India, and knew less about boys than mamma, who had been brought up with papa and my uncles, so she might really believe that everything was dangerous; and I have often seen her quite as much alarmed, or more, perhaps, about you—her consolations just showing that she was in a dreadful fright, and so making mamma twice as bad."

"Well," said Fred, sighing, "that is all over now, and she thought she was doing it all for the best."

"And," proceeded Henrietta, "I think, and Queen Bee thinks, that this perpetual staying on at Rocksand was more owing to her than to mamma. She imagined that mamma could not bear the sight of Knight Sutton, and that it was a great kindness to keep her from thinking of moving—"

"Ay, and that nobody can doctor her but Mr. Clarke," added Fred.

"Till now, I really believe," said Henrietta, "that the possibility of moving has entirely passed out of her mind, and she no more believes that she can do it than that the house can."

"Yes," said Fred, "I do not think a journey occurs to her among events possible, and yet without being very fond of this place."

"Fond! O no! it never was meant to be a home, and has nothing homelike about it! All her affections are really at Knight Sutton, and if she once went there, she would stay and be so much happier among her own friends, instead of being isolated here with me. In grandmamma's time it was not so bad for her, but now she has no companion at all but me. Rocksand has all the loneliness of the country without its advantages."

"There is not much complaint as to happiness, after all," said Fred.

"No, O no! but then it is she who makes it delightful, and it cannot be well for her to have no one to depend upon but me. Besides, how useless one is here. No opportunity of doing anything for the poor people, no clergyman who will put one into the way of being useful. O how nice it would be at Knight Sutton!"

"And perhaps she would be cured of her fears," added Fred; "she would find no one to share them, and be convinced by seeing that the cousins there come to no harm. I wish Uncle Geoffrey would recommend it!"

"Well, we will see what we can do," said Henrietta. "I do think we may persuade her, and I think we ought: it would be for her happiness and for yours, and on all accounts I am convinced that it ought to be done."

And as Henrietta came to this serious conclusion, they entered the steep straggling street of the little town of Rocksand, and presently were within the gates of the sweep which led to the door of the verandahed Gothic cottage, which looked very tempting for a summer's lodging, but was little fitted for a permanent abode.

In spite of all the longing wishes expressed during the drive, no ancestral home, beloved by inheritance, could have been entered with more affectionate rapture than that with which Frederick Langford sprang from the carriage, and flew to the arms of his mother, receiving and returning such a caress as could only be known by a boy conscious that he had done nothing to forfeit home love and confidence.

Turning back the fair hair that hung over his forehead, Mrs. Langford looked into his eyes, saying, half interrogatively, half affirmatively, "All right, Fred? Nothing that we need be afraid to tell Uncle Geoffrey? Well, Henrietta, he is grown, but he has not passed you yet. And now, Freddy, tell us about your examination," added she, as fondly leaning on his arm, she proceeded into the drawing-room, and they sat down together on the sofa, talking eagerly and joyously.

Mrs. Frederick Henry Langford (to give her her proper style) was in truth one whose peculiar loveliness of countenance well deserved the admiration expressed by her son. It was indeed pale and thin, but the features were beautifully formed, and had that expression of sweet placid resignation which would have made a far plainer face beautiful. The eyes were deep dark blue, and though sorrow and suffering had dimmed their brightness, their softness was increased: the smile was one of peace, of love, of serenity,—

of one who, though sorrow-stricken, as it were, before her time, had lived on in meek patience and submission, almost a child in her ways, as devoted to her mother, as little with a will and way of her own, as free from the cares of this work-a-day world. The long luxuriant dark brown hair, which once, as now with Henrietta, had clustered in thick glossy ringlets over her comb and round her face, was in thick braids beneath the delicate lace cap which suited with her plain black silk dress. Her figure was slender, so tall that neither her well-grown son nor daughter had yet reached her height, and, as Frederick said, with something queenlike in its unconscious grace and dignity.

As a girl she had been the merriest of the merry, and even now she had great playfulness of manner, and threw herself into the occupation of the moment with a life and animation that gave an uncommon charm to her manners, so that how completely sorrow had depressed and broken her spirit would scarcely have been guessed by one who had not known her in earlier days.

Frederick's account of his journey and of his school news was heard and commented on, a work of time extending far into the dinner ; the next matter in the regular course of conversation on the day of arrival was to talk over Uncle and Aunt Geoffrey's proceedings, and the Knight Sutton affairs.

"So, Uncle Geoffrey has been in the North ?" said Fred.

"Yes, on a special retainer," said Mrs. Langford, "and very much he seems to have enjoyed his chance of seeing York Cathedral."

"He wrote to me in court," said Fred, "to tell me what books I had better get up for this examination, and on a bit of paper scribbled all over one side with notes of the evidence. He said the Cathedral was beautiful beyond all he ever imagined."

"Had he never seen it before?" said Henrietta. "Lawyers seem made to travel in their vacations."

"Uncle Geoffrey could not be spared," said her mamma; "I do not know what Grandmamma Langford would do if he cheated her of any more of his holidays than he bestows upon us. He is far too valuable to be allowed to take his own pleasure."

"Besides, his own pleasure is at Knight Sutton," said Henrietta.

"He goes home just as he used from school," said Mrs. Langford. "Indeed, except a few grey hairs and 'crows-feet,' he is not in the least altered from those days : his work and play come just in the same way."

"And, as his daughter says, he is just as much the home pet," added Henrietta, "only rivalled by Busy Bee herself."

"No," said Fred, "according to Aunt Geoffrey, there are two suns in one sphere : Queen Bee is grandpapa's pet, Uncle Geoffrey grandmamma's. It must be great fun to see them."

"Happy people !" said Mrs. Langford.

"Henrietta says," proceeded Fred, "that there is a house to be let at Knight Sutton."

"The Pleasance : yes, I know it well," said his mother : "it is not actually in the parish, but close to the borders, and a very pretty place."

"With a pretty little stream in the garden, Fred," said Henrietta, "and looking into that beautiful Sussex coomb, that there is a drawing of in mamma's room."

"What size is it ?" added Fred.

"The comparative degree," said Mrs. Langford, "but my acquaintance with it does not extend beyond the recollection of a pretty-looking drawing-room with French windows, and a lawn where I used to be allowed to run about when I went with Grandmamma Langford to call on the old Miss

Drakes. I wonder your Uncle Roger does not take it, for those boys can scarcely, I should think, be wedged into Sutton Leigh when they are all at home."

"I wish some one else would take it," said Fred.

"Some one," added Henrietta, "who would like it of all things, and be quite at home there."

"A person," proceeded the boy, "who likes Knight Sutton and its inhabitants better than anything else."

"Only think," joined in the young lady, "how delightful it would be. I can just fancy you, mamma, sitting out on this lawn you talk of, on a summer's day, and nursing your pinks and carnations, and listening to the nightingales, and Grandpapa and Grandmamma Langford, and Uncle and Aunt Roger, and the cousins coming walking in at any time without ringing at the door ! And how nice to have Queen Bee and Uncle and Aunt Geoffrey all the vacation !"

"Without feeling as if we were robbing Knight Sutton," said Mrs. Langford. "Why, we should have you a regular little country maid, Henrietta, riding shaggy ponies, and scrambling over hedges, as your mamma did before you."

"And being as happy as a queen," said Henrietta ; "and the poor people, you know them all, don't you, mamma ?"

"I know their names, but my generation must have nearly passed away. But I should like you to see old Daniels the carpenter, whom the boys used to work with, and who was so fond of them. And the old schoolmistress in her spectacles. How she must be scandalised by the introduction of a noun and verb !"

"Who has been so cruel ?" asked Fred. "Busy Bee, I suppose."

"Yes," said Henrietta, "she teaches away with all her might ; but she says she is afraid they will forget it all while she is in London, for there is no one to keep it up. Now,

I could do that nicely. How I should like to be Queen Bee's deputy."

"But," said Fred, "how does Beatrice manage to make grandmamma endure such novelties? I should think she would disdain them more than the old mistress herself."

"Queen Bee's is not merely a nominal sovereignty," said Mrs. Langford.

"Besides," said Henrietta, "the new Clergyman approves of all that sort of thing; he likes her to teach, and puts her in the way of it."

CHAPTER II.

FROM this time forward everything tended towards Knight Sutton : castles in the air, persuasions, casual words which showed the turn of thought of the brother and sister, met their mother every hour. Nor was she, as Henrietta truly said, entirely averse to the change ; she loved to talk of what she still regarded as her home, but the shrinking dread of the pang it must give to return to the scene of her happiest days, to the burial-place of her husband, to the abode of his parents, had been augmented by the tender over-anxious care of her mother, Mrs. Vivian, who had strenuously endeavoured to prevent her from ever taking such a proposal into consideration, and fairly led her at length to believe it was out of the question.

A removal would in fact have been impossible during the latter years of Mrs. Vivian's life : but she had now been dead about eighteen months, her daughter had recovered from the first grief of her loss, and there was a general impression throughout the family that now was the time for her to come amongst them again. For herself, the possibility was but beginning to dawn upon her ; just at first she joined in building castles and imagining scenes at Knight Sutton, without thinking of their being realised, or that it only depended upon her, to find herself at home there ; and when Frederick and Henrietta, encouraged by this manner of talking pressed it upon her, she would reply with some vague intention of a return some time or other, but still thinking of it as something far away, and rather to be dreaded than desired.

It was chiefly by dint of repetition that it fully entered her mind that it was their real and earnest wish that she should engage to take a lease of the Pleasance, and remove almost immediately from her present abode; and from this time it might be perceived that she always shrank from entering on the subject in a manner which gave them little reason to hope.

"Yet, I think," said Henrietta to her brother one afternoon as they were walking together on the sands; "I think if she once thought it was right, if Uncle Geoffrey would tell her so, or if grandpapa would really tell her that he wished it, I am quite sure that she would resolve upon it."

"But why did he not do so long ago?" said Fred.

"Oh! because of grandmamma, I suppose," said Henrietta; "but he really does wish it, and I should not at all wonder if the Busy Bee could put it into his head to do it."

"Or if Uncle Geoffrey would advise her," said Fred; "but it never answers to try to make him propose anything to her. He never will do it; he always says he is not the Pope, or something to that effect." '

"If I was not fully convinced that it was right, and the best for all parties, I would not say so much about it," said Henrietta, in a tone rather as if she was preparing for some great sacrifice, instead of domineering over her mother.

To domineering, her temptation was certainly great. With all her good sense and ability, Mrs. Langford had seldom been called upon to decide for herself, but had always relied upon her mother for counsel; and during her long and gradual decline had learnt to depend upon her brother-in-law, Mr. Geoffrey Langford, for direction in great affairs, and in lesser ones upon her children. Girls are generally older of their age than boys, and Henrietta, a clever girl and her mother's constant companion, occupied a position in the family which amounted to something more than prime minister. Some one person must always be leader, and thus she had gradually attained, or had greatness thrust upon her; for justice requires it to be stated, that she more frequently tried to know her mamma's mind for her, than to carry her own point, though perhaps to do so always was more than could be expected of human nature at sixteen. The habit of being called on to settle whether they should use the britska or the pony carriage, whether satin or silk was best, or this or that book should be ordered, was, however, sufficient to make her very unwilling to be thwarted in other matters of more importance, especially in one on which were fixed the most ardent hopes of her brother, and the wishes of all the family.

Their present abode was, as she often said to herself, not the one best calculated for the holiday sports of a boy of sixteen, yet Frederick, having been used to nothing else, was very happy, and had tastes formed on their way of life. The twins, as little children, had always had the same occupations, Henrietta learning Latin, marbles, and trap-ball, and Frederick playing with dolls and working cross-stitch; and even now the custom was so far continued, that he gave lessons in Homer and Euclid in return for those which he received in Italian and music. For present amusement there was no reason to complain; the neighbourhood supplied many beautiful walks, while longer expeditions were made with Mrs. Langford in the pony carriage, and sketching, botanizing, and scrambling, were the order of the day. Boating too was a great delight, and had it not been for an occasional fretting recollection that he could not go out sailing without his mamma, and that most of his schoolfellows were spending their holidays in a very different manner, he would have been perfectly happy. Fortunately he had not sufficient acquaintance with the boys in the neighbourhood for the contrast to be often brought before him.

Henrietta did not do much to reconcile him to the anxious care with which he was guarded. She was proud of his talents, of his accomplishments, of his handsome features, and she would willingly have been proud of his excellence in manly sports, but in lieu of this she was proud of the spirit which made him long for them, and encouraged it by her full and entire sympathy. The belief that the present restraints must be diminished at Knight Sutton, was a moving spring with her, as much as her own wish for the scenes round which imagination had thrown such a brilliant halo. Of society they had hitherto seen little or nothing; Mrs. Langford's health and spirits had never been equal to visiting, nor was there much to tempt her in the changing inhabitants of a watering-place. Now and then, perhaps, an old acquaintance or distant connexion of some part of the family came for a month or six weeks, and a few calls were exchanged, and it was one of these visits that led to the following conversation.

"By-the-bye, mamma," said Fred, "I meant to ask you what that foolish woman meant about the St. Legers, and their not having thoroughly approved of Aunt Geoffrey's marriage."

"About the most ill-placed thing she could have said, Freddy," replied Mrs. Langford, "considering that I was always accused of having made the match."

"Made the match! O tell us, mamma; tell us all about it. Did you really?"

"Not consciously, Fred, and Frank St. Leger deserves as much of the credit as I do."

"Who was he? a brother of Aunt Geoffrey's?"

"O yes, Fred," said Henrietta, "to be sure you knew that. You have heard how mamma came home from India with General St. Leger and his little boy and girl. By-the-bye, mamma, what became of their mother?"

"Lady Beatrice? She died in India just before we came home. Well, I used to stay with them after we came back to England, and of course talked to my friend—"

"Call her Beatrice, mamma, and make a story of it."

"I talked to her about my Knight Sutton home and cousins, and on the other hand, Frank was always telling her about his school friend Geoffrey Langford. At last Frank brought him home with him from Oxford one Easter vacation. It was when the general was in command at ——, and Beatrice was in the midst of all sorts of gaieties, the mistress of the house, entertaining everybody, and all exactly what a novel would call brilliant."

"Were you there, mamma?"

"Yes, Beatrice had made a point of our coming to stay with her, and very droll it was to see how she and Geoffrey were surprised at each other; she to find her brother's guide, philosopher, and friend, the Langford who had gained every prize, a boyish-looking, boyish-mannered youth, very shy at first, and afterwards, excellent at giggling and making giggle; and he to find one with the exterior of a fine gay lady, so really simple in tastes and habits."

"Was Aunt Geoffrey ever pretty?" asked Fred.

"She is just what she was then, a little brown thing, with no actual beauty but in her animation and in her expression. I never saw a really handsome person who seemed to me nearly as charming. Then she had, and indeed has now, so much air and grace, so much of what, for want of a better word, I must call fashion in her appearance, that she was always very striking."

c

" Yes," said Henrietta, " I can quite see that ; it is not gracefulness, and it is not beauty, nor is it what she ever thinks of, but there is something distinguished about her. I should look twice at her if I met her in the street, and expect to see her get into a carriage with a coronet. And then and there they fell in love, did they ?"

" In long morning expeditions with the ostensible purpose of sketching, but in which I had all the drawing to myself, while the others talked either wondrous wisely or wondrous drolly. However, you must not suppose that anything of the novel kind was said then ; Geoffrey was only twenty, and Beatrice seemed as much out of his reach as the king's daughter of Hongarie."

" O yes, of course," said Henrietta, " but that only makes it more delightful ! Only to think of Uncle and Aunt Geoffrey having a novel in their history."

" That there are better novels in real life than in stories, is a truth or a truism often repeated, Henrietta," said her mother with a soft sigh, which she repressed in an instant, and proceeded : " Poor Frank's illness and death at Oxford brought them together the next year in a very different manner. Geoffrey was one of his chief nurses to the last, and was a great comfort to them all ; you may suppose how grateful they were to him. Next time I saw him, he seemed quite to have buried his youthful spirits in his studies : he was reading morn, noon, and night, and looking ill and overworked."

" O, Uncle Geoffrey ! dear good Uncle Geoffrey," cried Henrietta, in an ecstasy ; " you were as delightful as a knight of old, only as you could not fight tournaments for her, you were obliged to read for her ; and pining away all the time and saying nothing about it."

" Nothing beyond a demure inquiry of me when we were alone together, after the health of the general. Well, you know how well his reading succeeded : he took a double-first class, and very proud of him we were."

"And still he saw nothing of her," said Fred.

"Not till some time after he had been settled in his chambers at the Temple. Now you must know that General St. Leger, though in most matters a wise man, was not by any means so in money matters : and by some unlucky speculation which was to have doubled his daughter's fortune, managed to lose the whole of it, leaving little but his pay."

"Capital !" cried Frederick, "that brings her down to him."

"So it did," said his mother, smiling : "but the spectators did not rejoice quite so heartily as you do. The general's health was failing, and it was hard to think what would become of Beatrice ; for Lord St. Leger's family though very kind, were not more congenial then than they are now. As soon as all this was pretty well known, Geoffrey spoke, and the general, who was very fond of him, gave full consent. They meant to wait till it was prudent, of course, and were well contented ; but just after it was all settled, the general had a sudden seizure, and died. Geoffrey was with him, and he treated him like a son, saying it was his great comfort to know that her happiness was in his hands. Poor Beatrice, she went first to the St. Legers, stayed with them two or three months, then I would have her to be my bridesmaid, though"—and Mrs. Langford tried to smile, while again she strangled a sobbing sigh—"she warned me that her mourning was a bad omen. Well, she stayed with my mother while we went abroad, and on our return went with us to be introduced at Knight Sutton. Everybody was charmed, Mrs. Langford and Aunt Roger had expected a fine lady or a blue one, but they soon learnt to believe all her gaiety and all her cleverness a mere calumny, and grandpapa was delighted with her the first moment. How well I remember Geoffrey's coming home and thanking us for having managed so well as to make her like one of the family, while the truth was that she had fitted herself in, and found her place from the first moment. Now came a time of grave private conferences. A long engagement which might have been very well if the general had lived, was a dreary prospect now that Beatrice was without a home; but then your uncle was but just called to the bar, and had next to nothing of his own, present or to come. However, he had begun his literary works, and found them answer so well, that he believed he could maintain himself till briefs came in, and he had the sort of talent which gives confidence. He thought, too, that even in the event of his death she would be better off as one of us, than as a dependent on the St. Legers; and at last by talking to us, he nearly persuaded himself to believe it would be a very prudent thing to marry. It was a harder matter to persuade his father, but persuade him he did, and the wedding was at Knight Sutton that very summer."

"That's right," cried Fred, "excellent and glorious! A farthing for all the St. Legers put together."

"Nevertheless, Fred, in spite of your disdain, we were all of opinion that it was a matter of rejoicing that Lord St. Leger and Lady Amelia were present, so that no one had any reason to say that they disapproved. Moreover, lest you should learn imprudence from my story, I would also suggest that if your uncle and aunt had not been a couple *comme il y en a peu*, it would neither have been excellent nor glorious."

"Why, they are very well off," said Fred; "he is quite at the head of his profession. The first thing a fellow asks me when he hears my name is, if I belong to Langford the barrister."

" Yes, but he never would have been eminent, scarcely have had daily bread, if he had not worked fearfully hard, so hard that without the buoyant schoolboy spirit, which can turn from the hardest toil like a child to its play, his health could never have stood it."

· " But then it has been success and triumph," said Fred ; " one could work like a galley-slave with encouragement, and never feel it drudgery."

" It was not all success at first," said his mother ; "there was hard work, and disappointment, and heavy sorrow too ; but they knew how to bear it, and to win through with it."

" And were they very poor ?" asked Henrietta.

" Yes : but it was beautiful to see how she accommodated herself to it. The house that once looked dingy and deso-late, was very soon pretty and cheerful, and the *wirthschaft* so well ordered and economical, that Aunt Roger was struck dumb with admiration. I shall not forget Lady Susan's visit the last morning we spent with her in London, how amazed she was to find 'poor Beatrice' looking so bright and like herself, and how little she guessed at her morning's work, the study of shirt-making, and the copying out of a review of her husband's, full of Greek quotations."

" Well, the poverty is all over now," said Henrietta ; "but still they live in a very quiet way, considering Aunt Geof-frey's connections and the fortune he has made."

" Who put that notion into your head, my wise daughter?" said Mrs. Langford.

Henrietta blushed, laughed, and mentioned Lady Matilda St. Leger, a cousin of her Aunt Geoffrey's of whom she had seen something in the course of the last year.

" The truth is," said Mrs. Langford, "that your aunt had display and luxury enough in her youth to value it as it deserves, and he could not desire it except for her sake.

They had rather give with a free hand, beyond what any one knows or suspects."

"Ah! I know among other things that he sends Alexander to school," said Fred.

"Yes, and the improvements at Knight Sutton," said Henrietta, "the school, and all that grandpapa wished but could never afford. Well, mamma, if you made the match, you deserve to be congratulated on your work."

"There's nobody like Uncle Geoffrey, I have said, and shall always maintain," said Fred.

His mother sighed, saying, " I don't know what we should have done without him!" and became silent. Henrietta saw an expression on her countenance which made her unwilling to disturb her, and nothing more was said till it was discovered that it was bed-time.

CHAPTER III.

"WHERE is Madame?" asked Frederick of his sister, as she entered the breakfast room alone the next morning with the key of the tea-chest in her hand.

"A headache," answered Henrietta, "and palpitation!"

"A bad one?"

"Yes, very; and I am afraid it is our fault, Freddy: I am convinced it will not do, and we must give it up."

"How do you mean? The going to Knight Sutton? What has that to do with it? Is it the reviving old recollections that is too much for her?"

"Just listen what an effect last evening's conversation had upon her. Last night, after I had been asleep a long time, I woke up, and there I saw her kneeling before the table with her hands over her face. Just then it struck one, and soon after she got into bed. I did not let her know I was awake, for speaking would only have made it worse, but I am sure she did not sleep all night, and this morning has one of her most uncomfortable fits of palpitation. She had just fallen asleep, when I looked in after dressing, but I do not think she will be fit to come down to-day."

"And do you think it was talking of Uncle and Aunt Geoffrey that brought it on?" said Fred, with much concern; "yet it did not seem to have much to do with my father."

"O but it must," said Henrietta. "He must have been there all the time mixed up in everything. Queen Bee has told me how they were always together when they were children."

"Ah! perhaps; and I noticed how she spoke about her wedding," said Fred. "Yes, and to compare how differently it has turned out with Aunt Geoffrey and with her, after they had been young and happy together. Yes, no doubt it was he who persuaded the people at Knight Sutton into letting them marry!"

"And their sorrow that she spoke of must have been his death," said Henrietta. "No doubt the going over those old times renewed all those thoughts."

"And you think going to Knight Sutton might have the same effect. Well, I suppose we must give it up," said Fred, with a sigh. "After all, we can be very happy here!"

"O yes! that we can. It is more on your account than mine, that I wished it," said the sister.

"And I should not have thought so much of it, if I had not thought it would be pleasanter for you when I am away," said Fred.

"And so," said Henrietta, laughing yet sighing, "we agree to persuade each other that we don't care about it."

Fred performed a grimace, and remarked that if Henrietta continued to make her tea so scalding, there would soon be a verdict against her of fratricide; but the observation, being intended to conceal certain feelings of disappointment and heroism, only led to silence.

After sleeping for some hours, Mrs. Langford awoke refreshed, and got up, but did not leave her room. Frederick and Henrietta went to take a walk by her desire, as she declared that she preferred being alone, and on their return they found her lying on the sofa.

"Mamma has been in mischief," said Fred. "She did

not think herself knocked up enough already, so she has been doing it more thoroughly."

"Oh, mamma!" was Henrietta's reproachful exclamation, as she looked at her pale face and red swollen eyelids.

"Never mind, my dears," said she, trying to smile, "I shall be better now this is done, and I have it off my mind." They looked at her in anxious interrogation, and she smiled outright with lip and eye. "You will seal that letter with a good will, Henrietta," she said. "It is to ask Uncle Geoffrey to make inquiries about the Pleasance."

"Mamma!" and they stood transfixed at a decision beyond their hopes: then Henrietta exclaimed—

"No, no, mamma, it will be too much for you; you must not think of it."

"Yes," said Fred; "indeed we agreed this morning that it would be better not. Put it out of your head, mamma, and go on here in peace and comfort. I am sure it suits you best."

"Thank you, thank you, my dear ones," said she, drawing them towards her, and fondly kissing them, "but it is all settled, and I am sure it is better for you. It is but a dull life for you here."

"O no, no, no, dearest mamma : nothing can be dull with you," cried Henrietta, wishing most sincerely to undo her own work. "We are, indeed we are, as happy as the day is long. Do not fancy we are discontented; do not think we want a change."

Mrs. Langford replied by an arch though subdued smile.

"But we would not have you to do it on our account," said Fred. "Pray put it out of your head, for we do very well here, and it was only a passing fancy."

"You will not talk me out of it, my dears," said Mrs. Langford. "I know it is right, and it shall be done. It is only the making up my mind that was the struggle, and I shall look forward to it as much as either of you, when I know it is to be done. Now walk off, my dears, and do not let that letter be too late for the post."

"I do not half like it," said Fred, pausing at the door.

"I have not many fears on that score," said she, smiling. "No, do not be uneasy about me, my dear Fred, it is my proper place, and I must be happy there. I shall like to be near the Hall, and to see all the dear old places again."

"O, mamma, you cannot talk about them without your voice quivering," said Henrietta. "You do not know how I wish you would give it up!"

"Give it up! I would not for millions," said Mrs. Langford. "Now go, my dears, and perhaps I shall go to sleep again."

The spirits of the brother and sister did not just at first rise enough for rejoicing over the decision. Henrietta would willingly have kept back the letter, but this she could not do; and sealing it as if she were doing wrong, she sat down to dinner, feeling subdued and remorseful, something like a tyrant between the condemnation and execution of his victim. But by the time the first course was over, and she and Frederick had begun to recollect their long-cherished wishes, they made up their minds to be happy, and fell into their usual strain of admiration of the unknown haven of their hopes, and of expectations that it would in the end benefit their mother.

The next morning she was quite in her usual spirits, and affairs proceeded in the usual manner; Frederick's holidays came to an end, and he returned to school with many a fond lamentation from the mother and sister, but with cheerful auguries from both that the next meeting might be at Knight Sutton.

"Here, Henrietta," said her mother, as they sat at breakfast together a day or two after Frederick's departure, turning over to her the letter of which she had first broken the seal, while she proceeded to open some others. It was Uncle Geoffrey's writing, and Henrietta read eagerly :—

"My dear Mary,—I would not write till I could give you some positive information about the Pleasance, and that could not be done without a conference with Hardy, who was not at home. I am heartily glad that you think of coming among us again, but still I should like to feel certain that it is you that feel equal to it, and not the young ones who are set upon the plan. I suppose you will indignantly refute the charge, but you know I have never trusted you in that matter. However, we are too much the gainers to investigate motives closely, and I cannot but believe that the effort once over, you would find it a great comfort to be among your own people, and in your own country. I fully agree with you also in what you say of the advantage to Henrietta and Fred. My father is going to write, and I must leave him to do justice to his own cordiality, and proceed to business."

Then came the particulars of freehold and copyhold, purchase or lease, repair or disrepair, of which Henrietta knew nothing, and cared less; she knew that her mamma was considered a great heiress, and trusted to her wealth for putting all she pleased in her power : but it was rather alarming to recollect that Uncle Geoffrey would consider it right to make the best terms he could, and that the house might be lost to them while they were bargaining for it.

"O, mamma, never mind what he says about its being dear," said she, "I dare say it will not ruin us."

"Not exactly," said Mrs. Langford, smiling, "but gentlemen consider it a disgrace not to make a good bargain, and Uncle Geoffrey must be allowed to have his own way."

"O but, mamma, suppose some one else should take it."

"A village house is not like these summer lodgings, which are snapped up before you can look at them," said Mrs. Langford; "I have no fears but that it is to be had." But Henrietta could not help fancying that her mother would regard it somewhat as a reprieve, if the bargain was to go off independently of any determination of hers.

Still she had made up her mind to look cheerfully at the scheme, and often talked of it with pleasure, to which the cordial and affectionate letters of her father-in-law and the rest of the family, conduced not a little. She now fully perceived that it had only been from forbearance, that they had not before urged her return, and as she saw how earnestly it was desired by Mr. and Mrs. Langford, reproached herself as for a weakness for not having sooner resolved upon her present step. Henrietta's work was rather to keep up her spirits at the prospect, than to prevent her from changing her purpose, which never altered, respecting a return to the neighbourhood of Knight Sutton, though whether to the house of the tempting name, was a question which remained in agitation during the rest of the autumn, for as surely as Rome was not built in a day, so surely cannot a house be bought or sold in a day, especially when a clever and cautious lawyer acts for one party.

Matters thus dragged on, till the space before the Christmas holidays was reckoned by weeks, instead of months, and as Mrs. Frederick Langford laughingly said, she should be fairly ashamed to meet her boy again at their present home. She therefore easily allowed herself to be persuaded to accept Mr. Langford's invitation to take up her quarters at the Hall, and look about her a little before finally deciding upon the Pleasance. Christmas at Knight Sutton Hall had the greatest charms in the eyes of Henrietta and Frederick; for many a time had they listened to the descriptions given *con amore* by Beatrice Langford, to whom that place had ever been a home, perhaps the more beloved, because the other half of her life was spent in London.

It was a great disappointment, however, to hear that Mrs. Geoffrey Langford was likely to be detained in London by the state of health of her aunt, Lady Susan St. Leger, whom she did not like to leave, while no other of the family was at hand. This was a cruel stroke, but she could not bear that her husband should miss his yearly holiday, her daughter lose the pleasure of a fortnight with Henrietta, or Mr. and Mrs. Langford be deprived of the visit of their favourite son : and she therefore arranged to go and stay with Lady Susan, while Beatrice and her father went as usual to Knight Sutton.

Mr. Geoffrey Langford offered to escort his sister-in-law from Devonshire, but she did not like his holidays to be so wasted. She had no merely personal apprehensions, and new as railroads were to her, declared herself perfectly willing and able to manage with no companions but her daughter and maid, with whom she was to travel to his house in London, there to be met in a day or two by the two schoolboys, Frederick and his cousin Alexander, and then proceed all together to Knight Sutton.

Henrietta could scarcely believe that the long-wished-for time was really come, packing up actually commencing, and that her waking would find her under a different roof from that which she had never left. She did not know till now that she had any attachments to the place she had hitherto believed utterly devoid of all interest ; but she found she could not bid it farewell without sorrow. There was the old boatman with his rough kindly courtesy, and his droll ways of speaking ; there was the rocky beach where she and her brother had often played on the verge of the

ocean, watching with mysterious awe or sportive delight
the ripple of the advancing waves, the glorious sea itself,
the walks, the woods, streams, and rocks, which she now
believed, as mamma and Uncle Geoffrey had often told her,
were more beautiful than anything she was likely to find
in Sussex. Other scenes there were, connected with her
grandmother, which she grieved much at parting with, but
she shunned talking over her regrets, lest she should agitate
her mother, whom she watched with great anxiety.

She was glad that so much business was on her hands,
as to leave little time for dwelling on her feelings, to which
she attributed the calm quietness with which she went
through the few trying days that immediately preceded
their departure. Henrietta felt this constant employment
so great a relief to her own spirits, that she was sorry on
her own account, as well as her mother's, when every possible order had been given, every box packed, and nothing
was to be done, but to sit opposite to each other, on each
side of the fire, in the idleness which precedes candle-light.
Her mother leant back in silence, and she watched her
with an anxious gaze. She feared to say anything of sympathy with what she supposed her feelings, lest she should
make her weep. An indifferent speech would have been
out of place even if Henrietta herself could have made it,
and yet to remain silent was to allow melancholy thoughts
to prey upon her. So thought the daughter, longing at the
same time that her persuasions were all unsaid.

"Come here, my dear child," said her mother presently,
and Henrietta almost started at the calmness of the voice,
and the serenity of the tranquil countenance. She crossed
to her mother, and sat down on a low footstool, leaning
against her. "You are very much afraid for me," continued Mrs. Langford, as she remarked upon the anxious
expression of her face, far different from her own, "but you

need not fear, it is all well with me ; it would be wrong not
to be thankful for those who are not really lost to me as
well as for those who were given to me here."

All Henrietta's consideration for her mother could not
prevent her from bursting into tears. " O mamma, I did
not know it would be so like going away from dear grandmamma."

" Try to feel the truth, my dear, that our being near to
her depends on whether we are in our duty or not."

" Yes, yes, but this place is so full of her ; I do so love it !
I did not know it till now !"

" Yes, we must always love it, my dear child ; but we
are going to our home, Henrietta, to your father's home
in life and death, and it must be good for us to be there,
with your grandfather, who has wished for us. Knight
Sutton is our true home, the one where it is right for us
to be."

Henrietta still wept bitterly, and strange it was, that it
should be she, who stood in need of consolation, for the
fulfilment of her own most ardent wish, and from the very
person to whom it was the greatest trial. It was not, however, self-reproach that caused her tears. Her mother's
calmness prevented her from having any such misgivings.
But attachment to the place she was about to leave, and
the recollections, which she accused herself of having
slighted, had stirred her feelings. Her mother, who had
made up her mind to do what was right, found strength
and peace at the moment of trial, when the wayward and
untrained spirits of the daughter gave way. Not that she
blamed Henrietta, she was rather gratified to find that she
was so much attached to her home and her grandmother,
and felt so much with her ; and after she had succeeded in
some degree in restoring her to composure, they talked long
and earnestly over old times and deeper feelings.

CHAPTER IV.

THE journey to London was prosperously performed, and Mrs. Frederick Langford was not over-fatigued when she arrived at Uncle Geoffrey's house at Westminster. The cordiality of their greeting may be imagined, as a visit from Henrietta had been one of the favourite visions of her cousin Beatrice, through her whole life; and the two girls were soon deep in the delights of a conversation in which sense and nonsense had an equal share.

The next day was spent by the two Mrs. Langfords in quiet together, while Henrietta was conducted through a rapid whirl of sight-seeing by Beatrice and Uncle Geoffrey, the latter of whom, to his niece's great amazement, professed to find almost as much novelty in the sights as she did. A short December day, though not what they would have chosen, had this advantage, that the victim could not be as completely fagged and worn out as in a summer's day, and Henrietta was still fresh and in high spirits when they drove home and found to their delight that the two schoolboys had already arrived.

Beatrice met both alike as old friends and almost brothers, but Alexander, though returning her greeting with equal cordiality, looked shyly at the new aunt and cousin, and, as Henrietta suspected, wished them elsewhere. She had heard much of him from Beatrice, and knew that her brother regarded him as a formidable rival ; and she was therefore surprised to see that his broad honest face expressed more good humour than intellect, and his manners wanted polish. He was tolerably well-featured, with light eyes and dark hair, and though half a year older than his cousin, was much shorter,—more perhaps in appearance than reality, from the breadth and squareness of his shoulders, and from not carrying himself well.

Alexander was (as ought previously to have been recorded,) the third son of Mr. Roger Langford, the heir of Knight Sutton, at present living at Sutton Leigh, a small house on his father's estate, busied with farming, sporting, and parish business ; while his active wife contrived to make a narrow income feed, clothe, and at least half educate their endless tribe of boys. Roger, the eldest, was at sea ; Frederick, the second, in India ; and Alexander owed his more learned education to Uncle Geoffrey, who had been well recompensed by his industry and good conduct. Indeed his attainments had always been so superior to those of his brothers, that he might have been considered as a prodigy, had not his cousin Frederick been always one step before him.

Fred had greater talent, and had been much better taught at home, so that on first going to school, he took and kept the higher place ; but this was but a small advantage in his eyes, compared with what he had to endure out of school during his first half-year. Unused to any training or companionship save of womankind, he was disconsolate, bewildered, derided in that new rude world ; while Alex, accustomed to fight his way among rude brothers, instantly found his level, and even extended a protecting hand to his cousin, who requited it with little gratitude. Soon overcoming his effeminate habits, he grew expert and dexterous and was equal to Alex in all but main bodily strength ; but the spirit of rivalry once excited, had never died away, and with a real friendship and esteem for each other, their names or rather their nicknames had almost become party words among their schoolfellows.

Nor was it probable that this competition would be forgotten on this first occasion of spending their holidays together. Fred felt himself open to that most galling accusation of want of manliness, on account at once of his ignorance of country sports, and of his knowledge of accomplishments; but he did not guess at the feeling which made Alexander on his side regard those very accomplishments with a feeling which, if it were not jealousy, was at least very nearly akin to it.

Beatrice Langford had not the slightest claim to beauty. She was very little, and so thin that her papa did her no injustice when he called her " skin and bones;" but her thin brown face, with the aid of a pair of very large deep Italian-looking eyes, was so full of brilliant expression, and showed such changes of feeling from sad to gay, from sublime to ridiculous, that no one could have wished one feature otherwise. And if instead of being " like the diamond bright," they had been " dull as lead," it would have been little matter to Alex. Beatrice had been, she was still, his friend, his own cousin, more than what he could believe a sister to be if he had one,—in short his own little Queen Bee. He had had a monopoly of her; she had trained him in all the civilisation which he possessed, and it was with considerable mortification that he thought himself lowered in her eyes by comparison with his old rival, as old a friend of hers, with the same claim to cousinly affection; and instead of understanding only what she had taught him, familiar with the tastes and pursuits on which she set perhaps too great a value.

Fred did not care nearly as much for Beatrice's preference :

it might be that he took it as a matter of course, or perhaps that having a sister of his own, he did not need her sympathy, but still it was a point on which he was likely to be sensitive, and thus her favour was likely to be secretly quite as much a matter of competition as their school studies and pastimes.

For instance, dinner was over, and Henrietta was admiring some choice books of prints, such luxuries as Uncle Geoffrey now afforded himself, and which his wife and daughter greatly preferred to the more costly style of living which some people thought befitted them. She called to her brother who was standing by the fire, " Fred, do come and look at this beautiful Albert Durer, of Sintram."

He hesitated, doubting whether Alexander would scorn him for an acquaintance with Albert Durer, but Beatrice added, " Yes, it was an old promise that I would show it to you. There now, look, admire, or be pronounced insensible."

" A wonderful old fellow was that Albert," said Fred, looking, and forgetting his foolish false shame in the pleasure of admiration. " Yes; O how wondrously the expression on Death's face changes as it does in the story ! How easy it is to see how Fouqué must have built it up ! Have you seen it, mamma ?"

His mother came to admire. Another print was produced, and another, and Fred and Beatrice were eagerly studying the elaborate engravings of the old German, when Alex, annoyed at finding her too much engrossed to have a word for him, came to share their occupation, and took up one of the prints with no practised hand. " Take care, Alex, take care," cried Beatrice, in a sort of excruciated tone ; " don't you see what a pinch you are giving it ? Only the initiated ought to handle a print : there is a pattern for you," pointing to Fred.

She cut right and left : both looked annoyed, and retreated

from the table; Fred thinking how Alex must look down on fingers which possessed any tenderness; Alex provoked at once and pained. Queen Bee's black eyes perceived their power, and gave a flash of laughing triumph.

But Beatrice was not quite in her usual high spirits, for she was very sorry to leave her mother; and when they went up stairs for the night, she stood long over the fire talking to her, and listening to certain parting cautions.

"How I wish you could have come, mamma! I am so sure that grandmamma in her kindness will tease Aunt Mary to death. You are the only person who can guard her without affronting grandmamma. Now I—"

"Had better let it alone," rejoined Mrs. Geoffrey Langford. "You will do more harm than by letting things take their course. Remember, too, that Aunt Mary was at home there long before you or I knew the place."

"Oh, if that tiresome Aunt Amelia would but have had some consideration! To go out of town and leave Aunt Susan on our hands just when we always go home!"

"We have lamented that often enough," said her mother smiling. "It is unlucky, but it cannot be too often repeated, that wills and wishes must sometimes bend."

"You say that for me, mamma," said Beatrice. "You think grandmamma and I have too much *will* for each other."

"If you are conscious of that, Bec, I hope that you will bend that wilful will of yours."

"I hope I shall," said Beatrice, "but . . . Well, I must go to bed. Good night, mamma."

And Mrs. Geoffrey Langford looked after her daughter anxiously, but she well knew that Beatrice knew her besetting fault, and she trusted to the many fervent resolutions she had made against it.

The next morning the party bade adieu to Mrs. Geoffrey

Langford, and set out on their journey to Knight Sutton.
They filled a whole railroad carriage, and were a very cheerful party. Alexander and Beatrice sat opposite to each
other, talking over Knight Sutton delights with animation,
Beatrice ever and anon turning to her other cousins with
explanations, or referring to her papa, who was reading the
newspaper and talking to Mrs. Frederick Langford.

The day was not long enough for all the talk of the
cousins, and the early winter twilight came on before their
conversation was exhausted, or they had reached the Allonfield station.

" Here we are !" exclaimed Beatrice, as the train stopped,
and at the same moment a loud voice called out, " All
right ! where are you, Alex ?" upon which Alexander tumbled
across Henrietta to feel for the handle of the carriage-door,
replying, " Here, old fellow, let us out. Have you brought
Dumpling ?" And Uncle Geoffrey and Beatrice exclaimed,
" How d'ye do, Carey ?"

When Alexander had succeeded in making his exit, Henrietta beheld him shaking hands with a figure not quite his
own height, and in its rough great coat, not unlike a small
species of bear. Uncle Geoffrey and Fred handed out
the ladies, and sought their appurtenances in the dark,
and Henrietta began to give Alex credit for a portion of
that which maketh man, when he shoved his brother, ad-
monishing him that there was Aunt Mary, upon which Carey
advanced, much encumbered with sheepish shyness, presented a great rough driving-glove, and shortly and bluntly
replied to the soft tones which kindly greeted him, and
inquired for all at home.

" Is the Hall carriage come ?" asked Alex, and, receiving
a gruff affirmative, added, " then, Aunt Mary, you had better
come to it while Uncle Geoffrey looks after the luggage,"
offered his arm with tolerable courtesy, and conducted her

to the carriage. "There," said he, "Carey has driven in in our gig, and I suppose Fred and I had better go back with him."

"Is the horse steady?" asked his aunt, anxiously.

"Dumple? To be sure! Never does wrong! do you, old fellow?" said Alex, patting his old friend.

"And no lamps?"

"O, we know the way blindfold, and you might cross Sutton Heath a dozen times without meeting anything but a wheel-barrowful of peat."

"And how is the road now? It used to be very bad in my time."

"Lots of ruts," muttered Carey to his brother, who interpreted it, "A few ruts this winter, but Dumpling knows all the bad places."

By this time Uncle Geoffrey came up, and instantly perceiving the state of things, said, "I say, Freddy, do you mind changing places with me? I should like to have a peep at Uncle Roger before going up to the house, and then Dumpling's feelings won't be hurt by passing the turn to Sutton Leigh."

Fred could not object, and his mother rejoiced in the belief that Uncle Geoffrey would take the reins, nor did Beatrice undeceive her, though, as the vehicle rattled past the carriage at full speed, she saw Alexander's own flourish of the whip, and knew that her papa was letting the boys have their own way. She had been rather depressed in the morning on leaving her mother, but as she came nearer home her spirits mounted, and she was almost wild with glee. "Aunt Mary, do you know where you are?"

"On Sutton Heath, I presume, from the absence of land-marks."

"Yes, that we are. You dear old place, how d'ye do? You beginning of home! I don't know when it is best coming to you : on a summer's evening, all glowing with purple heath, or a frosty star-light night like this. There is the Sutton Leigh turn ! Hurrah ! only a mile further to the gate."

"Where I used to go to meet the boys coming home from school," said her aunt, in a low tone of deep feeling. But she would not sadden their blithe young hearts, and added cheerfully, "Just the same as ever, I see : how well I know the outline of the bank there !"

" Ay, it is your fatherland, too, Aunt Mary ! Is there not something inspiring in the very air ? Come, Fred, can't you get up a little enthusiasm ?"

"Oceans, without getting it up," replied Fred. " I never was more rejoiced in my whole life," and he began to hum Domum.

"Sing it, sing it ; let us join in chorus as homage to Knight Sutton," cried Henrietta.

And the voices began, "Domum, Domum, dulce Domum ;" even Aunt Mary herself caught the feelings of her young companions, felt herself coming to her own beloved home and parents, half forgot how changed was her situation, and threw herself into the delight of returning.

" Now, Fred," said Henrietta, " let us try those verses that you found a tune for, that begin ' What is home.' "

This also was sung, and by the time it was finished they had reached a gate leading into a long drive through dark beech woods. " This is the beautiful wood of which I have often told you, Henrietta," said Mrs. Frederick Langford.

" The wood with glades like cathedral aisles," said Henrietta. " O, how delightful it will be to see it come out in leaf !"

"Which I have never seen," said Beatrice. " I tell papa he has made his fortune, and ought to retire, and he says he is too young for it."

" In which I fully agree with him," said her aunt. " I should not like to see him with nothing to do."

" O, mamma, Uncle Geoffrey would never be anywhere with nothing to do," said Henrietta.

" No," said her mother, " but people are always happier with work made for them, than with what they make for themselves. Besides, Uncle Geoffrey has too much talent to be spared."

" Ay," said Fred, " I wondered to hear you so devoid of ambition, little Busy Bee."

" It is only Knight Sutton and thinking of May flowers that make me so," said Beatrice. " I believe after all, I should break my heart if papa did retire without—"

" Without what, Bee ?"

" Being Lord Chancellor, I suppose," said Henrietta very seriously. " I am sure I should."

" His being in Parliament will content me for the present," said Beatrice, " for I have been told too often that high principles don't rise in the world, to expect any more. We can be just as proud of him as if he was."

" You are in a wondrously humble and philosophic mood, Queen Bee," said Henrietta ; " but where are we now ?" added she, as a gate swung back.

" Coming into the paddock," said Beatrice ; " don't you see the lights in the house ? There, that is the drawing-room window to the right, and that large one the great hall window. Then upstairs, don't you see that red fire-light ? That is the south room, which Aunt Mary will be sure to have."

Henrietta did not answer, for there was something that subdued her in the nervous pressure of her mother's hand. The carriage stopped at the door, whence streamed forth light, dazzling to eyes long accustomed to darkness ; but in the midst stood a figure which Henrietta could not but have

recognised in an instant, even had not old Mr. Langford
paid more than one visit to Rocksand. Tall, thin, unbent,
with high bald forehead, clear eye, and long snowy hair;
there he was, lifting rather than handing his daughter-in-law
from the carriage, and fondly kissing her brow; then he
hastily greeted the other occupants of the carriage, while
she received the kiss of Mrs. Langford.

They were now in the hall, and turning again to his
daughter-in-law, he gave her his arm, and led her into the
drawing-room, where he once more embraced her, saying,
"Bless you, my own dear Mary!" She clung to him for a
moment as if she longed to weep with him, but recovering
herself in an instant, she gave her attention to Mrs. Langford, who was trying to administer to her comfort with a
degree of bustle and activity which suited well with the
alertness of her small figure and the vivacity of the black
eyes which still preserved their brightness, though her hair
was perfectly white. "Well, Mary, my dear, I hope you
are not tired. You had better sit down and take off your
furs, or will you go to your room? But where is Geoffrey?"

"He went with Alex and Carey, round by Sutton Leigh,"
said Beatrice.

"Ha! ha! my little Queen, are you there?" said grandpapa, holding out his arms to her. "And," added he, "is
not this your first introduction to the twins, grandmamma?
Why you are grown as fine a pair as I would wish to see
on a summer's day. Last time I saw you I could hardly
tell you apart, when you both wore straw hats and white
trousers. No mistake now, though. Well, I am right glad
to have you here."

"Won't you take off some of your wraps, Mary?" proceeded Mrs. Langford, and her daughter-in-law with a soft
"Thank you," passively obeyed. "And you too, my dear,"
she added to Henrietta.

"Off with that bonnet, Miss Henrietta," proceeded grand-papa. "Let me see whether you are as like your brother as ever. He has your own face, Mary."

"Do not you think his forehead like—" and she looked to the end of the room where hung the portraits of two young children, the brothers Geoffrey and Frederick. Henrietta had often longed to see it, but now she could attend to nothing but her mamma.

"Like poor dear Frederick?" said grandmamma. "Well, I can't judge by firelight, you know, my dear; but I should say they were both your very image."

"You can't be the image of any one I should like better," said Mr. Langford, turning to them cheerfully, and taking Henrietta's hand. "I wish nothing better than to find you the image of your mamma inside and out."

"Ah, there's Geoffrey!" cried Mrs. Langford, springing up and almost running to meet him.

"Well, Geoffrey, how d'ye do?" added his father with an indescribable tone and look of heartfelt delight. "Left all your cares behind you?"

"Left my wife behind me," said Uncle Geoffrey, making a rueful face.

"Ay, it is a sad business that poor Beatrice cannot come," said both the old people; "but how is poor Lady Susan?"

"As usual, only too nervous to be left with none of the family at hand. Well, Mary, you look tired."

Overcome, Uncle Geoffrey would have said, but he thought the other accusation would answer the same purpose and attract less attention, and it succeeded, for Mrs. Langford proposed to take her up stairs. Henrietta thought that Beatrice would have offered to save her the trouble, but this would not have been at all according to the habits of grandmamma or granddaughter, and Mrs. Langford briskly led the way to a large cheerful-looking room, talking

all the time and saying she supposed Henrietta would like
to be with her mamma. She nodded to their maid, who
was waiting there, and gave her a kindly greeting, stirred
the already bright fire into a blaze, and returning to her
daughter-in-law who was standing like one in a dream, she
gave her a fond kiss, saying, " There, Mary, I thought you
would like to be here."

" Thank you, thank you, you are always kind."

" There now, Mary, don't let yourself be overcome. You
would not bring him back again, I know. Come, lie down
and rest. There—that is right—and don't think of coming
down stairs. You think your mamma had better not, don't
you ?"

" Much better not, thank you, grandmamma," said Henrietta, as she assisted in settling her mother on the sofa.
" She is tired and overcome now, but she will be herself
after a rest."

" And ask for anything you like, my dear. A glass of
wine or cup of coffee ; Judith will get you one in a moment.
Won't you have a cup of coffee, Mary, my dear ?"

" Thank you, no, thank you," said Mrs. Frederick Langford, raising herself. " Indeed I am sorry—it is very foolish." Here the choking sob came again, and she was
forced to lie down. Grandmamma stood by, warming a
shawl to throw over her, and pitying her in audible whis-
pers. " Poor thing, poor thing ! it is very sad for her.
There ! a pillow, my dear ? I'll fetch one out of my room.
No ? Is her head high enough ? Some sal-volatile ? Yes,
Mary, would you not like some sal-volatile ?"

And away she went in search of it, while Henrietta, excessively distressed, knelt by her mother, who, throwing her
arms round her neck, wept freely for some moments, then
laid her head on the cushions again, saying, " I did not
think I was so weak !"

"Dearest mamma," said Henrietta, kissing her and feeling very guilty.

"If I have not distressed grandmamma!" said her mother anxiously. "No, never mind me, my dear, it was fatigue and—"

Still she could not finish, so painfully did the familiar voices, the unchanged furniture, recall both her happy childhood and the bridal days when she had last entered the house, that it seemed as it were a new thing, a fresh shock to miss the tone that was never to be heard there again. Why should all around be the same, when all within was altered? But it had been only the first few moments that had overwhelmed her, and the sound of Mrs. Langford's returning footsteps recalled her habit of self-control; she thanked her, held out her quivering hand, drank the sal-volatile, pronounced herself much better, and asked pardon for having given so much trouble. Mrs. Langford had tears in her eyes as she answered,

"Trouble? my dear child, no such thing! I only wish I could see you better. No doubt it is too much for you, this coming home the first time; but then you know poor Fred is gone to a better—Ah! well, I see you can't bear to speak of him, and perhaps after all quiet is the best thing. Don't let your mamma think of dressing and coming down, my dear."

There was a little combat on this point, but it ended in Mrs. Frederick Langford yielding, and agreeing to remain upstairs. Grandmamma would have waited to propose to her each of the dishes that were to appear at table, and hear which she thought would suit her taste: but very fortunately, as Henrietta thought, a bell rang at that moment, which she pronounced to be "the half-hour bell," and she hastened away, telling her granddaughter that dinner would be ready at half-past five, and calling the maid outside the door to give her full directions where to procure anything that her mistress might want.

"Dear grandmamma! just like herself!" said Mrs. Frederick Langford. "But Henrietta, my dear," she added with some alarm, "make haste and dress: you must never be too late in this house!"

Henrietta was not much accustomed to dress to a moment, and she was too anxious about her mamma to make speed with her whole will, and her hair was in no state of forwardness when the dinner-bell rang, causing her mamma to start and hasten her with an eager, almost alarmed manner. "You don't know how your grandmamma dislikes being kept waiting," said she.

At last she was ready, and running down, found all the rest assembled, evidently waiting for her. Frederick, looking anxious, met her at the door to receive her assurances that their mother was better; the rest inquired, and her apologies were cut short by grandmamma calling them to eat her turkey before it grew cold. The spirits of all the party were perhaps damped by Mrs. Frederick Langford's absence and its cause, for the dinner was not a very lively one, nor the conversation very amusing to Henrietta and Frederick, as it was chiefly on the news of the country neighbourhood, in which Uncle Geoffrey showed much interest.

As soon as she was released from the dining-room, Henrietta ran up to her mamma, whom she found refreshed and composed. "But, O mamma, is this a good thing for you?" said Henrietta, looking at the red case containing her father's miniature, which had evidently been only just closed on her entrance.

"The very best thing for me, dearest," was the answer now given in her own calm tones. "It does truly make me happier than anything else. No, don't look doubtful, my

Henrietta; if it were repining it might hurt me, but I trust it is not."

"And does this really comfort you, mamma?" said Henrietta, as she pressed the spring, and gazed thoughtfully on the portrait. "O, I cannot fancy that! the more I think, the more I try to realize what it might have been, think what Uncle Geoffrey is to Beatrice, till sometimes, O mamma, I feel quite rebellious!"

"You will be better disciplined in time, my poor child," said her mother, sadly. "As your grandmamma said, who could be so selfish as to wish him here?"

"And can you bear to say so, mamma?"

She clasped her hands and looked up, and Henrietta feared she had gone too far. Both were silent for some little time, until at last the daughter timidly asked, "And was this your old room, mamma?"

"Yes: look in that shelf in the corner; there are all our old childish books. Bring that one," she added, as Henrietta took one out, and opening it, she showed in the flyleaf the well-written "F. H. Langford," with the giver's name; and below in round hand, scrawled all over the page, "Mary Vivian, the gift of her cousin Fred." "I believe you may find that in almost all of them," said she. "I am glad they have been spared from the children at Sutton Leigh. Will you bring me a few more to look over, before you go down again to grandmamma?"

Henrietta did not like to leave her, and lingered while she made a selection for her among the books, and from that fell into another talk, in which they were interrupted by a knock at the door, and the entrance of Mrs. Langford herself. She sat a little time, and asked of health, strength, and diet, until she bustled off again to see if there was a good fire in Geoffrey's room, telling Henrietta that tea would soon be ready.

Henrietta's ideas of grandmammas were formed on the placid Mrs. Vivian, naturally rather indolent, and latterly very infirm, although considerably younger than Mrs. Langford; and she stood looking after her in speechless amazement, her mamma laughing at her wonder. "But, my dear child," she said, "I beg you will go down. It will never do to have you staying up here all the evening."

Henrietta was really going this time, when as she opened the door, she was stopped by a new visitor. This was an elderly respectable-looking maid-servant, old Judith, whose name was well known to her. She had been nursery-maid at Knight Sutton at the time "Miss Mary" arrived from India, and was now, what in a more modernized family would have been called ladies'-maid or housekeeper, but here was a nondescript office, if anything, upper housemaid. How she was loved and respected is known to all who are happy enough to possess a "Judith."

"I beg your pardon, miss," said she, as Henrietta opened the door just before her, and Mrs. Frederick Langford, on hearing her voice, called out, "O, Judith! is that you? I was in hopes you were coming to see me."

She advanced with a curtsey, at the same time affectionately taking the thin white hand stretched out to her. "I hope you are better, ma'am. It is something like old times to have you here again."

"Indeed I am very glad to be here, Judith," was the answer, "and very glad to see you looking like your own dear self."

"Ah! Miss Mary—I beg your pardon, ma'am; I wish I could see you looking better."

"I shall, I hope, to-morrow, thank you, Judith. But you have not been introduced to Henrietta, there."

"But I have often heard of you, Judith," said Henrietta, cordially holding out her hand. Judith took it, and looked

at her with affectionate earnestness. "Sure enough, miss,"
said she, "as Missus says, you are the very picture of your
mamma when she went away; but I think I see a look of
poor Master Frederick too."

"Have you seen my brother, Judith?" asked Henrietta,
fearing a second discussion on likenesses.

"Yes, Miss Henrietta; I was coming down from Missus's
room, when Mr. Geoffrey stopped me to ask how I did,
and said, 'Here's a new acquaintance for you, Judith,' and
there was Master Frederick. I should have known him
anywhere, and he spoke so cheerful and pleasant. A fine
young gentleman he is, to be sure."

"Why, we must be like your grandchildren!" said Henrietta; "but O! here comes Fred."

And Judith discreetly retreated as Fred entered bearing a
summons to his sister to come down to tea, saying that he
could scarcely prevail on grandmamma to let him take the
message instead of coming herself.

They found Queen Bee perched upon the arm of her
grandpapa's chair, with one hand holding by his collar. She
had been coaxing him to say Henrietta was the prettiest girl
he ever saw, and he was teasing her by declaring he should
never see anything like Aunt Mary in her girlish days.
Then he called up Henrietta and Fred, and asked them
about their home doings, showing so distinct a knowledge
of them, that they laughed and stood amazed. "Ah," said
grandpapa, "you forgot that I had a Queen Bee to enlighten
me. We have plenty to tell each other, when we go buzzing
over the ploughed fields together on a sunny morning,
haven't we, Busy, Busy Bee?"

Here grandmamma summoned them all to tea. She
liked every one to sit round the table, and put away work
and book, as for a regular meal, and it was rather a long
one. Then, when all was over, grandpapa called out,

"Come, young ladies, I've been wearying for a tune these three months. I hope you are not too tired to give us one."

"O no, no, grandpapa!" cried Beatrice: "but you must hear Henrietta. It is a great shame of her to play so much better than I do, with all my London masters too."

And in music the greater part of the evening passed away. Beatrice came to her aunt's room to wish her good night, and to hear Henrietta's opinions, which were of great delight and still greater wonder—grandmamma so excessively kind, and grandpapa, O, he was a grandpapa to be proud of!

CHAPTER V

IT was an agreeable surprise to Henrietta that her mother waked free from headache, very cheerful, and feeling quite able to get up to breakfast. The room looked very bright and pleasant by the first morning light that shone upon the intricate frost-work on the window; and Henrietta, as usual, was too much lost in gazing at the branches of the elms and the last year's rooks' nests, to make the most of her time; so that the bell for prayers rang long before she was ready. Her mamma would not leave her, and remained to help her. Just as they were going down at last, they met Mrs. Langford on her way up with inquiries for poor Mary. She would almost have been better pleased with a slight indisposition than with dawdling; but she kindly accepted Henrietta's apologies, and there was one exclamation of joy from all the assembled party at Mrs. Frederick Langford's unhoped-for entrance.

"Geoffrey, my dear," began Mrs. Langford, as soon as the greetings and congratulations were over, "will you see what is the matter with the lock of this tea-chest?—it has been out of order these three weeks, and I thought you could set it to rights."

While Uncle Geoffrey was pronouncing on its complaints, Atkins, the old servant, put in his head.

"If you please, sir, Thomas Parker would be glad to speak to Mr. Geoffrey about his son on the railway."

Away went Mr. Geoffrey to the lower regions, where Thomas Parker awaited him, and as soon as he returned was addressed by his father : "Geoffrey, I put those papers on the table in the study, if you will look over them when you have time, and tell me what you think of that turnpike trust."

A few moments after the door was thrown wide open, and in burst three boys, shouting with one voice—"Uncle Geoffrey, Uncle Geoffrey, you must come and see which of Vixen's puppies are to be saved !"

"Hush, hush, you rogues, hush !" was Uncle Geoffrey's answer ; "don't you know that you are come into civilised society ? Aunt Mary never saw such wild men of the woods."

"All crazy at the sight of Uncle Geoffrey," said grandmamma. "Ah, he spoils you all ! but, come here, Johnny, come and speak to your aunt. There, this is Johnny, and here are Richard and Willie," she added, as they came up and awkwardly gave their hands to their aunt and cousins.

Henrietta was almost bewildered by seeing so many likenesses of Alexander. "How shall I ever know them apart ?" said she to Beatrice.

"Like grandmamma's nest of teacups, all alike, only each one size below another," said Beatrice. "However, I don't require you to learn them all at once ; only to know Alex and Willie from the rest. Here, Willie, have you nothing to say to me ? How are the rabbits ?"

Willie, a nice looking boy of nine or ten years old, of rather slighter make than his brothers, and with darker eyes and hair, came to Queen Bee's side, as if he was very glad to see her, and only slightly discomposed by Henrietta's neighbourhood.

John gave the information that papa and Alex were just behind, and in another minute they made their appearance. "Good morning, sir; good morning, ma'am," were Uncle Roger's greetings, as he came in. "Ah, Mary, how d'ye do? glad to see you here at last; hope you are better.— Ah, good morning, good morning," as he quickly shook hands with the younger ones. "Good morning, Geoffrey; I told Martin to take the new drill into the out-field, for I want your opinion whether it is worth keeping."

And thereupon the three gentlemen began a learned discussion on drills, during which Henrietta studied her uncle. She was at first surprised to see him look so young— younger, she thought, than Uncle Geoffrey; but in a moment or two she changed her mind, for though mental labour had thinned and grizzled Uncle Geoffrey's hair, paled his cheek, and traced lines of thought on his broad high brow, it had not quenched the light that beamed in his eyes, nor subdued the joyous merriment that often played over his countenance, according with the slender active figure that might have belonged to a mere boy. Uncle Roger was taller, and much more robust and broad; his hair still untouched with grey, his face ruddy brown, and his features full of good nature, but rather heavy. In his plaid shooting coat and high gaiters, as he stood by the fire, he looked the model of a country squire; but there was an indescribable family likeness, and something of the same form about the nose and lip, which recalled to Henrietta the face she loved so well in Uncle Geoffrey.

The drill discussion was not concluded when Mrs. Langford gave the signal for the ladies to leave the breakfast table. Henrietta ran up stairs for her mother's work, and came down again laughing. "I am sure, Queenie," said she, "that your papa chose his trade rightly. He may well be called a great counsel. Besides all the opinions asked of him at breakfast, I have just come across a consultation on the stairs between him and Judith about—what was it? —some money in a savings' bank."

"Yes," said Beatrice, "Judith has saved a sum that is wondrous in these degenerate days of maids in silk gowns, and she is wise enough to give 'Master Geoffrey' all the management of it. But if you are surprised now, what will you be by the end of the day? See if his advice is not asked in at least fifty matters."

"I'll count," said Henrietta: "what have we had already?" and she took out pencil and paper—"Number one, the tea-chest; then the poor man, and the turnpike trust—"

"Vixen's puppies and the drill," suggested her mamma.

"And Judith's money," added Henrietta. "Six already"—

"To say nothing of all that will come by the post, and we shall not hear of," said Beatrice; "and look here, what I am going to seal for him, one, two, three—eight letters."

"Why! when could he possibly have written them?"

"Last night after we were gone to bed. It shows how much more grandmamma will let him do than any one else, that she can allow him to sit up with a candle after eleven o'clock. I really believe that there is not another living creature in the world who could do it in this house. There, you may add your own affairs to the list, Henrietta, for he is going to the Pleasance to meet some man of brick and mortar."

"O, I wish we could walk there!"

"I dare say we can. I'll manage. Aunt Mary, should you not like Henrietta to go and see the Pleasance?"

"Almost as much as Henrietta would like it herself, Busy Bee," said Aunt Mary; "but I think she should walk to Sutton Leigh to-day."

"Walk to Sutton Leigh!" echoed old Mrs. Langford, entering at the moment; "not you, surely, Mary?"

"O no, no, grandmamma," said Beatrice, laughing; "she was only talking of Henrietta's doing it."

"Well, and so do, my dears; it will be a very nice thing, if you go this morning before the frost goes off. Your Aunt Roger will like to see you, and you may take the little pot of black currant jelly that I wanted to send over for poor Tom's sore mouth."

Beatrice looked at Henrietta and made a face of disgust as she asked, "Have they no currant jelly themselves?"

"O no, they never can keep anything in the garden. I don't mean that the boys take the fruit; but between tarts and puddings and desserts, poor Elizabeth can never make any preserves."

"But," objected Queen Bee, "if one of the children is ill, do you think Aunt Roger will like to have us this morning? and the post girl could take the jelly."

"O nonsense, Bee," said Mrs. Langford, somewhat angrily; "you don't like to do it, I see plain enough. It is very hard you can't be as good-natured to your own little cousin as to one of the children in the village."

"Indeed, grandmamma, I did not mean that."

"Oh, no, no, grandmamma," joined in Henrietta, "we shall be very glad to take it. Pray let us."

"Yes," added Beatrice, "if it is really to be of any use, no one can be more willing."

"Of any use?" repeated Mrs. Langford. "No! never mind. I'll send some one."

"No, pray do not, dear grandmamma," eagerly exclaimed Henrietta; "I do beg you will let us take it. It will be making me at home directly to let me be useful."

Grandmamma was pacified. "When will you set out?" she asked, "you had better not lose this bright morning."

"We will go directly," said Queen Bee; "we will go by the west turning, so that Henrietta may see the Pleasance."

"My dear! the west turning will be a swamp, and I won't have you getting wet in your feet and catching cold."

"O, we have clogs : and besides, the road does not get so dirty since it has been mended. I asked Johnny this morning."

"As if he knew, or cared anything about it!—and you will be late for luncheon. Besides grandpapa will drive your aunt there the first day she feels equal to it, and Henrietta may see it then. But you will always have your own way."

Henrietta had seldom been more uncomfortable than during this altercation ; and but for reluctance to appear more obliging than her cousin, she would have begged to give up the scheme. Her mother would have interfered in another moment, but the entrance of Uncle Geoffrey gave a sudden turn to affairs.

"Who likes to go to the Pleasance?" said he, as he entered. "All whose curiosity lies that way may prepare their seven-leagued boots."

"Here are the girls dying to go," said Mrs. Langford, as well pleased as if she had not been objecting the minute before.

"Very well. We go by Sutton Leigh : so make haste, maidens." Then, turning to his mother, "Didn't I hear you say you had something to send to Elizabeth, ma'am?"

"Only some currant jelly for little Tom ; but if—"

"O grandmamma, that is my charge ; pray don't cheat me," exclaimed Henrietta. "If you will lend me a basket, it will travel much better with me than in Uncle Geoffrey's pocket."

"Ay, that will be the proper division of labour," said Uncle Geoffrey, looking well pleased with his niece; "but I thought you were off to get ready."

"Don't keep your uncle waiting, my dear," added her

mamma; and Henrietta departed, Beatrice following her to her room, and there exclaiming, "If there is a thing I can't endure, it is going to Sutton Leigh when one of the children is poorly! It is always bad enough—"

"Bad enough! O, Busy Bee!" cried Henrietta, quite unprepared to hear of any flaw in her paradise.

"You will soon see what I mean. The host of boys in the way; the wooden bricks and black horses spotted with white wafers that you break your shins over, the marbles that roll away under your feet, the whips that crack in your ears, the universal air of nursery that pervades the house. It is worse in the morning, too; for one is always whining over *sum*, *es*, *est*, and another over his spelling. O, if I had eleven brothers in a small house, I should soon turn misanthrope. But you are laughing instead of getting ready."

"So are you."

"My things will be on in a quarter of the time you take. I'll tell you what, Henrietta, the Queen Bee allows no drones, and I shall teach you to 'improve each shining hour;' for nothing will get you into such dire disgrace here as to be always behind time. Besides, it is a great shame to waste papa's time. Now, here is your shawl ready folded, and now I will trust you to put on your boots and bonnet by yourself."

In five minutes the Queen Bee flew back again, and found Henrietta still measuring the length of her bonnet strings before the glass. She hunted her down stairs at last, and found the two uncles and grandpapa at the door, playing with the various dogs, small and great, that usually waited there. Fred and the other boys had gone out together some time since, and the party now set forth, the three gentlemen walking together first. Henrietta turned as soon as she had gone a sufficient distance that she might study the aspect of the house. It did not quite fulfil her expectations; it was neither remarkable for age nor beauty; the masonry was in a sort of chessboard pattern, alternate squares of freestone and of flints, the windows were not casements as she thought they ought to have been, and the long wing, or rather ex-crescence, which contained the drawing-room, was by no means ornamental. It was a respectable, comfortable man-sion, and that was all that was to be said in its praise, and Beatrice's affection had so embellished it in description, that it was no wonder that Henrietta felt slightly disappointed. She had had some expectation, too, of seeing it in the midst of a park, instead of which the carriage-drive along which they were walking, only skirted a rather large grass field, full of elm trees, and known by the less dignified name of the Paddock. But she would not confess the failure of her expectations even to herself, and as Beatrice was evidently looking for some expressions of admiration, she said the road must be very pretty in summer.

"Especially when this bank is one forest of foxgloves," said Queen Bee. "Only think! Uncle Roger and the farmer faction wanted grandpapa to have this hedge-row grubbed up, and turned into a plain dead fence; but I carried the day, and I dare say Aunt Mary will be as much obliged to me as the boys, who would have lost their grand preserve of stoats and rabbits. But here are the out-field and the drill."

And going through a small gate at the corner of the pad-dock, they entered a large ploughed field, traversed by a footpath raised and gravelled, so as to be high and dry, which was well for the two girls, as the gentlemen left them to march up and down there by themselves, whilst they were discussing the merits of the brilliant blue machine which was travelling along the furrows. It was rather a trial of patience, but Beatrice was used to it, and Henrietta was in a temper to be pleased with anything.

At last the inspection was concluded, and Mr. Langford came to his granddaughters, leaving his two sons to finish their last words with Martin.

"Well, young ladies," said he, "this is fine drilling, in patience at least. I only wish my wheat may be as well drilled with Uncle Roger's newfangled machines."

"That is right, grandpapa," said Queen Bee; "you hate them as much as I do, don't you now?"

"She is afraid they will make honey by steam," said grandpapa, "and render bees a work of supererogation."

"They are doing what they can towards it," said Beatrice. "Why, when Mr. Carey took us to see his hives, I declare I had quite a fellow-feeling for my poor subjects, boxed up in glass, with all their privacy destroyed. And they won't even let them swarm their own way—a most unwarrantable interference with the liberty of the subject."

"Well done, Queenie," said Mr. Langford, laughing; "a capital champion. And so you don't look forward to the time when we are to have our hay made by one machine, our sheep washed by another, our turkeys crammed by a third—ay, and even the trouble of bird-starving saved us?"

"Bird-starving!" repeated Henrietta.

"Yes; or keeping a few birds, according to the mother's elegant diminutive," said Beatrice, "serving as live scare-crows."

"I should have thought a scarecrow would have answered the purpose," said Henrietta.

"This is one that is full of gunpowder, and fires off every ten minutes," said grandpapa: "but I told Uncle Roger we would have none of them here unless he was prepared to see one of his boys blown up at every third explosion."

"Is Uncle Roger so very fond of machines?" said Henrietta.

"He goes about to cattle shows and agricultural meetings,

and comes home with his pockets crammed with papers of new inventions, which I leave him to try as long as he does not empty my pockets too fast."

" Don't they succeed, then?" said Henrietta.

" Why—ay—I must confess we get decent crops enough. And once we achieved a prize ox,—such a disgusting over-grown beast, that I could not bear the sight of it; and told Uncle Roger I would have no more such waste of good victuals, puffing up the ox instead of the frog."

Henrietta was not quite certain whether all this was meant in jest or earnest; and perhaps the truth was, that though grandpapa had little liking for new plans, he was too wise not to adopt those which possessed manifest advantage, and only indulged himself in a good deal of playful grumbling, which greatly teased Uncle Roger.

" There is Sutton Leigh," said grandpapa, as they came in sight of a low white house among farm buildings. " Well, Henrietta, are you prepared for an introduction to an aunt and half-a-dozen cousins, and Jessie Carey into the bargain?"

" Jessie Carey!" exclaimed Beatrice, in a tone of dismay.

" Did you not know she was there? Why they always send Carey over for her with the gig if there is but a tooth-ache the matter at Sutton Leigh."

" Is she one of Aunt Roger's nieces?" asked Henrietta.

" Yes," said Beatrice. " And—O! grandpapa, don't look at me in that way. Where is the use of being your pet, if I may not tell my mind?"

" I won't have Henrietta prejudiced," said Mr. Langford. " Don't listen to her, my dear: and I'll tell you what Jessie Carey is. She is an honest, good-natured girl as ever lived; always ready to help every one, never thinking of trouble, without an atom of selfishness."

" Now for the *but*, grandpapa," cried Beatrice. " I allow all that, only grant me the *but*."

"But Queen Bee, chancing to be a conceited little Londoner, looks down on us poor country folks as unfit for her most refined and intellectual society."

"O grandpapa, that is not fair! Indeed, you don't really believe that. O, say you don't!" And Beatrice's black eyes were full of tears.

"If I do not believe the whole, you believe the half, Miss Bee," and he added, half whispering, "take care some of us do not believe the other half. But don't look dismal on the matter, only put it into one of your waxen cells, and don't lose sight of it. And if it is any comfort to you, I will allow that perhaps poor Jessie is not the most entertaining companion for you. Her vanity maggots are not of the same sort as yours."

They had by this time nearly reached Sutton Leigh, a building little altered from the farm-house it had originally been, with a small garden in front, and a narrow footpath up to the door. As soon as they came in sight there was a general rush forward of little boys in brown holland, all darting on Uncle Geoffrey, and holding him fast by legs and arms.

"Let me loose, you varlets," he cried, and disengaging one hand, in another moment drew from his capacious pocket a beautiful red ball, which he sent bounding over their heads, and dancing far away with all the urchins in pursuit.

At the same moment the rosy, portly, good-humoured Mrs. Roger Langford appeared at the door, welcoming them cordially, and, as usual, accusing Uncle Geoffrey of spoiling her boys. Henrietta thought she had never seen a happier face than hers in the midst of cares, and children, and a drawing-room which, with its faded furniture strewed with toys, had in fact, as Beatrice said, something of the appearance of a nursery.

Little Tom, the youngest, was sitting on the lap of his cousin, Jessie Carey, at whom Henrietta looked with some curiosity. She was a pretty girl of twenty, with a brilliant gipsy complexion, fine black hair, and a face which looked as good-natured as every other inhabitant of Sutton Leigh.

But it would be tedious to describe a visit which was actually very tedious to Beatrice, and would have been the same to Henrietta but for its novelty. Aunt Roger asked all particulars about Mrs. Frederick Langford, then of Aunt Geoffrey and Lady Susan St. Leger, and then gave the history of the misfortunes of little Tom, who was by this time on Uncle Geoffrey's knee looking at himself in the inside of the case of his watch. Henrietta's list, too, was considerably lengthened; for Uncle Geoffrey advised upon a smoky chimney, mended a cart of Charlie's, and assisted Willie in a puzzling Latin exercise.

It was almost one o'clock, and as a certain sound of clattering plates was heard in the next room, Aunt Roger begged her guests to come in to luncheon. Uncle Geoffrey accepted for the girls who were to walk on with him; but Mr. Langford, no eater of luncheons, returned to his own affairs at home. Henrietta found the meal was the family dinner. She had hardly ever been seated at one so plain, or on so long a table; and she was not only surprised, but tormented herself by an uncomfortable and uncalled-for fancy, that her hosts must be supposing her to be remarking on deficiencies. The younger children were not so perfect in the management of knife, fork, and spoon, as to be pleasant to watch; nor was the matter mended by the attempts at correction made from time to time by their father and Jessie. But Henrietta endured better than Beatrice, whose face ill concealed an expression of disgust and weariness, and who maintained a silence very unlike her usual habits.

At last Uncle Geoffrey, to the joy of both, proposed to pursue their walk, and they took leave. Queen Bee rejoiced as soon as they had quitted the house, that the boys were too well occupied with their pudding to wish to accompany them, but she did not venture on any further remarks before her papa. He gave a long whistle, and then turned to point out all the interesting localities to Henrietta. There was something to tell of every field, every tree, or every villager, with whom he exchanged his hearty greeting. If it were only a name, it recalled some story of mamma's, some tradition handed on by Beatrice. Never was walk more delightful; and the girls were almost sorry to find themselves at the green gate of the Pleasance, leading to a gravel road, great part of which had been usurped by the long shoots of the evergreens. Indeed, the place could hardly be said to correspond in appearance to its name, in its chilly, deserted, unfurnished state; but the girls were resolved to admire, and while Uncle Geoffrey was deep in the subject of repairs and deficiencies, they flitted about from garret to cellar, making plans, fixing on rooms, and seeing possibilities, in complete enjoyment. But even this could not last for ever; and, rather tired and very cold, they seated themselves on a step of the stairs, and there built a marvellous castle of delight for next summer; then talked over the Sutton Leigh household, discussed the last books they had read, and had just begun to yawn, when Uncle Geoffrey, being more merciful than most busy men, concluded his business, and summoned them to return home. Their homeward walk was by a different road, through the village of Knight Sutton itself, which Henrietta had not yet seen. It was a long straggling street, the cottages for the most part in gardens, and with a general look of comfort and neatness that showed the care of the proprietor.

"O, here is the church," said Henrietta, in a subdued voice, as they came to the low flint wall that fenced in the slightly rising ground occupied by the churchyard, surrounded by a whole grove of noble elm trees, amongst which could just be seen the small old church, with its large deep porch and curious low tower.

"The door is open," said Beatrice; "I suppose they are bringing in the holly for Christmas. Should you like to look in, Henrietta?"

"I do not know," said she, looking at her uncle. "Mamma—"

"I think it might be less trying if she has not to feel for you and herself too," said Uncle Geoffrey.

"I am sure I should wish it very much," said Henrietta; and they entered the low dark, solemn-looking building, the massive stone columns and low-browed arches of which had in them something peculiarly awful and impressive to Henrietta's present state of mind. Uncle Geoffrey led her on into the chancel, where, among numerous mural tablets recording the names of different members of the Langford family, was one chiefly noticeable for the superior taste of its Gothic canopy, and which bore the name of Frederick Henry Langford, with the date of his death, and his age,— only twenty-six. One of the large flat stones below also had the initials F. H. L., and the date of the year. Henrietta stood and looked in deep silence, Beatrice watching her earnestly and kindly, and her uncle's thoughts almost as much as hers, on what might have been. Her father had been so near to him in age, so constantly his companion, so entirely one in mind and temper, that he had been far more to him than his elder brother, and his death had been the one great sorrow of Uncle Geoffrey's life.

The first sound which broke the stillness was the opening of the door, as the old clerk's wife entered with a huge basket of holly, and dragging a mighty branch behind her. Uncle Geoffrey nodded in reply to her curtsey, and gave his daughter a glance which sent her to the other end of the church to assist in the Christmas decorations.

Henrietta turned her liquid eyes upon her uncle. "This is coming very near him!" said she in a low voice; "Uncle, I wish I might be quite sure that he knows me."

"Do not wish too much for certainty which has not been granted to us," said Uncle Geoffrey. "Think rather of 'I shall go to him, but he shall not return to me.'"

"But, uncle, you would not have me not believe that he is near to me and knows how—how I would have loved him, and how I do love him," she added, while the tears rose to her eyes.

"It may be so, my dear, and it is a thought which is not only most comforting, but good for us, as bringing us closer to the unseen world : but it has not been positively revealed, and it seems to me better to dwell on that time when the meeting with him is so far certain that it depends but on ourselves."

To many persons, Uncle Geoffrey would scarce have spoken in this way; but he was aware of a certain tendency in Henrietta's mind to merge the reverence and respect she owed to her parents, in a dreamy unpractical feeling for the father whom she had never known, whose voice she had never heard, and from whom she had not one precept to obey; while she lost sight of that honour and duty which was daily called for towards her mother. It was in honour, not in love, that Henrietta was wanting, and with how many daughters is it not the same? It was therefore, that though even to himself it seemed harsh, and cost him a pang, Mr. Geoffrey Langford resolved that his niece's first visit to her father's grave should not be spent in fruitless dreams of him or of his presence, alluring because involving neither self-reproach nor resolution; but in thoughts which might lead to action, to humility, and to the yielding up of self-will.

Henrietta looked very thoughtful, "That time is so far away!" said she.

"How do you know that?" said her uncle in the deep low tone that brought the full perception that "it is nigh, even at the doors."

She gave a sort of shuddering sigh, the reality being doubly brought home to her by the remembrance of the suddenness of her father's summons.

"It is awful," said she, "I cannot bear to think of it."

"Henrietta," said her uncle, solemnly, "guard yourself from being so satisfied with a dream of the present as to lose sight of the real, most real future." He paused, and as she did not speak, went on: "The present, which is the means of attaining to that future, is one not of visions and thoughts, but of deeds."

Again Henrietta sighed, but presently she said, "But, uncle, that would bring us back to the world of sense. Are we not to pray that we may in heart and mind ascend?"

"Yes, but to dwell with Whom? Not to stop short with objects once of earthly affection."

"Then would you not have me think of him at all?" said she, almost reproachfully.

"I would have you take care, Henrietta, lest the thought should absorb the love and trust due to your true and Heavenly FATHER, and at the same time you forget what on earth is owed to your mother. Do you think that is what your father would desire?"

"You mean," said she sadly, "that while I do not think enough of GOD, and while I love my own way so well, I have no right to dwell on the thought I love best,—the thought that he is near."

"'Take it rather as a caution than as blame," said Uncle Geoffrey. A long silence ensued, during which Henrietta thought deeply on the new idea opened to her. Her vision, for it could not be called her memory of her father, had in fact been too highly enshrined in her mind, too much worshipped, she had deemed this devotion a virtue, and fostered as it was by the solitude of her life, and the temper of her mother's mind, the truth was as Uncle Geoffrey had hinted, and she began to perceive it, but still it was most unwillingly, for the thought was cherished so as to be almost part of herself. Uncle Geoffrey's manner was so kind that she could not be vexed with him, but she was disappointed, for she had hoped for a narration of some part of her father's history, and for the indulgence of that soft sorrow which has in it little pain. Instead of this she was bidden to quit her beloved world, to soar above it, or to seek for a duty which she had rather not believe that she neglected, though—no, she did not like to look deeper.

Mr. Geoffrey Langford gave her time for thought, though of what nature it might be, he could not guess, and then said, "One thing more before we leave this place. Whether Fred cheerfully obeys the fifth commandment in its full extent, may often, as I believe, depend on your influence. Will you try to exert it in the right way?"

"You mean when he wishes to do things like other boys of his age," said Henrietta.

"Yes. Think yourself, and lead him to think, that obedience is better than what he fancies manliness. Teach him to give up pleasure for the sake of obedience, and you will do your work as a sister and daughter."

While Uncle Geoffrey was speaking, Beatrice's operations with the holly had brought her a good deal nearer to them,

and at the same time the church door opened, and a gentleman entered, whom the first glance showed Henrietta to
be Mr. Franklin, the clergyman of the parish, of whom she
had heard so much. He advanced on seeing Beatrice with
the holly in her hand. "Miss Langford! This is just what
I was wishing."

"I was just helping old Martha," said Beatrice, "we
came in to show my cousin the church, and—"

By this time the others had advanced.

"How well the church looks this dark afternoon," said
Uncle Geoffrey, speaking in a low tone, "it is quite the
moment to choose for seeing it for the first time. But you
are very early in beginning your adornments."

"I thought if I had the evergreens here in time, I might
see a little to the arrangement myself," said Mr. Franklin,
"but I am afraid I know very little about the matter. Miss
Langford, I wish you would assist us with your taste."

Beatrice and Henrietta looked at each other, and their
eyes sparkled with delight. "I should like it exceedingly,"
said the former; "I was just thinking what capabilities there
are. And Henrietta will do it beautifully."

"Then will you really be kind enough to come to-morrow,
and see what can be done?"

"Yes, we will come as soon as ever breakfast is over, and
work hard," said Queen Bee. "And we will make Alex
and Fred come too, to do the places that are out of reach."

"Thank you, thank you," said Mr. Franklin, eagerly; "I
assure you the matter was quite upon my mind, for the old
lady there, good as she is, has certainly not the best taste
in church-dressing."

"And pray, Mr. Franklin, let us have a step ladder, for
I am sure there ought to be festoons round those two columns of the chancel arch. Look, papa, do not you
think so?"

"You might put a twining wreath like the columns at Roslin chapel," said her papa, "and I should try how much I could cover the Dutch cherubs at the head of the tables of commandments."

"Oh, and don't you see," said Henrietta, "there in front of the altar is a space where I really think we might make the cross and 'i h c' in holly?"

"But could you, Henrietta?" asked Beatrice.

"O yes, I know I can; I made 'M. L.' in roses on mamma's last birthday, and set it up over the chimney-piece in the drawing-room, and I am sure we could contrive this. How appropriate it will look!"

"Ah!" said Mr. Franklin, "I have heard of such things, but I had always considered them as quite above our powers."

"They would be, without Henrietta," said Queen Bee, "but she was always excellent at wreath-weaving, and all those things that belong to choice taste and clever fingers. Only let us have plenty of the wherewithal, and we will do our work so as to amaze the parish."

"And now," said Uncle Geoffrey, "we must be walking home, my young ladies. It is getting quite dark."

It was indeed, for as they left the church the sunlight was fast fading on the horizon, and Venus was already shining forth in pure quiet beauty on the clear blue sky. Mr. Franklin walked a considerable part of the way home with them, adding to Henrietta's list by asking counsel about a damp spot in the wall of the church, and on the measures to be adopted with a refractory farmer.

By the time they reached home, evening was fast closing in; and at the sound of their entrance Mrs. Langford and Frederick both came to meet them in the hall, the former asking anxiously whether they had not been lingering in the cold and damp, inspecting the clogs to see that they were dry, and feeling if the fingers were cold. She then ordered

the two girls up stairs to dress before going into the drawing-
room with their things on, and told Henrietta to remember
that dinner would be at half-past five.

"Is mamma gone up?" asked Henrietta.

"Yes, my dear, long ago; she has been out with your
grandpapa, and is gone to rest herself."

"And how long have you been at home, Fred?" said
Queen Bee. "Why, you have performed your toilette already! Why did you not come to meet us?"

"I should have had a long spy-glass to see which way
you were gone," said Fred, in a tone which, to Henrietta's
ears, implied that he was not quite pleased, and then, following his sister up stairs, he went on to her, "I wish I had
never come in, but it was about three, and Alex and Carey
thought we might as well get a bit of something for luncheon,
and thereby they had the pleasure of seeing mamma send
her pretty dear up to change his shoes and stockings. So
there was an end of me for the day. I declare it is getting
too absurd! Do persuade mamma that I am not made of
sugar-candy."

With Uncle Geoffrey's admonitions fresh in her mind,
these complaints sounded painfully in Henrietta's ears, and
she would gladly have soothed away his irritation; but,
however convenient Judith might find the stairs for private
conferences, they did not appear to her equally appropriate,
especially when at the very moment grandpapa was coming
down from above and grandmamma up from below. Both
she and Fred therefore retreated into their mamma's room,
where they found her sitting on a low stool by the fire,
reading by its light one of the old childish books, of which
she seemed never to weary. Fred's petulance, to do him
justice, never could endure the charm of her presence, and
his brow was as bright and open as his sister's as he came
forward, hoping that she was not tired.

"Quite the contrary, thank you, my dear," said she, smiling ; "I enjoyed my walk exceedingly."

"A walk !" exclaimed Henrietta.

"A crawl, perhaps you would call it, but a delightful crawl it was with grandpapa up and down what we used to call the sun walk, by the kitchen garden wall. And now, Pussy-cat, Pussy-cat, where have you been ?"

" I've been to Sutton Leigh, with the good Queen," answered Henrietta, gaily. " I have seen everything—Sutton Leigh, and the Pleasance, and the church ! And, mamma, Mr. Franklin has asked us to go and dress the church for Christmas. Is not that what of all things is delightful ? Only think of church-decking ! What I have read and heard of, but I always thought it something too great and too happy for me ever to do."

"I hope you will be able to succeed in it," said her mamma. "What a treat it will be to see your work on Sunday."

"And you are to help, too, Fred ; you and Alexander are to come and reach the high places for us. But do tell us your adventures."

Fred had been all over the farm ; had been introduced to the whole live stock, including ferrets and the tame hedgehog ; visited the plantations, and assisted at the killing of a stoat ; cut his name out on the bark of the old pollard ; and, in short, had been supremely happy. He "was just going to see Dumpling and Vixen's puppies at Sutton Leigh, when—"

"When I caught you, my poor boy," said his mamma ; "and very cruel it was, I allow, but I thought you might have gone out again."

" I had no other thick shoes upstairs ; but really, mamma, no one thinks of minding those things."

" You should have seen him, Henrietta," said his mother ;

" his shoes looked as if he had been walking through the
river."

" Well, but so were all the others," said Fred.

" Very likely, but they are more used to it ; and, besides,
they are such sturdy fellows. I should as soon think of a
deal board catching cold. But you—if there is as much substance in you, it is all height ; and you know, Fred, you
would find it considerably more tiresome to be laid up with
a bad cold."

" I never catch cold," said Fred.

" Boys always say so," said Mrs. Frederick Langford ; " it
is a—what shall I call it ?—a puerile delusion, which their
mammas can always defeat when they choose by a formidable
list of colds and coughs ; but I won't put you in mind of
how often you have sat with your feet on the fender croaking
like an old raven, and solacing yourself with stick-liquorice
and Ivanhoe."

" You had better allow him to proceed in his pursuit of
a cold, mamma," said Henrietta, "just to see how grandmamma will nurse it."

A knock at the door here put an end to the conversation,
by announcing the arrival of Bennet, Mrs. Frederick Langford's maid ; who had come in such good time that Henrietta was, for once in her life, full dressed a whole quarter
of an hour before dinner time. Nor was her involuntary
punctuality without a reward, for the interval of waiting for
dinner, sitting round the fire, was particularly enjoyed by
Mr. and Mrs. Langford ; and Uncle Geoffrey, therefore,
always contrived to make it a leisure time ; and there was
so much merriment in talking over the walk, and discussing
the plans for the Pleasance, that Henrietta resolved never
again to miss such a pleasant reunion by her own tardiness.

Nor was the evening less agreeable. Henrietta pleased
grandmamma by getting her carpet-work out of some puzzle,

and by flying across the room to fetch the tea-chest : she
delighted grandpapa by her singing, and by finding his
spectacles for him ; she did quite a praiseworthy piece of
her own crochet purse, and laughed a great deal at the
battle that was going on between Queen Bee and Fred about
the hero of some new book. She kept her list of Uncle Geoffrey's manifold applicants on the table before her, and had
the pleasure of increasing it by two men, business unknown,
who sent to ask him to come and speak to them ; by a loud
and eager appeal from Fred and Beatrice to decide their
contest, by a question of taste on the shades of their grandmamma's carpet-work, and by her own query how to trans-
late a difficult German passage which had baffled herself,
mamma, and Fred.

However, Queen Bee's number, fifty, had not been attained, and her majesty was obliged to declare that she
meant in a week instead of a day, for which reason the cata-
logue was written out fair, to be continued.

Mrs. Frederick Langford thought herself well recompensed for the pain her resolution had cost her, by the
pleasure that Mr. and Mrs. Langford evidently took in her
son and daughter, by the brightness of her two children's
own faces, and especially when Henrietta murmured in her
sleep something about " delightful," " bright leaves and red
berries," and then, " and 'tis for my own dear papa."

And after all, in the attainment of their fondest wish,
were Henrietta and Frederick as serenely happy as she
was ?

CHAPTER VI

CHRISTMAS Eve, which was also a Saturday, dawned brightly on Henrietta, but even her eagerness for her new employment could not so far overcome her habitual dilatoriness as not to annoy her cousin, Busy Bee, even to a degree of very unnecessary fidgeting when there was any work in hand. She sat on thorns all breakfast time, devoured what her grandpapa called a sparrow's allowance, swallowed her tea scalding, and thereby gained nothing but leisure to fret at the deliberation with which Henrietta cut her bread into little square dice, and spread her butter on them as if each piece was to serve as a model for future generations.

The subject of conversation was not precisely calculated to soothe her spirits. Grandmamma was talking of giving a young party—a New-year's party on Monday week the second of January. "It would be pleasant for the young people," she thought, "if Mary did not think it would be too much for her."

Beatrice looked despairingly at her aunt, well knowing what her answer would be, that it would not be at all too much for her, that she should be very glad to see her former neighbours, and that it would be a great treat to Henrietta and Fred.

"We will have the carpet up in the dining-room," added

Mrs. Langford, "and Daniels, the carpenter, shall bring his violin, and we can get up a nice little set for a dance."

"O thank you, grandmamma," cried Henrietta eagerly, as Mrs. Langford looked at her.

"Poor innocent, you little know!" murmured Queen Bee to herself.

"That is right, Henrietta," said Mrs. Langford, "I like to see young people like young people, not above a dance now and then,—all in moderation."

"Above dancing," said grandpapa, who, perhaps, took this as a reflection on his pet, Queen Bee, "that is what you call being on the high rope, isn't it?"

Beatrice, though feeling excessively savage, could not help laughing.

"Are you on the high rope, Queenie?" asked Fred, who sat next her: "do you despise the light fantastic—?"

"I don't know: I do not mind it *much*," was all she could bring herself to say, though she could not venture to be more decidedly ungracious before her father. "Not much in itself," she added, in a lower tone, as the conversation grew louder, "it is the people, Philip Carey and all, —but hush! listen."

He did so, and heard Careys, Dittons, Evanses, &c., enumerated, and at each name Beatrice looked gloomier, but she was not observed, for her Aunt Mary had much to hear about the present state of the families, and the stream of conversation flowed away from the fête.

The meal was at last concluded, and Beatrice in great haste ordered Frederick off to Sutton Leigh, with a message to Alex to meet them at the church, and bring as much holly as he could, and his great knife. "Bring him safe," said she, "for if you fail, and prove a corbie messenger, I promise you worse than the sharpest sting of the most angry bee."

Away she ran to fetch her bonnet and shawl, while Henrietta walked up after her, saying she would just fetch her mamma's writing-case down for her, and then get ready directly. On coming down, she could not help waiting a moment before advancing to the table, to hear what was passing between her mother and uncle.

"Do you like for me to drive you down to the church to-day?" he asked.

"Thank you," she answered, raising her mild blue eyes, "I think not."

"Remember, it will be perfectly convenient, and do just what suits you," said he in a voice of kind solicitude.

"Thank you very much, Geoffrey," she replied, in an earnest tone, "but indeed I had better go for the first time to the service, especially on such a day as to-morrow, when thoughts *must* be in better order."

"I understand," said Uncle Geoffrey: and Henrietta, putting down the writing-case, retreated with downcast eyes, with a moment's perception of the higher tone of mind to which he had tried to raise her.

In the hall she found Mrs. Langford engaged in moving her precious family of plants from their night quarters near the fire to the bright sunshine near the window. Henrietta seeing her lifting heavy flower-pots, instantly sprang forward with, "O, grandmamma, let me help."

Little as Mrs. Langford was wont to allow herself to be assisted, she was gratified with the obliging offer, and Henrietta had carried the myrtle, the old-fashioned oak-leaved geranium, with its fragrant deeply-indented leaves, a grim-looking cactus, and two or three more, and was deep in the story of the orange-tree, the pip of which had been planted by Uncle Geoffrey at five years old, but which never seemed likely to grow beyond the size of a tolerable currant-bush, when Beatrice came down and beheld her with consternation

—" Henrietta! Henrietta! what are you about?" cried she, breaking full into the story. "Do make haste."

"I will come in a minute," said Henrietta, who was assisting in adjusting the prop to which the old daphne was tied.

"Don't stop for me, my dear," said Mrs. Langford: "there, don't let me be in your way."

"O, grandmamma, I like to do this very much."

"But, Henrietta," persisted the despotic Queen Bee, "we really ought to be there."

"What is all this about?" said grandmamma, not particularly well pleased. "There, go, go, my dear; I don't want any more, thank you: what are you in such a fuss for now, going out all day again?"

"Yes, grandmamma," said Beatrice, "did not you hear that Mr. Franklin asked us to dress the church for to-morrow? and we must not waste time in these short days."

"Dress the church! Well, I suppose you must have your own way, but I never heard of such things in my younger days. Young ladies are very different now!"

Beatrice drove Henrietta up stairs with a renewed "Do make haste!" and then replied in a tone of argument and irritation, "I do not see why young ladies should not like dressing churches for festivals better than dressing themselves for balls and dances!"

True as the speech was, how would Beatrice have liked to have seen her father or mother stand before her at that moment?

"Ah, well! it is all very well," said grandmamma, shaking her head, as she always did when out-argued by Beatrice, "you girls think yourselves so clever, there is no talking to you; but I think you had much better let old Martha alone: she has done it well enough before ever you were born, and such a litter as you will make! The church won't be fit to be seen to-morrow! All day in that cold damp place too! I wonder Mary could consent, Henrietta looks very delicate."

"O no, grandmamma, she is quite strong, very strong indeed."

"I am sure she is hoarse this morning," proceeded Mrs. Langford; "I shall speak to her mamma."

"O don't, pray, grandmamma; she would be so disappointed! And what would Mr. Franklin do?"

"O very well, I promise you, as he has done before," said Mrs. Langford, hastening off to the drawing-room, while her granddaughter darted up stairs to hurry Henrietta out of the house before a prohibition could arrive. It was what Henrietta had too often assisted Fred in doing to have many scruples, besides which she knew how grieved her mamma would be to be obliged to stop her, and how glad to find her safe out of reach; so she let her cousin heap on shawls, fur cuffs, and boas in a far less leisurely and discriminating manner than was usual with her.

"It would be absolute sneaking (to use an elegant word,) I suppose," said Beatrice, "to go down the back stairs."

"True," said Henrietta, "we will even take the bull by the horns."

"And trust to our heels," said Beatrice, stealthily opening the door; "the coast is clear, and I know both your mamma and my papa will not stop us if they can help it. One, two, three, and away!"

Off they flew, down the stairs, across the hall, and up the long green walk, before they ventured to stop for Henrietta to put on her gloves, and take up the boa that was dragging behind her like a huge serpent. And after all, there was no need for their flight; they might have gone openly and with clear consciences, had they but properly and submissively waited the decision of their elders. Mr. Geoffrey Langford, who did not know how ill his daughter had been behaving, would have been very sorry to interfere with the plan, and easily reconciled his mother to it, in his own cheerful pleasant way. Indeed her opposition had been entirely caused by Beatrice herself; she had not once thought of objecting when it had been first mentioned the evening before, and had not Beatrice first fidgeted and then argued, would only have regarded it as a pleasant way of occupying their morning.

"I could scold you, Miss Drone," said Beatrice when the two girls had set themselves to rights, and recovered breath; "it was all the fault of your dawdling."

"Well, perhaps it was," said Henrietta, "but you know I could not see grandmamma lifting those flower-pots without offering to help her."

"How many more times shall I have to tell you that grandmamma hates to be helped?"

"Then she was very kind to me," replied Henrietta.

"I see how it will be," said Beatrice, smiling, "you will be grandmamma's pet, and it will be a just division. I never yet could get her to let me help her in anything, she is so resolutely independent."

Queen Bee did not take into account how often her service was either grudgingly offered, or else when she came with a good will, it was also with a way, it might be better, it might be worse, but in which she was determined to have the thing done, and against which grandmamma was of course equally resolute.

"She is an amazing person!" said Henrietta, musingly. "Is she eighty yet?"

"Seventy-nine," said Beatrice; "and grandpapa eighty-two. I always say I think we should get the prize in a show of grandfathers and grandmothers, if there was one like Uncle Roger's fat cattle shows. You know she thinks

nothing of walking twice to church on a Sunday, and all
over the village besides when there is anybody ill. But
here is the Sutton Leigh path. Let me see if those boys
are to be trusted. Yes, yes, that's right! Capital!" cried
she, in high glee; "here is Birnam wood coming across the
field." And springing on one of the bars of the gate near
the top, she flourished her handkerchief chanting or singing,

> "Greet thee well, thou holly green,
> Welcome, welcome, art thou seen,
> With all thy glittering garlands bending,
> As to greet my—quick descending :"

she finished in an altered tone, as she was obliged to spring
precipitately down to avoid a fall. "It made a capital conclusion, however, though not quite what I had proposed.
Well, gentlemen," as four or five of the boys came up, each
bearing a huge holly bush—"Well, gentlemen, you are a
sight for sair een."

"With sair fingers, you mean," said Fred, "these bushes
scratch like half a dozen wild cats."

"It is in too good a cause for me to pity you," said Beatrice.

"Nor would I accept it if you would," said Fred.

His sister, however, seemed determined on bestowing it
whether he would or not,—"How your hands are bleeding!
Have you any thorns in them? Let me see, I have my
penknife."

"Stuff!" was Fred's gracious reply, as he glanced at Alex
and Carey.

"But why did you not put on your gloves?" proceeded
Henrietta.

"Gloves, nonsense!" said Fred, who never went without
them at Rocksand.

"He will take up the gauntlet presently," said Beatrice.

" By-the-bye, Alex, how many pairs of gloves have you had or lost in your life ?"

" O, I always keep a pair for Sundays and for Allonfield," said Alex.

" Jessie says she will never let me drive her again without them," said Carey, "but trust me for that : I hate them, they are such girl's things ; I tell her then she can't be driven."

Fred could not bear to hear of Carey's driving, a thing which he had not been permitted to attempt, and he hastily broke in, " You have not told the news yet."

" What news ?"

" The Euphrosyne is coming home," cried the boys with one voice. " Had we not told you ? The Euphrosyne is coming home, and Roger may be here any day !"

" That is something like news," said Queen Bee ; " I thought it would only be that the puppies could see, or that Tom's tooth was through. Grandpapa has not heard it ?"

" Papa is going up to tell him," said John. " I was going too, only Alex bagged me to carry his holly bush."

" And so the great Rogero is coming home !" said Beatrice. " How you will learn to talk sea slang ! And how happy grandmamma will be, especially if he comes in time for her great affair. Do you hear, Alex ? you must practise your steps, for grandmamma is going to give a grand party, Careys and Evanses, and all, on purpose to gratify Fred's great love of dancing."

" I love dancing ?" exclaimed Fred, in a tone of astonishment and contempt.

" Why, did you not look quite enraptured at breakfast when it was proposed ? I expected you every moment to ask the honour of my hand for the first quadrille, but I suppose you leave it for Philip Carey !"

" If it comes at all you must start me, Bee," said Alex, " for I am sure I can't dance with any one but you."

" Let me request it now," said Fred, " though why you should think I like dancing I cannot imagine ! I am sure nothing but your Majesty can make it endurable."

" There are compliments to your Majesty," cried Henrietta, laughing, " one will not or cannot dance at all without her, the other cannot find it endurable ! I long to see which is to be gratified."

" Time will show," said Beatrice ; " I shall ponder on their requests, and decide maturely, Greek against Prussian, lover of the dance against hater of the dance."

" I don't love it, I declare," exclaimed Fred.

" I don't mind it, if you dance with me," said Alex.

And Beatrice was in her glory, teasing them both, and feeling herself the object of attention to both.

Flirtation is not a pleasant word, and it is one which we are apt to think applies chiefly to the manners of girls, vain of their personal appearance, and wanting in sense or education. Beatrice would have thought herself infinitely above it ; but what else was her love of attention, her delight in playing off her two cousins against each other? Beauty, or the consciousness of beauty, has little to do with it. Henrietta, if ever the matter occurred to her, could not help knowing that she was uncommonly pretty, yet no one could be more free from any tendency to this habit. Beatrice knew equally well that she was plain, but that did not make the least difference ; if any, it was rather on the side of vanity, in being able without a handsome face, so to attract and engross her cousins. It was amusing, gratifying, flattering, to feel her power to play them off, and irritate the little feelings of jealousy which she had detected ; and thoughtless as to the right or wrong, she pursued her course.

G

On reaching the church they found that, as was usual
with her, she had brought them before any one was ready ;
the doors were locked, and they had to wait while Carey
and John went to old Martha's to fetch the key.   In a few
minutes more Mr. Franklin arrived, well pleased to see
them ready to fulfil their promise; the west door was
opened, and disclosed a huge heap of holly laid up under
the tower, ready for use.

The first thing the boys did was to go up into the belfry,
and out on the top of the tower, and Busy Bee had a great
mind to follow them ; but she thought it would not be fair
to Mr. Franklin, and the wide field upon which she had to
work began to alarm her imagination.

Before the boys came down again, she had settled the
plan of operations with Henrietta and Mr. Franklin, dragged
her holly bushes into the aisle, and brought out her knife
and string.   They came down declaring that they could be of
no use, and they should go away, and Beatrice made no objection to the departure of Carey and Johnny; who, as she
justly observed, would be only in the way ; but she insisted
on keeping Fred and Alex.

" Look at all those pillars !   How are we ever to twine
them by ourselves ?   Look at all those great bushes !   How
are we to lift them ?   No, no, indeed, we cannot spare you,
Fred.   We must have some stronger hands to help us, and
you have such a good eye for this sort of thing."

Had Alexander gone, Fred would have found some
excuse for following him, rather than he should leave
him with young ladies, doing young ladies' work ; but, as
Beatrice well knew, Alex would never withdraw his assistance when she asked Fred's, and she felt secure of them
both.

" There, Alex, settle that ladder by the screen, please.
Now will you see if there is anything to tie a piece of string

to ? for it is of no use to make a festoon if we cannot fasten it."

" I can't see anything."

" Here, give me your hand, and I'll look." Up tripped the little Bee, just holding by his hand. " Yes, to be sure there is ! Here is a great rough nail sticking out. Is it firm ? Yes, capitally. Now, Alex, make a sailor's knot round it. Help me down first though—thank you. Fred, will you trim that branch into something like shape ? You see how I mean. We must have a long drooping wreath of holly and ivy, to blend with the screen. How tough this ivy is ! Thank you—that's it. Well, Mr. Franklin, I hope we shall get on in time."

Mr. Franklin was sure of it ; and seeing all actively employed, and himself of little use, he took his leave for the present, hoping that the Misses Langford would not tire themselves.

Angels' work is church decoration—work fit for angels, that is to say ; but how pure should be the hands and hearts engaged in it ! Its greatness makes it solemn and awful. It is work immediately for the glory of GOD ; it is work like that of the children who strewed the palm-branches before the steps of the Redeemer ! Who can frame in imagination a more favoured and delightful occupation, than that of the four young creatures who were, in very deed, greeting the coming of their LORD with those bright glistening wreaths with which they were adorning His sanctuary ?

Angels' work ! but the angels veil their faces and tremble ; and we upon earth have still greater cause to tremble and bow down in awful reverence, when we are allowed to approach so near His shrine. And was that spirit of holy fear—that sole desire for His glory—the chief thought with these young people ?

Not that there was what even a severe judge could call

irreverence in word or deed; there was no idle laughter, and the conversation was in a tone and a style which showed that they were all well trained in respect for the sanctity of the place. Even in all the helping up and down ladders and steps, in the reaching over for branches, in all the little mishaps and adventures that befell them, their behaviour was outwardly perfectly what it ought to have been : and that is no small praise for four young people, under seventeen, left in church alone together for so many hours.

But still Beatrice's great aim was, unconsciously perhaps, to keep the two boys entirely devoted to herself, and to exert her power. Wonderful power it was in reality, which kept them interested in employment so little accordant with their nature; kept them amused without irreverence, and doing good service all the time. But it was a power of which she greatly enjoyed the exercise, and which did nothing to lessen the rivalry between them. As to Henrietta, she was sitting apart on a hassock, very happy, and very busy in arranging the Monogram and wreath which she had yesterday proposed. She was almost forgotten by the other three—certainly neglected—but she did not feel it so ; she had rather be quiet, for she could not work and talk like Queen Bee ; and she liked to think over the numerous verses and hymns that her employment brought to her mind. Uncle Geoffrey's conversation dwelt upon her too ; she began to realise his meaning, and she was especially anxious to fulfil his desire, by entreating Fred to beware of temptations to disobedience. Opportunities for private interviews were, however, very rare at Knight Sutton, and she had been looking forward to having him all to herself here, when he must wish to visit his father's grave with her. She was vexed for a moment that his first attention was not given to it; but she knew that his first thought was there, and boys never showed what was uppermost in their minds to any one but their sisters. She should have him by-and-by, and the present was full of tranquil enjoyment.

If Henrietta had been free from blame in coming to Knight Sutton at all, or in her way of leaving the house this morning, there would have been little or no drawback to our pleasure in contemplating her.

"Is it possible!" exclaimed Queen Bee, as the last reverberation of the single stroke of the deep-toned clock fell quivering on her ear. "I thought you would have given us at least eleven more."

"What a quantity remains to be done!" sighed Henrietta, laying down the wreath which she had just completed. "Your work looks beautiful, Queenie, but how shall we ever finish?"

"A short winter's day, too!" said Beatrice. "One thing is certain—that we can't go home to luncheon."

"What will grandmamma think of that?" said Henrietta doubtfully. "Will she like it?"

Beatrice could have answered, "Not at all;" but she said, "O never mind, it can't be helped; we should be late even if we were to set off now, and besides we might be caught and stopped."

"Oh, that would be worse than anything," said Henrietta, quite convinced.

"So you mean to starve," said Alex.

"See what slaves men are to creature comforts," said Beatrice; "what do you say, Henrietta?"

"I had much rather stay here," said Henrietta; "I want nothing."

"Much better fun to go without," said Fred, who had not often enough missed a regular meal not to think doing so an honour and a joke.

"I'll tell you what will do best of all!" cried Queen Bee. "You go to Dame Reid's, and buy us sixpennyworth of the gingerbread papa calls the extreme of luxury, and we will eat it on the old men's bench in the porch."

"Oho! her Majesty is descending to creature comforts," said Alex. "I thought she would soon come down to other mortals."

"Only to gratify her famishing subjects," said Beatrice, "you disloyal vassal, you! Fred is worth a dozen of you. Come, make haste. She is sure to have a fresh stock, for she always has a great baking when Mr. Geoffrey is coming."

"For his private eating?" said Fred.

"He likes it pretty well, certainly; and he seldom goes through the village without making considerable purchases for the benefit of the children in his path, who take care to be not a few. I found little Jenny Woods made small distinction between Mr. Geoffrey and Mr. Ginger. But come, Alex, why are not you off?"

"Because I don't happen to have a sixpence," said Alex, with an honest openness, overcoming his desire to add "in my pocket." It cost him an effort; for at school, where each slight advantage was noted, and comparisons perpetually made, Fred's superior wealth and larger allowance had secured him the adherence of some; and though he either knew it not, or despised such mammon worship, his rival was sufficiently awake to it to be uncomfortable in acknowledging his poverty.

"Every one is poor at the end of the half," said Fred, tossing up his purse and catching it again, so as to demonstrate its lightness. "Here is a sixpence, though, at her Majesty's service."

"And do you think she would take your last sixpence, you honour to loyalty?" said Beatrice, feeling in her pocket. "We are not fallen quite so low. But alas! the royal exchequer is, as I now remember, locked up in my desk at home."

"And my purse is in my workbox," said Henrietta.

"So, Fred, I must be beholden to you for the present," said Beatrice, "if it won't quite break you down."

"There are more where that came from," said Fred, with a careless air. "Come along, Alex."

Away they went. "That is unlucky," soliloquised Queen Bee: "if I could have sent Alex alone, it would have been all right, and he would have come back again; but now one will carry away the other, and we shall see them no more."

"No, no, that would be rather too bad," said Henrietta. "I am sure Fred will behave better."

"Mark what I say," said Beatrice. "I know how it will be; a dog or a gun is what a boy cannot for a moment withstand, and if we see them again 'twill be a nine days' wonder. But come, we must to the work; I want to look at your wreath."

She did not, however, work quite as cheerily as before, and lost much time in running backwards and forwards to peep out at the door, and in protesting that she was neither surprised nor annoyed at the faithlessness of her envoys. At last a droll little frightened knock was heard at the door. Beatrice went to open it, and a whitey-brown paper parcel was held out to her by a boy in a green canvas round frock, and a pair of round, hard, red, solid-looking cheeks; no other than Dame Reid's grandson.

"Thank you," said she. "Did Master Alexander give you this?"

"Ay."

"Thank you, that's right!" and away he went.

"You see," said Queen Bee, holding up the parcel to Henrietta, who came out to the porch, "Let us look. O, they have vouchsafed a note!" and she took out a crumpled envelope, directed in Aunt Mary's handwriting to Fred, on the back of which Alex had written, " Dear B., we beg pardon, but Carey and Dick are going up to Andrews's about his terrier.—A. L." " Very cool, certainly !" said Beatrice, laughing, but still with a little pique, " What a life I will lead them !"

" Well, you were a true prophet," said Henrietta, " and after all it does not much signify. They have done all the work that is out of reach ; but still I thought Fred would have behaved better."

" You have yet to learn the difference between Fred with you or with me, and Fred with his own congeners," said Beatrice ; " you don't know half the phases of boy nature."

Henrietta sighed ; for Fred had certainly not been quite what she expected him to-day. Not because he had appeared to forget her, for that was nothing—that was only appearance, and her love was too healthy and true even to feel it neglect ; but he had forgotten his father's grave. He was now neglecting the church ; and far from its consoling her to hear that it was the way with all boys when they came together, it gave her one moment's doubt whether they were not happier, when they were all in all to each other at Rocksand.

It was but for one instant that she felt this impression ; the next it had passed away, and she was sharing the ginger-bread with her cousin, and smiling at the great admiration in which it seemed to be held by the natives of Knight Sutton. They took a short walk up and down the church-yard while eating it, and then returned to their occupation, well pleased, on re-entering, to see how much show they had made already. They worked together very happily ; indeed, now that all thought of her squires was quite out of her head, Beatrice worked much more in earnest and in the right kind of frame ; something more of the true spirit of this service came over her, and she really possessed some of that temper of devotion which she fancied had been with her the whole day.

It was a beautiful thing when Henrietta raised her face, as she was kneeling by the font, and her clear sweet voice began at first in a low, timid note, but gradually growing fuller and stronger—

> " Hark! the herald angels sing
> Glory to the new-born King.
> Peace on earth, and mercy mild,
> GOD and sinners reconciled."

Beatrice took up the strain at the first line, and sweetly did their tones echo through the building; while their hearts swelled with delight and thankfulness for the "good tidings of great joy." Another and another Christmas hymn was raised, and never were carols sung by happier voices; and the decorations proceeded all the better and more suitably beneath their influence. They scarcely knew how time passed away, till Henrietta, turning round, was amazed to see Uncle Geoffrey standing just within the door watching them.

"Beautiful!" said he, as she suddenly ceased, in some confusion; "your work is beautiful! I came here prepared to scold you a little, but I don't think I can. Who made that wreath and Monogram?"

"She did, of course, papa," said Beatrice, pointing to her cousin. "Who else could?"

"It is a very successful arrangement," said Uncle Geoffrey, moving about to find the spot for obtaining the best view. "It is an arrangement to suggest so much."

Henrietta came to the place where he stood, and for the first time perceived the full effect of her work. It was placed in front of the altar, the dark crimson covering of which re-lieved the shining leaves and scarlet berries of the holly. The three letters, i h c, were in the centre, formed of small sprays fastened in the required shape; and around them was a large circle of holly, plaited and twined together, the many-pointed leaves standing out in every direction in their peculiar stiff gracefulness.

"I see it now!" said she, in a low voice full of awe. "Uncle, I did not mean to make it so!"

"How?" he asked.

"It is like Good Friday!" said she, as the resemblance to the crown of thorns struck her more and more strongly.

"Well, why not, my dear?" said her uncle, as she shrunk closer to him in a sort of alarm. "Would Christmas be worth observing if it were not for Good Friday?"

"Yes, it is right, uncle; but somehow it is melancholy."

"Where are those verses that say—let me see—

'And still Thy Church's faith
Shall link in all her prayer and praise,
Thy glory with Thy death.'

So you see, Henrietta, you have been guided to do quite right."

Henrietta gave a little sigh, but did not answer: and Beatrice said, "It is a very odd thing, whenever any work of art—or, what shall I call it?—is well done, it is apt to have so much more in it than the author intended. It is so in poetry, painting, and everything else."

"There is, perhaps, more meaning than we understand, when we talk of the spirit in which a thing is done," said her father: "but have you much more to do? Those columns look very well."

"O, are you come to help us, papa?"

"I came chiefly because grandmamma was a good deal concerned at your not coming home to luncheon. You must not be out the whole morning again just at present. I have some sandwiches in my pocket for you."

Beatrice explained how they had been fed, and her papa said, "Very well, we will find some one who will be glad of them; but mind, do not make her think you unsociable again. Do you hear and heed?"

It was that sort of tone which, while perfectly kind and gentle, shows that it belongs to a man who will be obeyed, and ready compliance was promised. He proceeded to give his very valuable aid at once in taste and execution, the adornment prospered greatly, and when Mr. Franklin came in, his surprise and delight were excited by the beauty which had grown up in his absence. The long, drooping, massive wreaths of evergreen at the east end, centring in the crown and letters; the spiral festoons round the pillars; the sprays in every niche; the tower of holly over the font—all were more beautiful both together and singly, than he had even imagined, and he was profuse in admiration and thanks.

The work was done; and the two Misses Langford, after one well-satisfied survey from the door, bent their steps homeward, looking forward to the pleasure with which grandpapa and Aunt Mary would see it to-morrow. As they went in the deepening twilight, the whole village seemed vocal: children's voices, shrill and tuneless near, but softened by distance, were ringing out here, there, and everywhere with—

"As shepherds watched their flocks by night."

And again as they walked on, the sound from another band of little voices was brought on the still frosty wind—

"Glad tidings of great joy I bring
To you and all mankind."

Imperfect rhymes, bad voices, no time observed; but how joyous,—how really Christmas-like—how well it suited the soft half-light, the last pale shine of sunset lingering in the south-west! the large solemn stars that one by one appeared! How Uncle Geoffrey caught up the lines and sang them over to himself! How light and free Beatrice walked!—and how the quiet happy tears would rise in Henrietta's eyes!

The singing in the drawing-room that evening, far superior as it was, with Henrietta, Beatrice, Frederick, and even Aunt Mary's beautiful voice, was not equal in enjoyment to that. Was it because Beatrice was teasing Fred all the time about his defection? The church singers came up to the Hall, and the drawing-room door was set open for the party to listen to them; grandpapa and Uncle Geoffrey went out to have a talk with them, and so passed the space till tea-time; to say nothing of the many little troops of young small voices outside the windows, to whom Mrs. Langford's plum buns, and Mr. Geoffrey's sixpences, were a very enjoyable part of the Christmas festivities.

CHAPTER VII.

THE double feast of Sunday and Christmas Day dawned upon Henrietta with many anxieties for her mother, to whom the first going to church must be so great a trial. Would that she could, as of old, be at her side the whole day ! but this privilege, unrecked of at Rocksand, was no longer hers. She had to walk to church with grandmamma and the rest of the party, while Mrs. Frederick Langford was driven in the open carriage by old Mr. Langford, and she was obliged to comfort herself with recollecting that no companion ever suited her better than grandpapa. It was a sight to be remembered when she came into church, leaning upon his arm, her sweet expression of peace and resignation, making her even more lovely than when last she entered there—her face in all its early bloom of youthful beauty, and radiant with innocent happiness.

But Henrietta knew not how to appreciate that "peace which passeth all understanding;" and all that she saw was the glistening of tears in her eyes, and the heaving of her bosom, as she knelt down in her place; and she thought that if she had calculated all that she would have to go through, and all her own anxieties for her, she should never have urged their removal. She viewed it however as a matter of expediency rather than of duty, and her feelings were not in the only right and wholesome channel. As on the former occasion, Knight Sutton Church seemed to her more full of her father's presence than of any other, so now, throughout the service, she was chiefly occupied with watching her mother; and entirely by the force of her own imagination, she contrived to work herself into a state of nervous apprehension, only equalled by her mamma's own anxieties for Fred.

Neither she nor any of her young cousins were yet confirmed, so they all left the church together. What would she not have given to be able to talk her fears over with either Frederick or Beatrice, and be assured by them that her mamma had borne it very well, and would not suffer from it. But though neither of them was indifferent or unfeeling, there was not much likelihood of sympathy from them just at present. Beatrice had always been sure that Aunt Mary would behave like an angel; and when Fred saw that his mother looked tranquil, and showed no symptoms of agitation, he dismissed anxiety from his mind, and never even guessed at his sister's alarms.

Nor in reality had he many thoughts for his sister of any kind; for he was, as usual, engrossed with Queen Bee, criticising the decorations which had been completed in his absence, and, together with Alex, replying to the scolding with which she visited their desertion.

Nothing could have been more eminently successful than the decorations, which looked to still greater advantage in the brightness of the morning sun than in the dimness of the evening twilight; and many were the compliments which the two young ladies received upon their handiwork. The old women had "had never seen nothing like it,"—the school children whispered to each other, "How pretty!" Uncle Geoffrey and Mr. Franklin admired even more than before; grandpapa and Aunt Mary were delighted; grandmamma herself allowed it was much better than she had expected; and Jessie Carey, by way of climax, said it "was like magic."

It was a very different Sunday from those to which Henrietta had been accustomed, in the complete quiet and retirement of Rocksand. The Hall was so far from the church, that there was but just time to get back in time for Evening Service. After which, according to a practice of which she had often heard her mamma speak with many agreeable reminiscences, the Langford family almost always went in a body on a progress to the farmyard, to visit the fatting oxen and see the cows milked.

Mrs. Roger Langford was at home with little Tom, and Mrs. Frederick Langford was glad to seek the tranquillity and repose of her own apartment; but all the rest went in procession, greatly to the amusement of Fred and Henrietta, to the large barn-like building, where a narrow path led them along the front of the stalls of the gentle-looking sweet-breathed cows, and the huge white-horned oxen.

Uncle Roger (as always happened) monopolized his brother, and kept him estimating the weight of the great Devon ox, which was next for execution. Grandmamma was escorting Charlie and Arthur (whom their grandfather was wont to call "penultimus and antepenultimus,") helping them to feed the cows with turnips, and guarding them from going behind their heels. Henrietta was extremely happy, for grandpapa himself was doing the honours for her, and instructing her in the difference between a Guernsey cow and a short-horn; and so was Alexander, for he had Queen Bee all to himself in a remote corner of the cow-house, rubbing old spotted Nancy's curly brow, catching at her polished black-tipped horn, and listening to his hopes and fears for the next half-year. Not so Frederick, as he stood at the door with Jessie Carey, who, having no love for the cow-house, especially when in her best silk, though always ready to take care of the children there, was very glad to secure a companion outside, especially one so handsome, so much more polished than any of her cousins, and so well able to reply to her small talk. Little did she guess how far off he wished her, or how he longed to be listening to his uncles, talking to Beatrice, sticking holly into the cows' halters with John and Richard, scrambling into the hay-loft with Carey and William—anywhere, rather than be liable to the imputation of being too fine a gentleman to enter a cow-house.

This accusation never entered the head of any one but himself; but still an attack was in store for him. After a few words to Martin the cowman, and paying their respects to the pigs, the party left the 'farm-yard, and the inhabitants of Sutton Leigh took the path to their own abode, while Beatrice turned round to her cousin, saying, "Well, Fred, I congratulate you on your politeness! How well you endured being victimised!"

"I victimised! How do you know I was not enchanted?"

"Nay, you can't deceive me while you have a transparent face. Trust me for finding out whether you are bored or not. Besides, I would not pay so bad a compliment to your taste as to think otherwise."

"How do you know I was not exercising the taste of Rubens himself? I was actually admiring you all, and thinking how like it all was to that great print from one of his pictures; the building with its dark gloomy roof, and open sides, the twilight, the solitary dispersed snow-flakes, the haze of dust, the sleek cattle, and their long white horns."

"Quite poetical," said Queen Bee, in a short, dry, satirical manner. "How charmed Jessie must have been!"

"Why?" said Fred, rather provoked.

"Such masterly eyes are not common among our young gentlemen. You will be quite her phœnix; and how much

'Thomson's Seasons' you will have to hear! I dare say you have had it already—

> 'Now, shepherds, to your helpless charge be kind!'"

"Well, very good advice, too," said Fred.

"I hate and detest Thomson," said Beatrice; "above all, for travestying Ruth into 'the lovely young Lavinia;' so whenever Jessie treated me to any of her quotations, I criticised him without mercy, and at last I said, by great good luck, that the only use of him was to serve as an imposition for young ladies at second-rate boarding schools. It was a capital hit, for Alex found out that it was the way she learnt so much of him, and since that time I have heard no more of 'Jemmy Thomson! Jemmy Thomson, O!'"

The laughter which followed this speech had a tone in it, which, reaching Mr. Geoffrey Langford, who was walking a little in front with his mother, made him suspect that the young people were getting into such spirits as were not quite Sunday-like; and, turning round, he asked them some trifling question, which made him a party to the conversation, and brought it back to a quieter, though not less merry tone.

Dinner was at five, and Henrietta was dressed so late that Queen Bee had to come up to summon her, and bring her down after every one was in the dining-room—an entrée all the more formidable, because Mr. Franklin was dining there, as well as Uncle Roger and Alexander.

Thanks in some degree to her own dawdling, she had been in a hurry the whole day, and she longed for a quiet evening; but here it seemed to her, as with the best intentions it usually is, in a large party, that, but for the laying aside of needlework, of secular books and secular music, it might as well have been any other day of the week.

Her mamma was very tired, and went to bed before tea,

H

the gentlemen had a long talk over the fire, the boys and Beatrice laughed and talked, and she helped her grandmamma to hand about the tea, answering her questions about her mother's health and habits, and heard a good deal that interested her, but still she could not feel as if it were Sunday. At Rocksand she used to sit for many a pleasant hour, either in the darkening summer twilight, or the bright red light of the winter fire, repeating or singing hymns, and enjoying the most delightful talks that the whole week had to offer, and now she greatly missed the conversation that would have "set this strange week to rights in her head," as she said to herself.

She thought over it a good deal whilst Bennet was brushing her hair at night, feeling as if it had been a week-day, and as if it would be as difficult to begin a new fresh week on Monday morning, as it would a new day after sitting up a whole night. How far this was occasioned by Knight Sutton habits, and how far it was her own fault, was not what she asked herself, though she sat up for a long time musing on the change in her way of life, and scarcely able to believe that it was only last Sunday that she had been sitting with her mother over their fire at Rocksand. Enough had happened for a whole month. Her darling project was fulfilled; the airy castle of former days had become a substance, and she was inhabiting it: and was she really so very much happier? There she went into a reverie—but musing is not meditating, nor vague dreamings wholesome reflections; she went on sitting there, chiefly for want of energy to move, till the fire burnt low, the clock struck twelve, and Mrs. Frederick Langford exclaimed in a sleepy voice, "My dear, are you going to sleep there?"

CHAPTER VIII

BREAKFAST was nearly over on Monday morning, when a whole party of the Sutton Leigh boys entered with the intelligence that the great pond in Knight's Portion was quite frozen over, and that skating might begin without loss of time.

"You are coming, are you not, Bee?" said Alex, leaning over the back of her chair.

"O yes," said she, nearly whispering, "only take care. It is taboo there,"—and she made a sign with her head towards Mrs. Langford, "and don't frighten Aunt Mary about Fred. O it is too late, Carey's doing the deed as fast as he can."

Carey was asking Fred whether he had ever skated, or could skate, and Fred was giving an account of his exploits in that line at school, hoping it might prove to his mother that he might be trusted to take care of himself since he had dared the danger before. In vain: the alarmed expression had come over her face, as she asked Alexander whether his father had looked at the ice.

"No," said Alex, "but it is perfectly safe. I tried it this morning, and it is as firm as this marble chimney-piece."

"He is pretty well to be trusted," said his grandfather, "more especially as it would be difficult to get drowned there."

"I would give a shilling to any one who could drown himself there," said Alex.

"The travelling man did," exclaimed at once Carey, John, and Richard.

"Don't they come in just like the Greek chorus?" said Beatrice, in a whisper to Fred, who gave a little laugh, but was too anxious to attend to her.

"I thought he was drowned in the river," said Alex.

"No, it was in the deep pool under the weeping willow, where the duckweed grows so rank in summer," said Carey.

Uncle Geoffrey laughed. "I am sorry to interfere with your romantic embellishments, Carey, or with the credit of your beloved pond, since you are determined not to leave it behindhand with its neighbours."

"I always thought it was there," said the boy.

"And thought wrong; the poor man was found in the river two miles off."

"I always heard it was at Knight's Pool," repeated Carey.

"I do not know what you may have heard," said Uncle Geoffrey; "but as it happened a good while before you were born, I think you had better not argue the point."

"Grandpapa," persisted Carey, "was it not in Knight's Pool?"

"Certainly not," was the answer drily given.

"Well," continued Carey, "I am sure you might drown yourself there."

"Rather than own yourself mistaken," said Uncle Geoffrey.

"Carey, Carey, I hate contradiction," said grandmamma, rising and rustling past where he stood with a most absurd, dogged, unconvinced face. "Take your arm off the mantelpiece, let that china cup alone, and stand like a gentleman —do!"

" All in vain !" said Beatrice. " To the end of his life he will maintain that Knight's Pool drowned the travelling man !"

" Well, never mind," said John, impatiently, " are we coming to skate this morning, or are we not ?"

" I really wish," said Aunt Mary, as if she could not help it, " without distrusting either old Knight's Pool or your judgment, Alexander, that you would ask some one to look at it."

" I should like just to run down and see the fun," said Uncle Geoffrey, thus setting all parties at rest for the moment. The two girls ran joyfully up to put on their bonnets, as Henrietta wished to see, Beatrice to join in, the sport. At that instant Mrs. Langford asked her son Geoffrey to remove some obstacle which hindered the comfortable shutting of the door, and though a servant might just as well have done it, he readily complied, according to his constant habit of making all else give way to her, replying to the discomfited looks of the boys, " I shall be ready by the time the young ladies come down."

So he was, long before Henrietta was ready, and just as she and Beatrice appeared on the stairs, Atkins was carrying across the hall what the boys looked at with glances of dismay, namely, the post-bag. Knight Sutton, being small and remote, did not possess a post-office, but a messenger came from Allonfield for the letters on every day except Sunday, and returned again in the space of an hour. A very inconvenient arrangement, as every one had said for the last twenty years, and might probably say for twenty years more.

As usual, more than half the contents were for G. Langford, Esq., and Fred's face grew longer and longer as he saw the closely-written business-like sheets.

" Fred, my poor fellow," said his uncle, looking up, " I

am sorry for you, but one or two must be answered by this day's post. I will not be longer than I can help."

" Then do let us come on," exclaimed the chorus.

" Come, Queenie," added Alex.

She delayed, however, saying, " Can I do any good, papa ?"

" Thank you, let me see. I do not like to stop you, but it would save time if you could just copy a letter."

" O thank you, pray let me," said Beatrice delighted. " Go on, Henrietta, I shall soon come."

Henrietta would have waited, but she saw a chance of speaking to her brother, which she did not like to lose.

Her mother had taken advantage of the various conversations going on in the hall, to draw her son aside, saying, " Freddy, I believe you think me very troublesome, but do let me entreat of you not to venture on the ice till one of your uncles has said it is safe."

" Uncle Roger trusts Alex," said Fred.

" Yes, but he lets all those boys take their chance, and a number of you together are likely to be careless, and I know there used to be dangerous places in that pond. I will not detain you, my dear," added she, as the others were preparing to start, " only I beg you will not attempt to skate till your uncle comes."

" Very well," said Frederick, in a tone of as much annoyance as ever he showed his mother, and with little suspicion how much it cost her not to set her mind at rest by exacting a promise from him. This she had resolutely forborne to do in cases like the present, from his earliest days, and she had her reward in the implicit reliance she could place on his word when once given. And now sighing that it had not been voluntarily offered, she went to her sofa, to struggle and reason in vain with her fears, and start at each approaching step, lest it should bring the tidings of some fatal accident, all the time blaming herself for the entreaties which might as she dreaded, place him in peril of disobedience.

In a few moments Mr. Geoffrey Langford was sitting in the great red leathern chair in the study, writing as fast as his fingers would move, apparently without a moment for thought, though he might have said, like the great painter, that what seemed the work of half an hour, was in fact the labour of years. His daughter, her bonnet by her side, sat opposite to him, writing with almost equal rapidity, and supremely happy, for to the credit of our little Queen Bee let it be spoken, that no talk with Henrietta, no walk with grandpapa, no new exciting tale, no, not even a flirtation with Fred and Alex, one, or both, was equal in her estimation to the pleasure and honour of helping papa, even though it was copying a dry legal opinion, instead of gliding about on the smooth hard ice, in the bright winter morning's sunshine.

The two pens maintained a duet of diligent scratching for some twenty or five and twenty minutes without intermission, but at last Beatrice looked up, and, without speaking, held up her sheet.

"Already? Thank you, my little clerk, I could think it was mamma. Now then, off to the skating. My compliments to Fred, and tell him I feel for him, and will not keep him waiting longer than I can avoid;" and muttering a resumption of his last sentence, on went the lawyer's indefatigable pen; and away flew the merry little Busy Bee, bounding off with her droll, tripping, elastic, short-stepped run, which suited so well with her little alert figure, and her dress, a small plain black velvet bonnet, a tight black velvet "jacket," as she called it, and a brown silk dress, with narrow yellow stripes, (chosen chiefly in joke, because it was the colour of a bee,) not a bit of superfluous shawl, boa, or ribbon about her, but all close and compact, fit for the diversion which she was eager to enjoy. The only girl among so many boys, she had learnt to share in many of their sports, and one of the prime favourites was skating, a diversion which owes as much of its charm to the caprices of its patron Jack Frost, as to the degree of skill which it requires.

She arrived at the stile leading to "Knight's Portion," as it was called, and a very barren portion must the poor Knight have possessed if it was all his property. It was a sloping chalky field, or rather corner of a down, covered with very short grass and thistles, which defied all the attacks of Uncle Roger and his sheep. On one side was a sort of precipice, where the chalk had been dug away, and a rather extensive old chalk pit formed a tolerable pond, by the assistance of the ditch at the foot of the hedge. On the glassy surface already marked by many a sharply traced circular line, the Sutton Leigh boys were careering, the younger ones with those extraordinary bends, twists, and contortions to which the unskilful are driven in order to preserve their balance. Frederick and Henrietta stood on the brink, neither of them looking particularly cheerful; but both turned gladly at the sight of the Busy Bee, and came to meet her with eager inquiries for her papa.

She was a very welcome sight to both, especially Henrietta, who had from the first felt almost out of place alone with all those boys, and who hoped that she would be some comfort to poor Fred, who had been entertaining her with every variety of grumbling for the last half hour, and perversely refusing to walk out of sight of the forbidden pleasure, or to talk of anything else. Such a conversation as she was wishing for, was impossible, whilst he was constantly calling out to the others, and exclaiming at their adventures, and in the intervals lamenting his own hard fate,

scolding her for her slowness in dressing, which had occasioned the delay, and magnifying the loss of his pleasure,
perhaps in a sort of secret hope that the temptation would
so far increase as to form in his eyes an excuse for yielding
to it. Seldom had he shown himself so unamiable towards
her, and with great relief and satisfaction she beheld her
cousin, descending the steep slippery path from the height
above, and while the cloud began to lighten on his brow,
she thought to herself, "It will be all right now, he is always
happy with Busy Bee!"

So he might have been had Beatrice been sufficiently un-
selfish for once to use her influence in the right direction,
and surrender an amusement for the sake of another; but
to give up or defer such a pleasure as skating with Alex
never entered her mind, though a moment's reflection might
have shown her how much more annoying the privation
would be rendered by the sight of a girl fearlessly enjoying
the sport from which he was debarred. It would, perhaps,
be judging too hardly to reckon against her as a fault that
her grandmamma could not bear to hear of anything so
"boyish," and had long ago entreated her to be more like a
young lady. There was no positive order in this case, and
her papa and mamma did not object. So she eagerly answered Alexander's summons, fastened on her skates, and
soon was gliding merrily on the surface of the Knight's Pool,
while her cousins watched her dexterity with surprise and
interest; but soon Fred once more grew gloomy, sighed,
groaned, looked at his watch, and recommenced his complaints. At first she had occupation enough in attending to
her own security to bestow any attention on other things,
but in less than a quarter of an hour, she began to feel at
her ease, and her spirits rising to the pitch where consideration is lost, she "could not help," in her own phrase,
laughing at the disconsolate Fred.

"How wobegone he looks !" said she, as she whisked past, "but never mind, Fred, the post must go some time or other."

"It must be gone," said Fred. "I am sure we have been here above an hour !"

"Henrietta looks blue with cold, like an old hen obliged to follow her ducklings to the water !" observed Beatrice, again gliding near, and in the midst of her next circular sweep she chanted—

> "Although their feet are pointed, and my feet are round,
> Pray, is that any reason why I should be drowned ?"

It was a great aggravation of Fred's calamities to be obliged to laugh, nor were matters mended by the sight of the party now advancing from the house, Jessie Carey, with three of the lesser boys.

"What news of Uncle Geoffrey ?"

"I did not see him," said Jessie : "I think he was in the study, Uncle Roger went to him there."

"No hope then !" muttered the unfortunate Fred.

"Can't you skate, Fred ?" asked little Arthur with a certain most provoking face of wonder and curiosity.

"Presently," said Fred.

"He must not," cried Richard, in a tone which Fred thought malicious, though it was only rude.

"Must not ?" and Arthur looked up in amazement to the boy so much taller than his three brothers, creatures in his eyes privileged to do what they pleased.

"His mamma won't let him," was Dick's polite answer. Fred could have knocked him down with the greatest satisfaction, but in the first place he was out of reach, in the second, the young ladies were present, in the third he was a little boy, and a stupid one, and Fred had temper enough left to see that there would be nothing gained by quarrelling with him, so contenting himself with a secret but most ardent wish that he had him as his fag at school, he turned to Jessie, and asked her what she thought of the weather, if the white frost would bring rain, &c. &c.

Jessie thought the morning too bright not to be doubtful, and the hoar-frost was so very thick and white that it was not likely to continue much longer.

"How beautiful these delicate white crests are to every thorn in the hedge!" said Henrietta; "and look, these pieces of chalk are almost cased in glass."

"O I do love such a sight!" said Jessie. "Here is a beautiful bit of stick crusted over."

"It is a perfect little Giant's Causeway," said Henrietta; "do look at these lovely little columns, Fred."

"Ah!" said Jessie,

> "Myriads of little salts, or hook'd or shaped
> Like double wedges.—"

She thought Beatrice safe out of hearing, but that very moment by she came, borne swiftly along, and catching the cadence of that one line, looked archly at Fred, and shaped with her lips rather than uttered—

"O Jemmy Thomson! Jemmy Thomson, O!"

It filled up the measure. That Beatrice, Alexander, and Chorus should be making him a laughing-stock, and him pinned to Miss Carey's side, was more than he could endure. He had made up his mind that Uncle Geoffrey was not coming at all, his last feeble hold of patience and obedience gave way, and he exclaimed, "Well, I shan't wait any longer, it is not of the least use."

"O, Fred, consider!" said his sister.

"That's right, Freddy," shouted Carey, "he'll not come now, I'll answer for it."

"You know he promised he would," pleaded Henrietta.

"Uncle Roger has got hold of him, and he is as bad as the old man of the sea," said Fred, "the post has been gone this half hour, and I shall not wait any longer."

"Think of mamma."

"How can you talk such nonsense, Henrietta?" exclaimed Fred impatiently, "do you think that I am so awfully heavy that the ice that bears them must needs break with me?"

"I do not suppose there is any danger," said Henrietta, "but for the sake of poor mamma's entreaties!"

"Do you think I am going to be kept in leading strings all the rest of my life?" said Fred, obliged to work himself into a passion in order to silence his sister and his conscience. "I have submitted to such absurd nonsense a great deal too long already, I will not be made a fool of in the sight of everybody; so here goes!"

And breaking away from her detaining arm, he ran down to the verge of the pond, and claimed the skates which he had lent to John. Henrietta turned away, her eyes full of tears.

"Never mind, Henrietta," shouted the good-natured Alexander, "I'll engage to fish him out if he goes in."

"It is as likely I may fish you out, Mr. Alex," returned Fred, slightly affronted.

"Or more likely still there will be no fishing in the case," said the naughty little siren, who felt all the time a secret satisfaction in the consciousness that it was she who had made the temptation irresistible, then adding, to pacify Henrietta and her own feelings of compunction, "Aunt Mary must be satisfied when she hears with what exemplary patience he waited till papa was past hope, and the pond past fear."

Whether Alex smiled at the words "past fear," or whether Fred only thought he did is uncertain, the effect was that he exclaimed, "I only wish there was a place in this pond that you did not like to skate over, Alex."

"Well, there is one," said Alex, laughing, "where Carey drowns the travelling man : there is a spring there, and the ice is never so firm, so you may try—"

"Don't, Fred—I beg you won't !" cried Beatrice.

"O, Fred, Fred, think, think if anything should happen !" implored Henrietta.

"I shan't look, I can't bear it !" exclaimed Jessie, turning away.

Fred without listening skated triumphantly towards the hedge, and across the perilous part, and fortunately it was without disaster. In the midst of the shout of applause with which the chorus celebrated his achievement, a gate in the hedge suddenly opened, and the two uncles stood before them. The first thing Uncle Geoffrey did was to take a short run, and slide right across the middle of the pond, while Uncle Roger stood by laughing and saying, "Well done, Geoffrey, you are not quite so heavy as I am."

Uncle Geoffrey reaching the opposite side, caught up little Charley by the arms and whirled him round in the air, then shouted in a voice that had all the glee and blithe exultation of a boy just released from school, "I hereby certify to all whom it may concern, the pond is franked ! Where's Fred ?"

Fred wished himself anywhere else, and so did Henrietta. Even Queen Bee's complacency gave way before her father, and it was only Alexander who had spirit to answer, "We thought you were not coming at all."

"Indeed !" said Uncle Geoffrey ; and little Willy exclaimed, "Why, Alex, Uncle Geoffrey always comes when he promises," a truth to which every one gave a mental assent.

Without taking the smallest notice of Frederick by word or look, Uncle Geoffrey proceeded to join the other boys, to the great increase of their merriment, instructing them in making figures of eight, and in all the other mysteries of the skating art, which they could scarcely enjoy more than he seemed to do. Henrietta, cold and unhappy, grieved at her brother's conduct, and still more grieved at the displeasure of her uncle, wished to return to the house, yet could not make up her mind to do so, for fear of her mamma's asking about Fred; and whilst she was still doubting and hesitating, the church bell began to ring, reminding her of the saint's day service, one of the delights of Knight Sutton to which she had so long looked forward. Yet here was another disappointment. The uncles and the two girls immediately prepared to go. Jessie said she must take Arthur and Charley home, and set off. The boys could do as they pleased, and Willy holding Uncle Geoffrey's hand was going with him, but the rest continued their sport, and among them Fred. He had never disobeyed a church bell before, and had rather not have done so now, but as he saw none of his male companions setting off, he fancied that to attend a week-day service in the holidays might be reckoned a girlish proceeding, imagined his cousins laughing at him as soon as his back was turned, and guessed from Uncle Geoffrey's grave looks that he might be taken to task when no longer protected by the presence of the rest.

He therefore replied with a gruff short " No" to his sister's anxious question whether he was not coming, and flourished away to the other end of the pond; but a few seconds after he was not a little surprised and vexed at finding himself mistaken after all—at least so far as regarded Alex, who had been only going on with his sport to the last moment, and now taking off his skates, vaulted over the gate, and ran at full speed after the rest of the party, overtaking them before they reached the village.

Henrietta was sadly disappointed when, looking round at

the sound of footsteps, she saw him instead of her brother. His refusal to go to church grieved her more than his disobedience, on which she did not in general look with sufficient seriousness, and for which in the present case there were many extenuating circumstances, which she longed to plead to Uncle Geoffrey, who would, she thought, relax in his severity towards her poor Fred, if he knew how long he had waited, and how much he had been teased. This, however, she could not tell him without complaining of his daughter, and in fact it was an additional pain that Queen Bee should have used all her powerful influence in the wrong direction.

It was impossible to be long vexed with the little Busy Bee, even in such circumstances as these, especially when she came up to her, put her arm into hers, and looked into her face with all the sweetness that could sometimes reside in those brown features of hers, saying, "My poor Henrietta, I am afraid we have been putting you to torture all this time, but you know that it is quite nonsense to be afraid of anything happening."

"O yes, I know that, but really, Queenie, you should not have persuaded him."

"I? Well, I believe it was rather naughty of me to laugh at him, for persuade him I did not, but if you had but seen him in the point I did, and known how absurd you two poor disconsolate creatures looked, you would not have been able to help it. And how was I to know that he would go into the only dangerous place he could find, just by way of bravado? I could have beaten myself when I saw that, but it's all safe, and no harm done."

"There is your papa displeased with him."

"O, I will settle that; I will tell him it was half of it my fault, and beg him to say nothing about it. And as for Fred—I should like to make a charade of fool-hardy, with a personal application. Did you ever act a charade, Henrietta?"

"Never; I scarcely know what it is."

"O charming, charming! What rare fun we will have! I wish I had not told you of fool-hardy, for now we can't have that, but this evening, O, this evening, I am no Queen Bee if you do not see what will amaze you! Alex! Alex! Where is the boy? I must speak to you this instant."

Pouncing upon Alexander, she drew him a little behind the others, and was presently engaged in an eager low-voiced conference, apparently persuading him to something much against his inclination, but Henrietta was not sufficiently happy to bestow much curiosity on the subject. All her thoughts were with Fred, and she had not long been in church before all her mother's fears seemed to have passed to her. Her mother had recovered her serenity, and was able to trust her boy in the hands of his Heavenly FATHER, while Henrietta, haunted by the remembrance of many a moral tale, was tormenting herself with the expectation of retribution, and dwelling on a fancied figure of her brother lifted senseless out of the water, with closed eyes and dripping hair.

CHAPTER IX

WITH all her faults, Queen Bee was a good-natured, generous little thing, and it was not what every one would have done, when, as soon as she returned from church, she followed her father to the study, saying, "Papa, you must not be displeased with Fred, for he was very much plagued, and he only had just begun when you came."

"The other boys had been teasing him?"

"Dick had been laughing at him, saying his mamma would not let him go on the ice, and that, you know, was past all bearing. And honestly, it was my fault too; I laughed, not at that joke, of course, for it was only worthy of Dick himself, but at poor Fred's own disconsolate looks."

"Was not his case unpleasant enough, without your making it worse?"

"Of course, papa, I ought to have been more considerate, but you know how easily I am run away with by high spirits."

"And I know you have the power to restrain them, Beatrice. You have no right to talk of being run away with, as if you were helpless."

"I know it is very wrong; I often think I will check myself, but there are many speeches which, when once they come to my lips, are irresistible, or seem so. However, I will not try to justify myself; I know I was to blame, only

I

you must not be angry with Fred, for it really did seem rather unreasonable to keep him there parading about with Henrietta and Jessie, when the ice was quite safe for everybody else."

"I am not angry with him, Bee; I cannot but be sorry that he gave way to the temptation, but there was so much to excuse him, that I shall not show any further displeasure. He is often in a very vexatious position for a boy of his age. I can imagine nothing more galling than these restraints."

"And cannot you—" said Beatrice, stopping short.

"Speak to your aunt? I will not make her miserable. Anything she thinks right she will do, at whatever cost to herself, and for that very reason I will not interfere. It is a great deal better for Fred that his amusement should be sacrificed to her peace, than her peace to his amusement."

"Yet surely this cannot go on for life," said Beatrice, as if she was half afraid to hazard the remark.

"Never mind the future. She will grow more used to the other boys, and gain more confidence in Fred. Things will right themselves, if we do not set them wrong. And now, mark me. You are not a mere child, who can plead the excuse of thoughtlessness for leading him into mischief; you know the greatness of the sin of disobedience, and the fearful responsibility incurred by conducing to it in others. Do not help to lead him astray for the sake of—of vanity—of amusement."

Something in the manner in which he pronounced these words conveyed to Beatrice a sense of the emptiness and worthlessness of her motives, and she answered earnestly, "I was wrong, papa; I know it is a love of saying clever things that often leads me wrong. It was so to-day, for I could have stopped myself, but for the pleasure of making fun. It is vanity, and I will try to subdue it."

Beatrice had a sort of candid way of reasoning about her

faults, and would blame herself, and examine her motives in a manner which disarmed reproof by forestalling it. She was perfectly sincere, yet it was self-deception, for it was not as if it was herself whom she was analysing, but rather as if it was some character in a book; indeed, she would have described herself almost exactly as she is here described, except that her delineation would have been much more clever and more exact. She would not have spared herself—for this reason, that her own character was more a study to her than a reality, her faults rather circumstances than sins; it was her mind, rather than her soul, that reflected and made resolutions, or more correctly, what would have been resolutions, if they had possessed any real earnestness, and not been done, as it were, mechanically, because they became the occasion.

The conversation was concluded by the sound of the luncheon bell, and she ran up to take off her bonnet, her thoughts taking the following course: "I am very sorry; it is too bad to tease poor Fred, cruel and wrong, and *all that*, only if he would not look absurd! It is too droll to see how provoked he is, when I take the least notice of Alex, and after all, I don't think he cares for me half as much as Alex does, only it flatters his vanity. Those great boys are really quite as vain as girls, not Alex though, good down-right fellow, who would do anything for me, and I have put him to a hard proof to-night. What a capital thought those charades are! Fred will meet the others on common, nay, on superior ground, and there will be none of these foolish questions who can be most manly mad. Fred is really a fine spirited fellow though, and I thought papa could not find it in his heart to be angry with him. How capitally he will act, and how lovely Henrietta will look! I *must* make them take to the charades, it will be so very delightful, and keep Fred quite out of mischief, which will set Aunt Mary at ease. And how amused grandpapa will be ! What shall it be to-night? What Alex can manage to act tolerably. *Ce n'est que le premier pas qui coute,* and the *premier pas* must be with our best foot foremost. I give myself credit for the thought ; it will make all smooth."

These meditations occupied her during a hasty toilette and a still more rapid descent, and were abruptly concluded by her alighting from her swinging jump down the last four steps close to Fred himself, who was standing by the hall fire with a gloomy expression of countenance, which, with inconsiderate good-nature she hastened to remove. " Don't look dismal, Freddy ; I have told papa all about it, and he does not *mind* it. Cheer up, you adventurous knight, I have some glorious fun for you this evening."

Not mind it ! The impression thus conveyed to one but too willing to receive it, was that Uncle Geoffrey, that external conscience, thought him excused from attending to unreasonable prohibitions. Away went all the wholesome self-reproach which he had begun to feel, away went all fear of Uncle Geoffrey's eye, all compunction in meeting his mother, and he entered the dining-room in such lively spirits that his uncle was vexed to see him so unconcerned, and his mother felt sure that her entreaty had not been disregarded. She never heard to the contrary, for she liked better to trust than to ask questions, and he, like far too many boys, did not think concealment blameable where there was no actual falsehood.

All the time they were at table Queen Bee was in one of her states of wild restlessness, and the instant she was at liberty she flew away, and was seen no more that afternoon, except in certain flittings into different apartments, where she appeared for a moment or two with some extraordinary and mysterious request. First, she popped upon grandpapa, and with the expense of a little coaxing and teasing, obtained from him the loan of his Deputy-Lieutenant's uniform; then she darted into the drawing-room, on hearing Uncle Roger's voice, and conjured him not to forget to give a little note to Alex, containing these words, "Willy must wear his cap without a peak. Bring Roger's dirk, and above all, beg, borrow, or steal, Uncle Roger's fishing boots." Her next descent was upon Aunt Mary, in her own room : " Aunt, would you do me a great favour, and ask no questions, nor tell Henrietta? Do just lend me the three little marabout feathers which you had in your cap yesterday evening. Only for this one evening, and I'll take great care."

" I am sure, my dear, you are very welcome to them; I do not feel like myself in such finery," said Mrs. Frederick Langford, smiling, as Beatrice took possession of the elegant little white cap, which she had the discretion to carry to Bennet, its lawful protector, to be reft of its plumed honours. Bennet, an old friend of nursery days, was in the secret of her plans for the evening; her head-quarters were in the work-room, which had often served her as a play-room in days gone by, and Judith, gratified by a visit from " Miss Bee," dived for her sake into boxes and drawers, amid hoards where none but Judith would have dared to rummage.

All this might ultimately be for Henrietta's entertainment, but at present it did not much conduce towards it, as she was left to her own resources in the drawing-room. She practised a little, worked a little, listened to a consultation between grandpapa and Uncle Roger, about the new pig-sty, wrote it down in her list when they went into the study to ask Uncle Geoffrey's advice, tried to talk over things in general with her mamma, but found it impossible with grandmamma continually coming in and out of the room, yawned, wondered what Busy Bee was about, felt deserted, gave up work, and had just found an entertaining book, when grandmamma came in, and invited her to visit the poultry-yard. She readily accepted, but for want of Queen Bee to hurry her, kept grandmamma waiting longer than she liked, and had more of a scolding than was agreeable. The chickens were all gone to roost by the time they arrived, the cock just peering down at them with his coral-bordered eye, and the ducks waddling stealthily in one by one, the feeding was over, the hen-wife gone, and Mrs. Langford vexed at being too late.

Henrietta was annoyed with herself and with the result of the day, but she had some consolation, for as they were going towards the house, they met Mr. Langford, who called out, "So you have been walking with grandmamma! Well, if you are not tired, come and have a little turn with grandpapa. I am going to speak to Daniels, the carpenter, and my ' merry Christmas ' will be twice as welcome to his old father, if I take you with me."

Henrietta might be a little tired, but such an invitation was not to be refused, and she was at her grandpapa's side in an instant, thanking him so much that he laughed and said the favour was to him. "I wish we had Fred here too," said he, as they walked on, "the old man will be very glad to see you."

" Was he one of mamma's many admirers in the village ?"

" All the village admired Miss Mary, but it was your father who was old Daniels' chief friend. The boys used to have a great taste for carpentry, especially your father, who was always at his elbow when he was at work at the Hall. Poor old man, I thought he would never have held up his head again when our great trouble came on us. He used to touch his hat, and turn away without looking me in the face. And there you may see stuck up over the chimney-piece in his cottage the new chisel that your father gave him when he had broken his old one."

"Dear old man!" said Henrietta, warmly, "I am so very glad that we have come here, where people really care for us, and are interested in us, and not for our own sake. How delightful it is! I feel as if we were come out of banishment."

"Well, it is all the better for you," said Mr. Langford; "if we had had you here, depend upon it, we should have spoilt you. We have so few granddaughters that we cannot help making too much of them. There is that little Busy Bee—by-the-bye, what is her plan this evening, or are not you in her secret?"

"O no, I believe she is to surprise us all. I met her, just before I came out, dragging a huge bag after her: I wanted to help her, but she would not let me."

"She turns us all round her finger," said grandpapa. "I never found the person who could resist Queen Bee, except grandmamma. But I am glad you do not take after her, Henrietta, for one such grandchild is enough, and it is better for womankind to have *leadable* spirits than leading."

"O, grandpapa!"

"That is a dissentient O. What does it mean? Out with it."

"Only that I was thinking about weakness; I beg your pardon, grandpapa."

"Look here!" and Mr. Langford bent the slender cane in his hand (he disdained a stronger walking-stick) to its full extent of suppleness. "Is this weak?"

"No, it is strong in energy," said Henrietta, laughing, as the elastic cane sprang back to its former shape.

"Yet to a certain point you can bend it as far as you please. Well that should be the way with you: be turned any way but the wrong, and let your own determination be only to keep upright."

"But women are admired for influence."

" Influence is a good thing in its way, but only of a good sort when it is unconscious. At any rate, when you set to work to influence people, take care it is only with a view to their good and not to your own personal wishes, or influencing becomes a dangerous trade, especially for young ladies towards their elders."

Grandpapa, who had only seen Henrietta carried about by Beatrice, grandmamma, or Fred, and willing to oblige them all, had little idea how applicable to her case was his general maxim, nor indeed did she at the moment take it to herself, although it was one day to return upon her. It brought them to the neat cottage of the carpenter, with the thatched workshop behind, and the garden in front, which would have looked neat but for the melancholy aspect of the yellow frost-bitten cabbages.

This was Henrietta's first cottage visit, and she was all eagerness and interest, picturing to herself a venerable old man, almost as fine-looking as her grandfather, and as eloquent as old men in cottages always are in books ; but she found it rather a disappointing meeting. It was a very nice trim-looking daughter-in-law who opened the door, on Mr. Langford's knock, and the room was neatness itself, but the old carpenter was not at all what she had imagined. He was a little stooping old man, with a shaking head, and weak red eyes under a green shade, and did not seem to have anything to say beyond " Yes, sir," and " Thank you, sir," when Mr. Langford shouted into his deaf ears some of the " compliments of the season." Looking at the young lady, whom he evidently mistook for Beatrice, he hoped that Mr. and Mrs. Geoffrey were quite well. His face lighted up a little for a moment when Mr. Langford told him this was Mr. Frederick's daughter, but it was only for an instant, and in a somewhat querulous voice he asked if there was not a young gentleman too.

"O yes," said Mr. Langford, "he shall come and see you some day."

"He would not care to see a poor old man," said Daniels, turning a little away, while his daughter-in-law began to apologise for him by saying, "He is more lost than usual to-day, sir; I think it was getting tired going to church, yesterday morning; he did not sleep well, and he has been so fretful all the morning, a body did not know what to do with him."

Mr. Langford said a few more cheerful words to the poor old man, then asked the daughter where her husband was, and, hearing that he was in the workshop, refused offers of fetching him in, and went out to speak to him, leaving Henrietta to sit by the fire and wait for him. A weary waiting time she found it; shy as she was of poor people, as of a class with whom she was utterly unacquainted, feeling bound to make herself agreeable, but completely ignorant how to set about it, wishing to talk to the old man, and fearing to neglect him, but finding conversation quite impossible except with Mrs. Daniels, and not very easy with her—she tried to recollect what storied young ladies did say to old men, but nothing she could think of would do, or was what she could feel herself capable of saying. At last she remembered, in "Gertrude," the old nurse's complaint that Laura did not inquire after the rheumatism, and she hazarded her voice in expressing a hope that Mr. Daniels did not suffer from it. Clear as the sweet voice was, it was too tremulous (for she was really in a fright of embarrassment) to reach the old man's ear, and his daughter-in-law took it upon her to repeat the inquiry in a shrill sharp scream, that almost went through her ears: then while the old man was answering something in a muttering maundering way, she proceeded with a reply, and told a long story about his ways with the doctor, in her Sussex dialect, almost incom-

prehensible to Henrietta. The conversation dropped, until
Mrs. Daniels began hoping that every one at the Hall was
quite well, and as she inquired after them one by one, this
took up a reasonable time; but then again followed a silence. Mrs. Daniels was not a native of Knight Sutton, or
she would have had more to say about Henrietta's mother;
but she had never seen her before, and had none of that
interest in her that half the parish felt. Henrietta wished
there had been a baby to notice, but she saw no trace in
the room of the existence of children, and did not like to
ask if there were any. She looked at the open hearth, and
said it was very comfortable, and was told in return that it
made a great draught, and smoked very much. Then she
bethought herself of admiring an elaborately worked frame
sampler, that hung against the wall; and the conversation
this supplied lasted her till, to her great joy, grandpapa
made his appearance again, and summoned her to return, as
it was already growing very dark.

She thought he might have made something of an apology
for the disagreeableness of his friend; but, being used to it,
and forgetting that she was not, he did no such thing; and
she was wondering that cottage visiting could ever have been
represented as so pleasant an occupation, when he began
on a far more interesting subject, asking about her mother's
health, and how she thought Knight Sutton agreed with
her, saying how very glad he was to have her there again,
and how like his own daughter she had always been. He
went on to tell of his first sight of his two daughters-in-law,
when, little guessing that they would be such, he went to
fetch home the little Mary Vivian, who had come from
India under the care of General St. Leger. "There they
were," said he: "I can almost see them now, as their black
nurse led them in; your aunt a brown little sturdy thing,
ready to make acquaintance in a moment, and your mamma

such a fair, shrinking, fragile morsel of a child, that I felt quite ashamed to take her among all my great scrambling boys."

"Ah! mamma says her recollection is all in bits and scraps; she recollects the ship, and she remembers sitting on your knee in a carriage; but she cannot remember either the parting with Aunt Geoffrey or the coming here."

"I do not remember about the parting with Aunt Geoffrey; they managed that in the nursery, I believe, but I shall never forget the boys receiving her,—Fred and Geoffrey, I mean,—for Roger was at school. How they admired her like some strange curiosity, and played with her like a little girl with a new doll. There was no fear that they would be too rough with her, for they used to touch her as if she was made of glass. And what a turn out of old playthings there was in her service!"

"That was when she was six," said Henrietta, "and papa must have been ten."

"Yes, thereabouts, and Geoffrey a year younger. How they did pet her and come down to all their old baby-plays again for her sake, till I was almost afraid that cricket and hockey would be given up and forgotten."

"And were they?"

"No, no, trust boys for that. Little Mary came to be looker on, if she did not sometimes play herself. She was distressed damsel, and they knight and giant, or dragon, or I cannot tell what, though many's the time I have laughed over it. Whatever they pleased was she: never lived creature more without will of her own."

"Never," responded Henrietta; but that for which Mr. Langford might commend his little Mary at seven years old, did not appear so appropriate a subject of observation in Mrs. Frederick Langford, and by her own daughter.

"Eh!" said her grandfather. Then answering his mental

objection in another tone, " Ay, ay, no will for her own pleasure ; that depends more on you than on any one else."

" I would do anything on earth for her !" said Henrietta, feeling it from the bottom of her heart.

" I am sure you would, my dear," said Mr. Langford, "and she deserves it. There are few like her, and few that have gone through so much. To think of her as she was when last she was here and to look at her now ! Well, it won't do to talk of it ; but I thought when I saw her face yesterday, that I could see, as well as believe, it was all for the best for her, as I am sure it was for us."

He was interrupted just as they reached the gate by the voice of his eldest son calling " Out late, sir," and looking round, Henrietta saw what looked in the darkness like a long procession, Uncle and Aunt Roger, and their niece, and all the boys, as far down as William, coming to the Hall for the regular Christmas dinner-party.

Joining company, Henrietta walked with Jessie and answered her inquiries whether she had got wet or cold in the morning ; but it was in an absent manner, for she was all the time dwelling on what her grandfather had been saying. She was calling up in imagination the bright scenes of her mother's youth ; those delightful games of which she had often heard, and which she could place in their appropriate setting now that she knew the scenes. She ran up to her room, where she found only Bennet, her mother having dressed and gone down ; and sitting down before the fire, and resigning her curls to her maid, she let herself dwell on the ideas the conversation had called up, turning from the bright to the darker side. She pictured to herself the church, the open grave, her uncles and her grandfather round it, the villagers taking part in their grief, the old carpenter's averted head—she thought what must have been the agony of the moment, of laying in his untimely grave one so fondly loved, on whom the world was just opening so brightly,—and the young wife—the infant children—how fearful it must have been! "It was almost a cruel dispensation," thought Henrietta. "O, how happy and bright we might have been! What would it not have been to hold by his hand, to have his kiss, to look for his smile! And mamma, to have had her in all her joyousness and blitheness, with no ill health, and no cares! O, why was it not so? And yet grandpapa said it was for the best! And in what a manner he did say it, as if he really felt and saw, and knew the advantage of it! To dear papa himself I know it was for the best, but for us, mamma, grandpapa—no, I never shall understand it. They were good before; why did they need punishment? Is this what is called saying 'Thy will be done?' Then I shall never be able to say it, and yet I ought!"

"Your head a little higher, if you please, Miss Henrietta," said Bennet; "it is that makes me so long dressing you, and your mamma has been telling me that I must get you ready faster."

Henrietta slightly raised her head for the moment, but soon let it sink again in her musings, and when Bennet reminded her, replied, "I can't, Bennet, it breaks my neck." Her will was not with her mother's, in a trifling matter of which the reasonableness could not but approve itself to her. How, then, was it likely to be bent to that of her Heavenly Parent, in what is above reason?

The toilet was at length completed, and in time for her to be handed in to dinner by Alexander, an honour which she owed to Beatrice having already been secured by Frederick, who was resolved not to be again abandoned to Jessie. Alex did not favour her with much conversation, partly because he was thinking with perturbation of the task set him for the evening, and partly because he was trying to hear what Queen Bee was saying to Fred, in the midst of the clatter of knives and forks, and the loud voice of Mr. Roger Langford, which was enough to drown most other sounds. Some inquiries had been made about Mrs. Geoffrey Langford and her aunt Lady Susan St. Leger, which had led Beatrice into a great lamentation for her mother's absence, and from thence into a description of what Lady Susan exacted from her friends. "Aunt Susan is a regular fidget," said she; "not such a fidget as some people," with an indication of Mrs. Langford. "Some people are determined to make others comfortable in a way of their own, and that is a fidget to be regarded with considerable respect; but Aunt Susan's fidgeting takes the turn of sacrificing the comfort of every one else to her own and her little dog's."

"That is very hard on Aunt Geoffrey," said Fred.

"Frightfully. Any one who was less selfish would have insisted on mamma's coming here, instead of which Aunt Susan only complains of her sister and brother, and everybody else, for going out of London, when she may be taken suddenly ill at any time. She is in such a nervous state that Mr. Payton cannot tell what might be the consequence," said Beatrice, in an imitative tone, which made Fred laugh.

"I am sure I should leave her to take care of herself," said he.

"So do the whole family except ourselves; they are all worn out by her querulousness, and are not particularly given to patience and unselfishness either. But mamma is really fond of her, because she was kind to her when she came home from India, and she manages to keep her quiet better than any one else can. She can very seldom resist mamma's cheerful voice, which drives off half her nerves at once. You cannot think how funny it is to see how Aunt

Amelia always seems to stroke the cat the wrong way, and mamma to smooth her down the right."

A lull in the conversation left these last words audible, and Mr. Langford said, "What is that about stroking the cat, Queenie?"

"O you are telling it all—O don't, Bee!" cried Willy.

And with certain jokes about cats and bags, which seemed excessively to discomfit Willy, who protested the cat was not in the bag at all—it was the partridges—the conversation drifted away again from the younger party.

As soon as dinner was over, Beatrice again disappeared, after begging her grandmamma to allow the great Indian screen to remain as it at present stood, spread out so as to cut off one end of the room, where there was a door opening into the study. Behind this screen frequent rustlings were heard, with now and then a burst of laughing or whispering, and a sound of moving furniture, which so excited Mrs. Langford, that, starting up, she exclaimed that she must go and see what they could be doing.

"We are taking great care, grandmamma," called Alexander. "We won't hurt it."

This, by showing so far that there was something to be hurt, was so far from reassuring her, that she would certainly have set out on a voyage of discovery, but for Mr. Langford, who professed himself convinced that all was right, and said he would not have the Busy Bee disturbed.

She came in to tea, bringing Alex and Willy with her,— the latter, in a marvellous state of mystery and excitement, longing to tell all himself, and yet in great terror lest the others should tell.

As soon as the tea was despatched, the three actors departed, and presently there was a call from behind the screen, "Are you ready, good people?"

"Go it," answered Carey.

"Are the elders ready?" said Beatrice's voice.

"Papa, don't go on talking to Uncle Geoffrey!" cried Willy.

"Ay, ay, all attention," said grandpapa. "Now for it!"

The screen was folded back, and discovered Alex in a pasteboard crown, ermine tippet, and purple mantle, sitting enthroned with Beatrice (a tiara and feathers on her head) at his side, and kneeling before them a nondescript article, consisting chiefly of a fur cloak, a fur cap, adorned with a pair of grey squirrel cuffs, sewn ingeniously into the form of ears, a boa by way of tail, and an immense pair of boots. As Uncle Geoffrey said, the cat was certainly out of the bag, and it proceeded in due form to take two real partridges from the bag, and present them to the king and princess in the name of the Marquis Carabbas.

The king and princess made some consultation as to who the marquis might be, the princess proposing to send for the Peerage, and the king cross-examining puss in an incredulous way which greatly puzzled him, until at length he bethought himself of exclaiming in a fierce manner, "I've told you the truth, Mr. King, and if you won't believe me, I can't help it!" and walked off on his hind legs in as dignified and resentful a manner as his boots would let him; repairing to the drawing-room to have his accoutrements admired, while the screen was again spread in preparation for Scene II.

Scene II. presented but a half-length, a shawl being hung in front, so as to conceal certain incongruities. A great arm-chair was wheeled close to the table, on which stood an aged black jack out of the hall, a quart measure, and a silver tankard; while in the chair, a cushion on his head, and a great carving-knife held like a sceptre in his hand, reclined Alex, his bulk enlarged by at least two pillows, over which an old, long-breasted white satin waistcoat, embroidered with silver, had with some difficulty been brought to meet. Before him stood a little figure in a cloth cap, set jauntily on one side, decorated with a fox's brush, and with Mrs. Frederick Langford's three feathers, and a coat bearing marvellous resemblance to Beatrice's own black velvet spencer, crossed over one shoulder by a broad blue ribbon, which Henrietta knew full well. "Do thou stand for my father," began this droll little shape, "and examine me in the particulars of my life."

It was not badly carried out; Prince Henry when he did not giggle, acted beautifully; and Falstaff really did very well, though his eyes were often directed downwards, and the curious, by standing on tiptoe, obtained not only a view of Prince Hal's pink petticoat, but of a great Shakespeare laid open on the floor : and a very low bow on the part of the heir apparent, when about to change places with his fat friend, was strongly suspected of being for the purpose of turning over a leaf. It was with great spirit that the parting appeal was given, "Banish fat Jack, and banish all the world!" And there was great applause when fat Jack and Prince Hal jumped up and drew the screen forward again; though Uncle Geoffrey and Aunt Mary were cruel enough to utter certain historical and antiquarian doubts as to whether the Prince of Wales was likely to wear the three feathers and ribbon of the garter in his haunts at Eastcheap.

In the concluding scene the deputy lieutenant's uniform made a great figure, with the addition of the long-breasted waistcoat, a white scarf, and the white cockade, adorning Alex, who, with a boot-jack under his arm, looked as tall and as rigid as he possibly could, with a very low bow, which was gracefully returned by a royal personage in a Scottish bonnet, also bearing the white cockade, a tartan scarf, and the blue ribbon. Altogether, Prince Charles

Edward and the Baron of Bradwardine stood confessed; the charter was solemnly read, and the shoe pulled off, or supposed to be, as the lower screen still remained to cut off the view; and then the Baron indulged in a lengthy yawn and stretch, while Prince Charley, skipping into the midst of the audience, danced round Mr. Langford, asking if he had guessed it.

CHAPTER X

BEATRICE had not judged amiss when she thought charade-acting an amusement likely to take the fancy of her cousins. The great success of her *boot-jack* inspired both Frederick and Henrietta with eagerness to imitate it; and nothing was talked of but what was practicable in the way of scenes, words, and decorations. The Sutton Leigh party were to dine at the Hall again on Thursday, and it was resolved that there should be a grand charade, with all the splendour that due preparation could bestow upon it. "It was such an amusement to grandpapa," as Beatrice told Henrietta, "and it occupied Fred so nicely," as she said to her father; both which observations being perfectly true, Mr. Geoffrey Langford was very willing to promote the sport, and to tranquillise his mother respecting the dis-arrangement of her furniture.

But what should the word be? Every one had predilec-tions of their own—some for comedy, others for tragedy; some for extemporary acting, others for Shakespeare. Bea-trice, with her eye for drawing, already grouped her *dramatis personæ*, so as to display Henrietta's picturesque face and figure to the greatest advantage, and had designs of making her and Fred represent Catherine and Henry Seyton, whom, as she said, she had always believed to be exactly like them. Fred was inclined for "another touch at Prince Hal," and devised numerous ways of acting Anonymous, for the sake of " Anon, anon, sir." Henrietta wanted to contrive something in which Queen Bee might appear as an actual fairy bee, and had very pretty visions of making her a beneficent spirit in a little fanciful opera, for which she had written three or four verses, when Fred put an end to it by pronouncing it " nonsense and humbug."

So passed Tuesday, without coming to any decision, and Henrietta was beginning to fear that they would never fix at all, when on Wednesday morning Beatrice came down in an ecstasy with the news, that by some chance a wig of her papa's was in the house, and a charade they must and would have which would bring in the wig. " Come and see it," said she, drawing her two cousins into the study after breakfast : the study being the safest place for holding counsel on these secret subjects. " There now, is it not charming? O, a law charade we must have, that is certain !"

Fred and Henrietta, who had never chanced to see a barrister's wig before, were greatly diverted with its little tails, and tried it on in turn. Whilst Henrietta was in the midst of her laugh at the sight of her own fair ringlets hanging out below the tight grey rolls, the door suddenly opened, and gave entrance to its owner, fiercely exclaiming, " What ! nothing safe from you, you impertinent kittens?"

" O, Uncle Geoffrey, I beg your pardon !" cried Henrietta, blushing crimson.

" Don't take it off till I have looked at you," said Uncle Geoffrey. " Why, you would make a capital Portia !"

" Yes, yes !" cried Queen Bee, " that is it : Portia she shall be, and I'll be Nerissa."

" Oh, no, Queenie, I could never be Portia !" said Henrietta : " I am sure I can't."

" But I have set my heart on being the ' little scrubby lawyer's clerk,' " said Busy Bee; " it is what I am just fit for; and let me see—Fred shall be Antonio, and that will make you plead from your very heart, and you shall have Alex for your Bassanio."

"But the word. Do you mean to make it fit in with Falstaff and Catherine Seyton?" said Henrietta.

"Let me see," said Beatrice; "bond—bondage, jew—jeweller, juniper,—"

"Lawsuit," said Fred. "Ay, don't you see, all the scenes would come out of the 'Merchant of Venice.' There is 'law' when the old Jew is crying out for his ducats, and —but halloo!" and Fred stood aghast at the sight of his uncle, whose presence they had all forgotten in their eagerness.

"Traitor!" said Beatrice; "but never mind, I believe we must have let him into the plot, for nobody else can be Shylock."

"O, Bee," whispered Henrietta, reproachfully, "don't tease him with our nonsense. Think of asking him to study Shylock's part, when he has all that pile of papers on the table."

> "Jessica, my girl,
> Look to my house. I am right loath to go;
> There is some ill a-brewing to my rest,
> For I did dream of money-bags to-night."

Such was Uncle Geoffrey's reply; his face and tone so suddenly altered to the snarl of the old Jew, that his young companions at first started, and then clapped their hands in delighted admiration.

"Do you really know it all?" asked Henrietta, in a sort of respectful awe.

"It won't cost me much trouble to get it up," said Mr. Geoffrey Langford; "Shylock's growls stick in one's memory better than finer speeches."

"Then will you really be so very kind?"

"Provided you will leave the prompter of Monday night on the table this morning," said Uncle Geoffrey, smiling in that manner which, to a certain degree, removed any feeling of obligation, by making it seem as if it was entirely for his own diversion. Nor could it be denied that he did actually enjoy it.

The party took up their quarters in the study, which really was the only place fit for consultations and rehearsals, since Fred and Alex could not be taken to the maids' work-room, and none of the downstairs apartments could be made subject to the confusion incidental to their preparations. Henrietta had many scruples at first about disturbing Uncle Geoffrey, but his daughter laughed at them all; and they were soon at an end when she perceived that he minded their chattering, spouting, and laughing, no more than if they had been so many little sparrows twittering on the eaves, but pursued the even tenour of his writing uninterruptedly, even while she fitted on his head a yellow pointed cap, which her ingenious fingers had compounded of the lining of certain ugly old curtains.

His presence in this silent state served, too, as a protection in Mrs. Langford's periodical visitations to stir the fire; but for him, she would assuredly have found fault, and probably Beatrice have come to a collision with her, which would have put an end to the whole scheme.

It formed a considerable addition to Henrietta's list of his avocations, and really by making the utmost of everything he did for other people during that whole week, she made the number reach even to seventy-nine by the next Thursday morning. The most noted of these employments were the looking over a new Act of Parliament with the County Member, the curing grandmamma's old gander of a mysterious lameness, the managing of an emigration of a whole family to New Zealand, the guessing a riddle supposed "to have no answer," and the mending of some extraordinary spring that was broken in Uncle Roger's new drill. Beatrice was charmed with the list; Aunt Mary said it was delightful to be so precious to every one; and grandpapa, shaking his head at his son, said he was ashamed to find that his family contained such a "Jack of all trades:" to which Uncle Geoffrey replied, that it was too true that "all work and no play make Jack a very dull boy."

The breaking up of the frost, with a succession of sleet, snow and rain, was much in favour of Beatrice and her plans, by taking away all temptation from the boys to engage in out-of-door amusements; and Antonio and Bassanio studied their parts so diligently, that Carey was heard to observe that it might just as well be the half year. They had, besides their own proper parts, to undertake those of the Princes of Aragon and Morocco, since Queen Bee, willing to have as much of Nerissa as possible, had determined to put their choice, and that of Bassanio, all into the one scene belonging to "suit." It was one of those occasions on which she showed little consideration, for she thus gave Portia an immense quantity to learn in only two days; persuading herself all the time that it was no such hard task, since the beautiful speech about mercy Henrietta already knew by heart, and she made no difficulties about the rest. Indeed, Beatrice thought herself excessively amiable in doing all she could to show off her cousin's beauty and acting, whilst taking a subordinate part herself; forgetting that humility is not shown in choosing a part, but in taking willingly that which is assigned us.

Henrietta was rather appalled at the quantity she had to learn, as well as at the prominent part she was to take; but she did not like to spoil the pleasure of the rest with objections, and applied herself in good earnest to her study. She walked about with a little Shakspeare in her hand; she learnt while she was dressing, working, waiting; sat up late, resisting many a summons from her mother to come to bed, and long before daylight, was up and learning again.

The great evening had come, and the audience were thus arranged : grandmamma took up her carpet work, expressing many hopes to Aunt Roger that it would be over now, and out of the children's heads, for they turned the house upside down, and for her part, she thought it very like play-acting. Aunt Roger returning the sentiment with interest took out one of the little brown-holland frocks, which she seemed to be always making. Uncle Roger composed himself to sleep in the arm-chair for want of his brother to talk to; grand-papa moved a sofa to the front for Aunt Mary, and sat down by her, declaring that they would see something very pretty, and hoping it would not be too hard a nut for his old wits to crack; Jessie, and such of the boys as could not be persuaded to be magnificoes found themselves a convenient station and the scene opened.

It was a very short one, but it made every one laugh greatly, thanks to Shylock's excellent acting, and the chorus of boys, who greatly enjoyed chasing him across the stage, crying, "The law, his ducats, and his daughter !"

Then, after a short interval, appeared Portia, a silver arrow in her hair, almost lovely enough for the real Portia; though the alarmed expression in her glowing face was little accordant with the calm dignified self-possession of the noble Venetian heiress. Nerissa, a handkerchief folded squarely over her head, short petticoats, scarlet lambs'-wool worked into her stockings, and a black apron trimmed with bright ribbon, made a complete little Italian waiting-maid; her quick, pert reply to her lady's first faltering speech, seemed wonderfully to restore Portia to herself, and they got on well and with spirit through the description of the suitors, and the choice of the two first caskets. Portia looked excessively dignified, and Nerissa's by-play was capital. Whether it was owing to Bassanio's awkwardness or her own shyness, she did not prosper quite so well when the leaden casket was chosen; Bassanio seemed more afraid of her than rejoiced, and looked much more at Nerissa than at her, whilst she moved as slowly, and spoke in as cold and measured a way, as if it had been the Prince of Morocco who had unfortunately hit upon the right casket.

In the grand concluding scene she was however all that could be wished. She really made a very pretty picture, in the dark robes, the glowing carnation of her cheek contrasting with the grey wig, beneath which a few bright ringlets still peeped out; one little white hand raised, and the other holding the parchment, and her eyes fixed on the Jew, as if she either imagined herself Portia, or saw her brother in Antonio's case, for they glistened with tears, and her voice had a tremulous pleading tone, which fairly made her grandfather and mother both cry heartily.

"Take, then, thy bond; take thou thy pound of flesh!"

The Duke (little Willy) was in an agony, and was forcibly withheld by Bassanio from crying "No, he shan't!" Nerissa was so absorbed as even to have forgotten herself; Shylock could hardly keep his countenance up to the necessary expression of malice and obduracy; even Johnny and Dick were hanging with breathless attention on the "but," when suddenly there was a general start throughout the party; the door opened; Atkins, with a voice and face full of delight, announced "Master Roger," and there entered a young man, in a pea jacket and worsted comforter.

Such confusion, such rapture as ensued! The tumultuous welcomes and handshakings before the sailor had time to distinguish one from another, the actors assuming their own characters, grandmamma and Mrs. Roger Langford asking dozens of questions in a breath, and Mr. Roger Langford fast asleep in his great arm-chair, till roused by Dick tugging at his arm, and Willy hammering on his knee, he slowly arose, saying, "What, Roger, my boy, is it you? I thought it was all their acting!"

"Ah! Miss Jessie," exclaimed Roger; "that is right. I have not seen such a crop of shining curls since I have been gone. So you have not lost your pink cheeks with pining for me. How are they all at home?"

"Here, Roger, your Aunt Mary," said his mother; and instantly there was a subduing of the young sailor's boisterous mirth, as he turned to answer her gentle welcome. The laugh arose the next moment at the appearance of the still half-disguised actors: Alex without Bassanio's short black cloak and slouched hat and feather, but still retaining his burnt-cork eyebrows and moustache, and wondering that Roger did not know him; Uncle Geoffrey still in Shylock's yellow cap, and Fred somewhat grim with the Prince of Morocco's complexion.

"How d'ye do, Phil?" said Roger, returning his cousinly shake of the hand with interest. "What! are not you Philip Carey?"

"O, Roger, Roger!" cried a small figure, in whom the Italian maiden predominated.

"What, Aunt Geoffrey masquerading too? How d'ye do, aunt?"

"Well done, Roger! That's right! Go on!" cried his father, laughing heartily.

"Is it not my aunt? No? Is it the little Bee, then? Why you are grown as like her! But where is Aunt Geoffrey then? Not here? That is a bore. I thought you would have all been in port here at Christmas. And is not this Philip? Come tell me, some of you, instead of standing laughing there. Are you Fred Langford, then?"

"Right this time," said Fred, "so now you must shake hands with me in my own name."

"Very glad to do so, and see you here at last," said Roger, cordially. "And now tell me, what is all this about? One would think you were crossing the Line."

"You shall hear what it is all about, and see too," said Mr. Langford. "We must have that wicked old Jew disappointed, must not we, Willy? But where is my little Portia? What is become of her?"

"Fled, I suspect," said her mother, "gone to turn into herself before her introduction."

"O, Roger, it was so jolly," Carey was now heard to say above the confusion of voices. "Uncle Geoffrey was an old Jew, going to cut a pound of flesh out of Fred, and Henrietta was making a speech, in a lawyer's wig, and had just found such a dodge!"

"Ha! like the masks in the carnival at Rio! Ferrars and I went ashore there, and—"

"Have you been at Sutton Leigh, Roger?" "Have you dined?" "Cold turkey—excellent Christmas pie, only too much pepper—a cup of tea—no, but we will have the beef in—"

Further conversation was suspended by these propositions, with the answers and thanks resulting therefrom, but in the midst grandpapa exclaimed, "Ah! here she is! Here is the counsellor! Here is a new cousin for you, Roger; here is the advocate for you when you have a tough lawsuit! Lucky for you, Master Geoffrey, that she is not a man, or your nose would soon be put out of joint. You little rogue! How dared you make your mother and grandfather cry their hearts out?"

"I was very glad to see you as bad as myself, sir," said Mrs. Frederick Langford. "I was very much ashamed of being so foolish, but then, you know, I could hardly ever read through that scene without crying."

"Ah! you are a prudent mamma, and will not let her be conceited. But to see Geoffrey, with his lips quivering, and yet frowning and looking savage with all his might and main! Well, you are a capital set of actors, all of you, and we must see the end of it."

This was the great desire of Beatrice, and she was annoyed with Henrietta for having thrown aside her borrowed garments, but the Fates decreed otherwise. The Christmas pie came in, grandpapa proceeded to carve it, and soon lost the remembrance of the charade in talking to his eldest grandson about his travels. A sailor just returned from four years on the South American coast, who had doubled Cape Horn, shot condors on the Andes, caught goats at Juan Fernandez, fished for sharks in the Atlantic, and heard parrots chatter in the Brazilian woods, could not fail to be very entertaining, even though he cared not for the Incas of Peru, and could tell little about the beauties of an iceberg; and accordingly every one was greatly entertained except the Queen Bee, who sat in a corner of the sofa, playing with her watch-chain, wondering how long Roger would go on eating pie, looking at the time-piece and strangling the yawns induced by her inability to attract the notice of either of her squires, whose eyes and ears were all for the new comer. She was not even missed; if she had been, it would have been some consolation; but on they went, listening and laughing, as if the course of the Euphrosyne, her quick sailing, and the adventures of her crew, were the only subjects of interest in the world. He was only at home for a week, but so much the worse; that would be till the end of Beatrice's own visit, and she supposed it would be nothing but Euphrosyne the whole time.

There was at last a change : Roger had half a hundred questions to ask about his cousins and all the neighbours.

"And has Philip Carey set up for himself at Allonfield?

Does he get any practice? I have a great mind to be ill; it would be such a joke to be doctored by Master Philip!"

"Ah! to think of your taking Mr. Frederick for poor Philip," said Jessie. "I assure you," nodding to Fred, "I take it as a great compliment, and so will Philip."

"And is Fanny Evans as pretty as ever?"

"Oh! grown quite fat and coarse," said Jessie; "but you may judge for yourself on Monday. Dear Mrs. Langford is so kind as to give us a regular Christmas party, and all the Evanses and Dittons are coming. And we are to dance in the dining-room, the best place for it in the county; the floor is so much better laid down than in the Allonfield assembly-room."

"No such good place for dancing as the deck of a frigate," said Roger. "This time last year we had a ball on board the Euphrosyne at Rio. I took the prettiest girl there in to supper—don't be jealous, Jessie, she had not such cheeks as yours. She was better off there than in the next ball where I met her, in the town. She fancied she had got rather a thick sandwich at supper: she peeped in, and what do you think she found? A great monster of a cockroach, twice as big as any you ever saw."

"O, you horrid wretch!" cried Jessie, "I am sure it was your doing. I am sure you will give me a scorpion, or some dreadful creature! I won't let you take me in to supper on Monday, I declare."

"Perhaps I won't have you. I mean to have Cousin Henrietta for my partner, if she will have me."

"Thank you, Cousin Roger," faltered Henrietta blushing crimson, with the doubt whether she was saying the right thing, and fearing Jessie might be vexed. Her confusion was increased the next moment, as Roger, looking at her more fully than he had done before, went on, "Much honoured, cousin. Now, all of you wish me joy. I am safe

to have the prettiest girl in the room for my partner.   But
how slow of them all not to have engaged her before.   Eh !
Alex, what have you to say for yourself?"

"I hope for Queen Bee," said Alex.

"And Jessie must dance with me, because I don't know
how," said Carey.

"My dears, this will never do !" interposed grandmamma.
"You can't all dance with each other, or what is to become
of the company?   I never heard of such a thing.   Let me
see; Queen Bee must open the ball with little Henry Har-
grave, and Roger must dance with Miss Benson."

"No, no," cried Roger, "I won't give up my partner,
ma'am ; I am a privileged person, just come home.   Knight
Sutton has not had too much of Henrietta or me, so you
must let us be company.   Come, Cousin Henrietta, stick
fast to your engagement; you can't break the first promise
you ever made me.   Here," proceeded he, jumping up, and
holding out his hand, "let us begin this minute; I'll show
you how we waltz with the Brazilian ladies."

"Thank you, Cousin Roger, I cannot waltz," said Henrietta.

"That's a pity.   Come, Jessie, then."

If the practice of waltzing was not to be admired, there
was something which was very nice in the perfect good
humour with which Jessie answered her cousin's summons,
without the slightest sign of annoyance at his evident preference of Henrietta's newer face.

"If I can't waltz, I can play for you," said Henrietta, willing not to seem disobliging; and going to the piano, she
played whilst Roger and Jessie whirled merrily round the
room, every now and then receiving shocks against the
furniture, and minding them not the least in the world, till
at last, perfectly out of breath, they dropped laughing upon
the sofa.

The observations upon the wild spirits of sailors ashore then sank into silence; Mrs. Roger Langford reproved her son for making such a racket, as was enough to kill his Aunt Mary; with a face of real concern he apologised from the bottom of his heart, and Aunt Mary in return assured him that she enjoyed the sight of his merriment.

Grandmamma announced in her most decided tone that she would have no waltzes and no polkas at her party. Roger assured her that there was no possibility of giving a dance without them, and Jessie seconded him as much as she ventured; but Mrs. Langford was unpersuadable, declaring that she would have no such things in her house. Young people in her days were contented to dance country dances; if they wanted anything newer, they might have quadrilles, but as to these new romps, she would not hear of them.

And here, for once in her life, Beatrice was perfectly agreed with her grandmamma, and she came to life again, and sat forward to join in the universal condemnation of waltzes and polkas that was going on round the table.

With this drop of consolation to her, the party broke up, and Jessie, as she walked home to Sutton Leigh, found great solace in determining within herself that at any rate waltzing was not half so bad as dressing up and play-acting, which she was sure her mamma would never approve.

Beatrice came to her aunt's room, when they went up stairs, and petitioned for a little talk, and Mrs. Frederick Langford, with kind pity for her present motherless condition, accepted her visit, and even allowed her to outstay Bennet, during whose operations the discussion of the charade, and the history of the preparations and contrivances, gave subject to a very animated conversation.

Then came matters of more interest. What Beatrice seemed above all to wish for, was to relieve herself by the expression of her intense dislike to the ball, and all the company, very nearly without exception, and there were few elders to whom a young damsel could talk so much without restraint as to Aunt Mary.

The waltzing, too, how glad she was that grandmamma had forbidden it, and here Henrietta chimed in. She had never seen waltzing before; had only heard of it as people in their quiet homes hear and think of the doings of the fashionable world, and in her simplicity was perfectly shocked and amazed at Jessie, a sort of relation, practising it and pleading for it.

"My dear!" said Beatrice, laughing, "I do not know what you would do if you were me, when there is Matilda St. Leger *polka-ing* away half the days of her life."

"Yes, but Lady Matilda is a regular fashionable young lady."

"Ay, and so is Jessie at heart. It is the elegance and the air, and the society that are wanting, not the will. It is the circumstances that make the difference, not the temper."

"Quite true, Busy Bee," said her aunt, "temper may be the same in very different circumstances."

"But it is very curious, mamma," said Henrietta, "how people can be particular in one point, and not in another. Now, Bee, I beg your pardon, only I know you don't mind it, Jessie did not approve of your skating."

"Yes," said Beatrice, "every one has scruples of his own, and laughs at those of other people."

"Which I think ought to teach Busy Bees to be rather less stinging," said Aunt Mary.

"But then, mamma," said Henrietta, "we must hold to the right scruples, and what are they? I do not suppose that in reality Jessie is less—less desirous of avoiding all that verges towards a want of propriety than we are, yet she waltzes. Now we were brought up to dislike such things."

"O, it is just according to what you are brought up to," said Beatrice. "A Turkish lady despises us for showing our faces : it is just as you think it."

"No, that will not do," said Henrietta. "Something must be actually wrong. Mamma, do say what you think."

"I think, my dear, that woman has been mercifully endowed with an instinct which discerns unconsciously what is becoming or not, and whatever at the first moment jars on that sense is unbecoming in her own individual case. The fineness of the perception may be destroyed by education, or wilful dulling, and often on one point it may thus be silent, though alive and active on others."

"Yes," said Henrietta, as if satisfied.

"And above all," said her mother, "it, like other gifts, grows dangerous, it may become affectation."

"Pruding," said Beatrice, "showing openly that you like it to be observed how prudent and proper you are."

"Whereas true delicacy would shrink from showing that it is conscious of anything wrong," said Henrietta. "Wrong I do not exactly mean, but something on the borders of it."

"Yes," said Aunt Mary, "and above all, do not let this delicacy show itself in the carping at other people, which only exalts our own opinion of ourselves, and very soon turns into 'judging our neighbour.'"

"But there is false delicacy, aunt."

"Yes, but it would be false kindness to enter on a fresh discussion to-night, when you ought to be fast asleep."

CHAPTER XI.

THE Queen Bee, usually undisputed sovereign of Knight Sutton, found in her cousin Roger a formidable rival. As son and heir, elder brother, and newly arrived after five years' absence, he had considerable claims to attention, and his high spirits, sailor manners, sea stories, and bold open temper, were in themselves such charms that it was no wonder that Frederick and Alexander were seduced from their allegiance, and even grandpapa was less than usual the property of his granddaughter.

This, however, she might have endured, had the sailor himself been amenable to her power, for his glories would then have become hers, and have afforded her further opportunities of coquetting with Fred. But between Roger and her there was little in common : he was not, and never had been, accessible to her influence ; he regarded her indeed with all the open-hearted affection of cousinly intercourse, but for the rest, thought her much too clever for him, and far less attractive than either Henrietta or Jessie.

If she would, Henrietta might have secured his devotion, for he was struck with her beauty, and considered it a matter of credit to himself to engross the prettiest person present. Had Beatrice been in her place, it may be doubted how far love of power, and the pleasure of teasing, might have carried her out of her natural character in the style that suited him; but Henrietta was too simple, and her mind too full of her own affairs even to perceive that he distinguished her. She liked him, but she showed none of the little airs which would have seemed to appropriate him. She was ready to be talked to, but only as she gave the attention due to any one, nay, showing, because she felt, less eagerness than if it had been grandpapa, Queen Bee, or Fred, a talk with the last of whom was a pleasure now longed for, but never enjoyed. To his stories of adventures, or accounts of manners, she lent a willing and a delighted ear; but all commonplace jokes tending to flirtation fell flat; she either did not catch them, or did not catch at them. She might blush and look confused, but it was uncomfortable, and not gratified embarrassment, and if she found an answer, it was one either to change the subject, or honestly manifest that she was not pleased.

She did not mortify Roger, who liked her all the time; and if he thought at all, only considered her as shy or grave, and still continued to admire her, and seek her out, whenever his former favourite, Jessie, was not in the way to rattle with in his usual style. Jessie was full of enjoyment, Henrietta was glad to be left to her own devices, her mamma was still more rejoiced to see her act so properly without self-consciousness or the necessity of interference, and the Queen Bee ought to have been duly grateful to the one faithful vassal who was proof against all allurements from her side and service.

She ought, but the melancholy fact is that the devotion of womankind is usually taken as a matter of course. Beatrice would have despised and been very angry with Henrietta had she deserted to Roger, but she did not feel in the least grateful for her adherence, and would have been much more proud of retaining either of the boys. There was one point on which their attention could still be commanded, namely, the charades ; for though the world may be of opinion that they had had quite a sufficiency of that amusement, they were but the more stimulated by their success on Thursday, and the sudden termination in the very height of their triumph.

They would, perhaps, have favoured the public with a repetition of Shylock's trial the next evening, but that, to the great consternation, and, perhaps, indignation of Beatrice, when she came down to breakfast in the morning, she found their tiring room, the study, completely cleared of all their various goods and chattels, Portia's wig in its box, the three caskets gone back to the dressing-room, the duke's throne safe in its place in the hall, and even Shylock's yellow cap picked to pieces, and rolled up in the general hoard of things which were to come of use in seven years' time.　Judith, who was putting the finishing touches to the re-arrangement by shaking up the cushions of the great chair, and restoring the inkstand to its place in the middle of the table, gave in answer to her exclamations the information that " Missus had been up since seven o'clock, helping to put away the things herself, for she said she could not bear to have Mr. Geoffrey's room not fit for anybody to sit in." This might certainly be considered as a tolerably broad hint that they had better discontinue their representations, but they were arrived at that state of eagerness which may be best illustrated by the proverb referring to a blind horse. Every one, inclined to that same impetuosity, and want of soberness, can remember the dismay with which hosts of such disregarded checks will recur to the mind when too late, and the poor satisfaction of the self-justification which truly answers that their object was not even comprehended. Henrietta, accustomed but little to heed such indications of dissent from her will, did not once think of her grandmamma's dislike, and Beatrice with her eyes fully open to it, wilfully despised it as a fidgety fancy.

Henrietta had devised a series of scenes for the word assassin, and greatly delighted the imagination of her partners by a proposal to make a pair of asses' ears of cotton velvet for the adornment of Bottom the weaver. Fred fell back in his chair in fits of laughing at the device, and Queen Bee capered and danced about the room, declaring her worthy to be her own "*primest* of viziers."

" And," said Beatrice, " what an exquisite interlude it will make to relieve the various plagues of Monday evening."

" Why you don't mean to act then !" exclaimed Henrietta.

" Why not? You don't know what a relief it will be. It will be an excuse for getting away from all the stupidity."

" To be sure it will," cried Fred. " A bright thought, Mrs. Bee. We shall have it all to ourselves in the study in comfort."

" But would grandmamma ever let us do it ?" said Henrietta.

" I will manage," said Beatrice. " I will make grandpapa agree to it, and then she will not mind. Think how he enjoyed it."

" Before so many people !" said Henrietta. " O, Queenie, it will never do ! It would be a regular exhibition."

" My dear, what nonsense !" said Beatrice. " Why, it is all among friends and neighbours."

" Friends and neighbours to you," said Henrietta.

" And yours too. Fred, she is deserting ! I thought you meant to adopt or inherit all Knight Sutton and its neighbourhood could offer."

" A choice inheritance that neighbourhood, by your account," said Fred. " But come, Henrietta, you must not spoil the whole affair by such nonsense and affectation."

"Affectation! O, Fred!"

"Yes, to be sure it is," said Fred: "to set up such scruples as these. Why, you said yourself that you forgot all about the spectators when once you get into the spirit of the thing."

"And what is affectation," said Beatrice, seeing her advantage, "but thinking what other people will think?"

There are few persuasions to which a girl who claims to possess some degree of sense is more accessible, than the imputation of affectation, especially when brought forward by a brother, and enforced by a clever and determined friend. Such a feeling is no doubt often very useful in preventing folly, but it may sometimes be perverted to the smothering of wholesome scruples. Henrietta only pressed one point more, she begged not to be Titania.

"O, you must, you silly child," said Beatrice. "I have such designs for dressing you! Besides, I mean to be Mustardseed, and make grandpapa laugh by my by-play at the giant Oxbeef."

"But consider, Bee," said Henrietta, "how much too tall I am for a fairy. It would be too absurd to make Titania as large as Bottom himself—spoil the whole picture. You might surely get some little girls to be the other fairies, and take Titania yourself."

"Certainly it might conciliate the people to have their own children made part of the show," said Beatrice. "Little Anna Carey has sense enough, I think; ay, and the two Nevilles, if they will not be shy. We will keep you to come out in grand force in the last scene—Queen Eleanor sucking the poison. Aunt Mary has a certain black-lace scarf that will make an excellent Spanish mantilla. Or else suppose you are Berengaria, coming to see King Richard when he was 'old-man-of-the-mountained.' "

"No, no," cried Fred, "stick to the Queen Eleanor scene.

We will have no more blacking of faces. Yesterday I was too late down stairs, because I could not get the abominable stuff out of my hair."

"And it would be a cruel stroke to be taken for Philip Carey again, in the gentleman's own presence too," said Beatrice. "Monsieur is apparemment the apothecaire de famille. Do you remember, Henrietta, the French governess in Miss Edgeworth's book?"

"Jessie smiled and nodded as if she was perfectly enchanted with the mistake," said Henrietta.

"And I do not wonder at it," said Beatrice, "the mistake, I mean. Fred's white hands there have just the look of a doctor's; of course Roger thought the only use for them could be to feel pulses, and Philip, for want of something better to do, is always trying for a genteel look."

"You insulting creature!" said Fred. "Just as if I tried to look genteel."

"You do, then, whether you try or not. You can't help it, you know, and I am very sorry for you; but you do stand and walk and hold out your hand just as Philip is always trying to do, and it is no wonder Roger thought he had succeeded in attaining his object."

"But what a goose the man must be to make such absurdity his object," said Henrietta.

"He could not be a Carey and be otherwise," said Busy Bee. "And besides, what would you have him do? As to getting any practice, unless his kith and kin choose to victimise themselves philanthropically according to Roger's proposal, I do not see what chance he has, where every one knows the extent of a Carey's intellects; and what is left for the poor man to do but to study the cut of his boots?"

"If you say much more about it, Queenie," said Henrietta, "you will make Fred dance in Bottom's hob-nailed shoes."

"Ah! it is a melancholy business," said Beatrice; "but it cannot be helped. Fred cannot turn into a clodhopper. But what earthquake is this?" exclaimed she, as the front door was dashed open with such violence as to shake the house, and the next moment Alexander rushed in, heated and almost breathless. "Rats! rats!" was his cry; "Fred, that's right. But where is Uncle Geoffrey?"

"Gone to Allonfield."

"More's the pity. There are a whole host of rats in the great barn at home. Pincher caught me one just now, and they are going to turn the place regularly out, only I got them to wait while I came up here for you and Uncle Geoffrey. Come, make haste, fly—like smoke—while I go and tell grandpapa."

Off flew Fred to make his preparation, and off to the drawing-room hurried Alex to call grandpapa. He was greeted by a reproof from Mrs. Langford for shaking the house enough to bring it down, and grandpapa laughed, thanked him, and said he hoped to be at Sutton Leigh in time for the rat hunt, as he was engaged to drive grandmamma and Aunt Mary thither and to the Pleasance that afternoon.

Two seconds more, and Fred and Alex were speeding away together, and the girls went up to put on their bonnets to walk and meet their elders at Sutton Leigh. For once Beatrice let Henrietta be as slow as she pleased, for she was willing to let as much of the visit as possible pass before they arrived there. They walked along merrily concocting their arrangements for Monday evening, until at length they came to the gates of Sutton Leigh, and already heard the shouts of triumph, the barking of dogs, and the cackle of terrified poultry, which proclaimed that the war was at its height.

"O! the glories of a rat hunt!" cried Beatrice. "Come,

Henrietta, here is a safe place whence to contemplate it, and really it is a sight not to be lost."

Henrietta thought not indeed when she looked over a gate leading into the farm-yard on the side opposite to the great old barn, raised on a multitude of stone posts, a short ladder reaching to the wide doors which were folded back so as to display the heaps of straw thrown violently back and forward; the dogs now standing in attitudes of ecstatic expectation, tail straight out, head bent forward, now springing in rapture on the prey; the boys rushing about with their huge sticks, and coming down now and then with thundering blows, the labourers with their white shirt sleeves and pitchforks pulling down the straw, Uncle Roger with a portentous-looking club in the thick of the fight. On the ladder, cheering them on, stood grandpapa, holding little Tom in his arms, and at the bottom, armed with small sticks, were Charlie and Arthur, consoling themselves for being turned out of the melée, by making quite as much noise as all those who were doing real execution, thumping unmercifully at every unfortunate dead mouse or rat that was thrown out, and charging fiercely at the pigs, ducks, and geese that now and then came up to inspect proceedings, and perhaps, for such accidents will occur in the best regulated families, to devour a share of the prey.

Beatrice's first exclamation was, "O! if papa was but here!"

"Nothing can go on without him, I suppose," said Henrietta. "And yet, is this one of his great enjoyments?"

"My dear, don't you know it is a part of the privilege of a free-born Englishman to delight in hunting 'rats and mice and such small deer,' as much or more than the grand chasse? I have not the smallest doubt that all the old cavaliers were fine old farm-loving fellows, who liked a rat hunt, and enjoyed turning out a barn with all their hearts."

"There goes Fred!" cried Henrietta.

"Ah! capital. He takes to it by nature, you see. There —there! O what a scene it is! Look how beautifully the sun comes in, making that solid sort of light on the mist of dust at the top."

"And how beautifully it falls on grandpapa's head! I think that grandpapa with little Tom is one of the best parts of the picture, Bee."

"To be sure he is, that noble old head of his, and that beautiful gentle face; and to see him pointing, and soothing the child when he gets frightened at the hubbub, and then enjoying the victories over the poor rats as keenly as anybody!"

"Certainly," said Henrietta, "there is something very odd in man's nature; they can like to do such cruel-sounding things without being cruel! Grandpapa, or Fred, or Uncle Roger, or Alex now, they are as kind and gentle as possible: yet the delight they can take in catching and killing—"

"That is what town-people never can understand," said Beatrice, "that hunting-spirit of mankind. I hate above all things to hear it cried down, and the nonsense that is talked about it. I only wish that those people could have seen what I did last summer—grandpapa calling Carey, and holding the ladder for him while he put the young birds into their nest that had fallen out. And O the uproar that there was one day when Dick did something cruel to a poor rabbit; it was two or three years ago, and Alex and Carey set upon him and thrashed him so that they were really punished for it; bad as it was of Dick; it was one of those bursts of generous indignation."

"It is a very curious thing," said Henrietta, "the soldier spirit it must be, I suppose—"

"What are you philosophizing about, young ladies?"

asked Mr. Langford, coming up as Henrietta said these last words.

"Only about the spirit of the chace, grandpapa," said Beatrice, "what the pleasure can be of the field of slaughter there."

"Something mysterious, you may be sure, young ladies," said grandpapa. "I have hunted rats once or twice a year now these seventy years or more, and I can't say I am tired yet. And there is Master Fred going at it, for the first time in his life, as fiercely as any of us old veterans, and he has a very good eye for a hit, I can tell you, if it is any satisfaction to you. Ha! hoigh Vixen! hoigh Carey! that's it—there he goes!"

"Now, grandpapa," said Beatrice, catching hold of his hand, "I want just to speak to you. Don't you think we might have a little charade-acting on Monday to enliven the evening a little?"

"Eh? what? More charades? Well, they are very pretty sport, only I think they would astonish the natives here a little. Are we to have the end of Shylock?"

"No," said Beatrice, "we never condescend to repeat ourselves. We have a new word and a beauty, and don't you think it will do very well?"

"I am afraid grandmamma will think you are going to take to private theatricals."

"Well, it won't be nearly such regular acting as the last," said Beatrice, "I do not think it would do to take another half-play for so many spectators, but a scene or two mostly in dumb show would make a very nice diversion. Only say that you consent, grandpapa."

"Well, I don't see any harm in it," said grandpapa, "so long as grandmamma does not mind it. I suppose your mamma does not, Henrietta?"

"O no," said Henrietta, with a certain mental reservation

that she would make her not mind it, or at any rate not
gainsay it. Fred's calling her affected was enough to make
her consent, and bring her mamma to consent to anything;
for so little is it really the nature of woman to exercise power,
that if she domineers, it is sure to be compensated by some
subjection in some other manner: and if Henrietta ruled
her mother, she was completely under the dominion of Fred
and Beatrice. Themistocles' wife might rule Athens, but
she was governed by her son.

After this conversation they went in, and found Aunt
Roger very busy, recommending servants to Aunt Mary,
and grandmamma enforcing all she said. The visit soon
came to an end, and they went on to the Pleasance, where
the inspection did not prove quite as agreeable as on the
first occasion; for grandmamma and Beatrice had very different views respecting the appropriation of the rooms, and
poor Mrs. Frederick Langford was harassed and wearied by
her vain attempts to accede to the wishes of both, and vex
neither. Grandmamma was determined too to look over
every corner, and discuss every room, and Henrietta, in
despair at the fatigue her mother was obliged to go through,
kept on seeking in vain for a seat for her, and having at last
discovered a broken-backed kitchen chair in some of the
regions below, kept diligently carrying it after her in all her
peregrinations. She was constantly wishing that Uncle
Geoffrey would come, but in vain; and between the long
talking at Sutton Leigh, the wandering about the house, and
the many discussions, her mamma was completely tired out,
and obliged, when they came home, to confess that she
had a headache. Henrietta fairly wished her safe at Rocksand.

While Henrietta was attending her mother to her own
room, and persuading her to lay up for the evening, Beatrice,
whose head was full of but one matter, pursued Mrs. Lang-

ford into the study, and propounded her grand object. As
she fully expected, she met with a flat refusal, and sitting
down in her arm-chair, Mrs. Langford very earnestly began
with "Now listen to me, my dear child," and proceeded
with a long story of certain private theatricals some forty
years ago, which, to her certain knowledge, ended in a young
lady eloping with a music-master. Beatrice set to work to
argue : in the first place it was not probable that either she
or Henrietta would run away with their cousins ; secondly,
that the former elopement was not chargeable on poor
Shakespeare ; thirdly, that these were not theatricals at all.

"And pray what are they, then—when you dress yourselves up, and speak the speeches out as boldly as Mrs.
Siddons, or any of them ?"

"You pay us a great compliment," said Beatrice, who
could sometimes be pert when alone with grandmamma ;
and then she went on with her explanation of how very far
this was from anything that could be called theatrical ; it
was the guessing the word, not their acting, that was the
important point. The distinction was too fine for grandmamma ; it was play-acting, and that was enough for her,
and she would not have it done. "But grandpapa liked it,
and had given full consent." This was a powerful piece of
ordnance which Beatrice had kept in reserve, but at the first
moment the shot did not *tell.*

Ladies were the best judges in such a case as this, said
Mrs. Langford, and let who would consent, she would never
have *her* granddaughters standing up, speaking speeches out
of Shakespeare, before a whole room full of company.

"Well, then, grandmamma, I'll tell you what : to oblige
you, we will not have one single scene out of Shakespeare—
not one. Won't that do ?"

"You will go to some other play-book, and that is worse,"
said Mrs. Langford.

"No, no, we will not: we will do every bit out of our own heads, and it shall be almost all Fred and Alex; Henrietta and I will scarcely come in at all. And it will so shorten the evening, and amuse every one so nicely! and grandpapa has said we may."

Mrs. Langford gave a sort of sigh. "Ah, well! you always will have your own way, and I suppose you must; but I never thought to see such things in my house. In my day, young people thought no more of a scheme when their elders had once said, No."

"Yes, only you must not say so, grandmamma. I am sure we would give it up if you did; but pray do not—we will manage very well."

"And put the whole house in a mess, as you did last time; turn everything upside down. I tell you, Beatrice, I can't have it done. I shall want the study to put out the supper in."

"We can dress in our own rooms, then," said Beatrice; "never mind that."

"Well, then, if you will make merry-andrews of yourselves, and your fathers and mothers like to let you, I can't help it—that's all I have to say," said Mrs. Langford, walking out of the room; while Fred entered from the other side a moment after. "Victory, victory, my dear Fred!" cried Beatrice, darting to meet him in an ecstasy, "I have prevailed: you find me in the hour of victory. The Assassin for ever! announced for Monday night, before a select audience!"

"Well, you are an irresistible Queen Bee," said Fred; "why Alex has just been telling me ever so much that his mother told him about grandmamma's dislike to it. I thought the whole concern a gone 'coon, as they say in America."

"I got grandpapa first," said Beatrice, "and then I persuaded her; she told me it would lead to all sorts of mischief, and gave me a long lecture which had nothing to do with it. But I found at last that the chief points which alarmed her were poor Shakespeare and the confusion in the study; so by giving up those two I gained everything."

"You don't mean that you gave up Bully Bottom?"

"Yes, I do; but you need not resign your asses' ears. You shall wear them in the character of King Midas."

"I think," said the ungrateful Fred, "that you might as well have given it all up together as Bottom."

"No, no; just think what capabilities there are in Midas. We will decidedly make him King of California, and I'll be the priestess of Apollo; there is an old three-legged epergne-stand that will make a most excellent tripod. And only think of the whispering into the reeds, 'King Midas has the ears of an ass.' I would have made more of a fight for Bottom, if that had not come into my head."

"But you will have nothing to do."

"That helped to conciliate. I promised we girls should appear very little, and for the sake of effect, I had rather Henrietta broke on the world in all her beauty at the end. I do look forward to seeing her as Queen Eleanor; she will look so regal."

Fred smiled, for he delighted in his sister's praises. "You are a wondrous damsel, busy one," said he, "to be content to play second fiddle."

"Second fiddle! As if I were not the great moving spring! Trust me, you would never write yourself down an ass but for the Queen Bee. How shall we ever get your ears from Allonfield? Saturday night, and only till Monday evening to do everything in!"

"Oh, you will do it," said Fred. "I wonder what you

and Henrietta cannot do between you! Oh, there is Uncle Geoffrey come in," he exclaimed, as he heard the front door open.

"And I must go and dress," said Beatrice, seized with a sudden haste, which did not speak well for the state of her conscience.

Uncle Geoffrey was in the hall, taking off his mud-bespattered gaiters. "So you are entered with the vermin, Fred," called he, as the two came out of the drawing-room.

"O how we wished for you, Uncle Geoffrey! but how did you hear it?"

"I met Alex just now. Capital sport you must have had. Are you only just come in?"

"No, we were having a consultation about the charades," said Fred; "the higher powers consent to our having them on Monday."

"Grandmamma approving?" asked Uncle Geoffrey.

"O yes," said Fred, in all honesty, "she only objected to our taking a regular scene in a play, and 'coming it as strong' as we did the other night; so it is to be all extemporary, and it will do famously."

Beatrice, who had been waiting in the dark at the top of the stairs, listening, was infinitely rejoiced that her project had been explained so plausibly, and yet in such perfect good faith, and she flew off to dress in high spirits. Had she mentioned it to her father, he would have doubted, taken it as her scheme, and perhaps put a stop to it: but hearing of it from Frederick, whose pleasures were so often thwarted, was likely to make him far more unwilling to object. For its own sake, she knew he had no objection to the sport; it was only for that of his mother; and since he had heard of her as consenting, all was right. No, could Beatrice actually say so to her own secret soul?

She could not; but she could smother the still small voice that checked her, in a multitude of plans, and projects, and criticisms, and airy castles, and, above all, the pleasure of triumph and dominion, and the resolution not to yield, and the delight of leading.

CHAPTER XII.

"OUR hearts and all our members, being mortified from all worldly and carnal lusts :" so speaks the collect with which we begin the new year—such the prayer to which the lips of the young Langfords said, "Amen :" but what was its application to them? What did they do with the wicked world in their own guarded homes? There was Uncle Geoffrey, he was in the world. It might be for him to pray for that spirit which enabled him to pass unscathed through the perils of his profession, neither tempted to grasp at the honours nor the wealth which lay in his way, unhardened and unsoured by the contact of the sin and selfishness on every side. This might indeed be the world. There was Jessie Carey, with her love of dress, and admiration, and pleasure; she should surely pray that she might live less to the vanities of the world; there were others, whose worn countenances spoke of hearts devoted to the cares of the world; but those fair, fresh, happy young things, early taught how to prize vain pomp and glory, their minds as yet free from anxiety, looking from a safe distance on the busy field of trial and temptation—were not they truly kept from that world which they had renounced?

Alas! that they did not lay to heart that the world is everywhere; that if education had placed them above being tempted by the poorer, cheaper, and more ordinary attractions, yet allurements there were for them also. A pleasure pursued with headlong vehemence because it was of their own devising, love of rule, the spirit of rivalry, the want of submission; these were of the world. Other temptations had not yet reached them, but if they gave way to those which assailed them in their early youth, how could they expect to have strength to bear up against the darker and stronger ones which would meet their riper years?

Even before daylight had fully found its way into Knight Sutton Hall, there was many a note of preparation, and none clearer or louder than those of the charade actors. Beatrice was up long before light, in the midst of her preparations, and it was not long after, as lamp in hand, she whisked through the passages, Frederick's voice was heard demanding whether the Busy Bee had turned into a firefly, and if the paste was made wherewith Midas was to have his crown stuck with gold paper. Zealous indeed were the workers, and heartily did old Judith wish them anywhere else, as she drove them, their lamps, their paste, and newspaper, from one corner of the study to the other, and at last, fairly out into the hall, threatening them with what Missus would say to them. At last, grandmamma came down with a party of neat little notes in her hand, to be immediately sent off by Martin and the cart to Allonfield, and Martin came to the door leading to the kitchen regions to receive his directions.

"O, how lucky!" cried Queen Bee, springing up. "The cotton velvet for the ears! I'll write a note in a second!" Then she paused. "But I can't do it without Henrietta; I don't know how much she wants. Half a yard must do, I suppose; but then, how to describe it? Half a yard of donkey-coloured velvet! It will never do; I must see Henrietta first."

"Have not you heard her bell?" said Fred.

"No: shall I go and knock at the door? She must be up by this time."

"You had better ask Bennet," said Fred; "she sometimes gets up quietly, and dresses herself without Bennet, if mamma is asleep, because it gives her a palpitation to be disturbed in the morning."

Bennet was shouted for, and proved not to have been into her mistress's room. The charade mania was not strong enough to make them venture upon disturbing Mrs. Frederick Langford, and to their great vexation, Martin departed bearing no commission for the asinine decorations.

About half an hour after, Henrietta made her appearance, as sorry as any one that the opportunity had been lost, more especially as mamma had been broad awake all the time, and the only reason she had not rung the bell was, that she was not ready for Bennet.

As usual, she was called an incorrigible dawdle, and made humble confession of the same, offering to do all in her power to make up for the morning's laziness. But what would Midas be without his ears?

The best plan that Queen Bee could devise, was, that, whilst Henrietta was engaged with the other preparations, she should walk to Sutton Leigh with Frederick, to despatch Alexander to Allonfield. No sooner said than done, and off they set, but neither was this plan fated to meet with success; for just as they came in sight of Sutton Leigh, they were hailed by the loud hearty voice of Roger, and beheld him at the head of four brothers, marching off to pay his respects to his Aunt Carey, some three miles off. Alex came to hold counsel at Queen Bee's summons, but he could do nothing for her, for he had that morning been taken to task for not having made a visit to Mrs. Carey, since he came home, and especially ordered off to call upon her, before meeting her at the party that evening.

"How abominably provoking!" cried Beatrice; "just as if it signified. If I had but a fairy!"

"Carey!" called Alex, "here! Bee wants to send over to Allonfield: won't you take Dumple, and go?"

"Not I," responded Carey; "I want to walk with Roger. But there's Dumple, let her go herself."

"What, ride him?" asked Beatrice, "thank you, Carey."

"Fred might drive you," said Carey; "O no, poor fellow, I suppose he does not know how."

Fred coloured with anger. "I do," said he; "I have often driven our own horses."

"Ay," said Beatrice, "with the coachman sitting by you, and Aunt Mary little guessing what you were doing."

"I assure you, Queen," said Fred, very earnestly, "I do really know how to drive, and if we may have the gig, and you will trust yourself with me, I will bring you home quite safe."

"I know you can have the gig," said Carey, "for papa offered it to Roger and Alex this morning; only we chose all to walk together. To think of doubting whether to drive old Dumple!"

"I don't question," said Fred; "I only want to know if Busy Bee will go. I won't break your neck, I promise you."

Beatrice was slightly mistrustful, and had some doubts about Aunt Mary, but poor Alex did much to decide her, though intending quite the reverse.

"I don't advise you, Bee," said he.

"O, as to that," said she, pleased to see that he disliked the plan, "I have great faith in Dumple's experience, and I can sit tight in a chay, as the boy said to grandpapa when he asked him if he could ride. My chief doubt is about Aunt Mary."

Fred's successful disobedience in the matter of skating had decidedly made him less scrupulous about showing open disregard of his mother's desires, and he answered in a certain superior patronising manner, "O, you know I only give way sometimes, because she does make herself so intensely miserable about me; but as she will be spared all that now, by knowing nothing about it, I don't think it need be considered."

Beatrice recollected what her father had said, but eluded it the next moment, by replying to herself, that no commands had been given in this case.

Alex stood fumbling with the button of his great-coat, looking much annoyed, and saying nothing; Roger called out to him that they could not wait all day, and he exerted himself to take Beatrice by the arm, and say, "Bee, I wish you would not, I am sure there will be a blow-up about it at home."

"O, you think nobody can or may drive me but yourself, Master Alex," said Beatrice, laughing. "No, no, I know very well that nobody will care when it is done, and there are no commands one way or the other. I love my own neck, I assure you, Alex, and will not get that into a scrape. Come, if that will put you into a better humour, I'll dance with you first to-night."

Alex turned away, muttering, "I don't like it—I'd go myself, but—well, I shall speak to Fred."

Beatrice smiled with triumph at the jealousy which she thought she had excited, and watched to see the effect of the remonstrance.

"You are sure now," said he, "that you can drive safely? Remember it would be a tolerable piece of work if you were to damage that little Bee."

This eloquent expostulation might have had some weight, if it had come from any one else; but Fred was too much annoyed at the superiority of his rival to listen with any patience, and he replied rather sullenly, that he could take as good care of her as Alex himself, and he only wished that their own horses were come from Rocksand.

"Well, I have no more to say," said Alex, "only please to mind this, Langford junior, you may do just as you please with our horse, drive him to Jericho for what I care. It was for your own sake and Beatrice's that I spoke."

"Much obliged, Langford senior," replied Fred, making himself as tall as he could, and turning round to Carey with a very different tone, "Now, Carey, we won't stop you any longer, if you'll only just be so good as to tell your man to get out the gig."

Carey did so, and Beatrice and Frederick were left alone, but not long, for Uncle Roger presently came into the yard, with Willy and Arthur running after him. To take possession of his horse and carriage, in his very sight, without permission, was quite impossible, and, besides, Beatrice knew full well that her dexterity could obtain a sanction from him, which might be made to parry all blame. So, tripping up to him, she explained in a droll manner the distress in which the charade actors stood, and how the boys had said that they might have Dumple to drive to Allonfield. Good-natured Uncle Roger, who did not see why Fred should not drive as well as Alex or any of his other boys, knew little or nothing of his sister-in-law's fears, and would, perhaps, have taken Fred's side of the question if he had, did exactly as she intended, declared them perfectly welcome to the use of Dumple, and sent Willy into the house for the driving whip. Thus authorised, Beatrice did not fear even her father, who was not likely to allow in words what a nonentity the authority of Uncle Roger might really be esteemed.

Willy came back with a shilling in his hand, and an entreaty that he might go with Queen Bee and Fred, to buy a cannon for the little ships, of which Roger's return always produced a whole fleet at Sutton Leigh. His cousins were in a triumphant temper of good-nature, and willingly consenting, he was perched between them; but for one moment Beatrice's complacency was diminished, as Uncle Roger called out, "Ha! Fred, take care! What are you doing?—you'll be against the gate-post—don't bring his head so short round. If you don't take more care, you'll certainly come to a smash before you get home."

If honour and credit had not been concerned, both Beatrice and Frederick would probably have been much better satisfied to have given up their bold design after this *début*, but they were far too much bent on their own way to yield, and Fred's pride would never have allowed him to acknowledge that he felt himself unequal to the task he had so rashly undertaken. Uncle Roger, believing it to be only carelessness instead of ignorance, and too much used to dangerous undertakings of his own boys to have many anxieties on their account, let them go on without further question, and turned off to visit his young wheat without the smallest uneasiness respecting the smash he had predicted, as he had done, by way of warning, at least twenty times before.

Busy Bee was in that stage of girlhood which is very sensible on some points, in the midst of great folly upon others, and she was quite wise enough to let Fred alone, to give full attention to his driving all the way to Allonfield. Dumple knew perfectly well what was required of him, and went on at a very steady well-behaved pace, up the hill, across the common, and into the town, where, leaving him at the inn, they walked into the street, and Beatrice, after an infinity of searching, succeeded in obtaining certain grey cotton velvet, which, though Fred asserted that donkeys had a tinge of lilac, was certainly not unfit to represent their colour. As Fred's finances were in a much more flourishing state since New Year's day, he proceeded to delight the very heart of Willy by a present of a pair of little brass cannon, on which his longing eyes had often before been fixed, and they then returned to the carriage, in some dismay on perceiving that it was nearly one o'clock.

"We must go straight home," said Beatrice, "or this velvet will be of no use. There is no time to drive to Sutton Leigh and walk from thence."

Unfortunately, however, there was an influential personage who was by no means willing to consent to this arrangement, namely, Dumple, who, well aware that an inexperienced hand held the reins, was privately determined that his nose should not be turned away from the shortest road to his own stable.

As soon, therefore, as he came to the turning towards Sutton Leigh, he made a decided dash in that direction. Fred pulled him sharply, and a little nervously; the horse resisted; Fred gave him a cut with the whip, but Dumple felt that he had the advantage, and, replying with a demonstration of kicking, suddenly whisked round the corner, and set off over the rough jolting road at a pace very like running away. Fred pulled hard, but the horse went the faster. He stood up. "Sit still," cried Beatrice, now speaking for the first time, "the gate will stop him;" but ere the words were uttered, Frederick, whether by a movement of his own, or the rapid motion of the carriage, she knew not, was thrown violently to the ground; and as she was whirled on, she saw him no more. Instinct, rather than presence of mind, made her hold fast to the carriage with one hand, and throw the other arm round little Willy, to prevent him from being thrown out, as they were shaken from side to side by the ruts and stones over which they were jolted. A few minutes more, and their way was barred by a gate—that which she had spoken of—the horse, used to stopping there, slackened his pace, and stood still, looking over it as if nothing had happened.

Trembling in every limb, Beatrice stood safely on the

ground, and Willy beside her. Without speaking, she hurried back to seek for Fred, her steps swifter than they had ever before been, though to herself it seemed as if her feet were of lead, and the very throbbing of her heart dragged her back. In every bush she fancied she saw Fred coming to meet her, but it was only for a moment, and at length she saw him but too plainly. He was stretched at full length on the ground, senseless—motionless. She sank rather than knelt down beside him, and called him; but not a token was there that he heard her. She lifted his hand, it fell powerless, and clasping her own, she sat in an almost unconscious state of horror, till roused by little Willy, who asked in a terrified breathless whisper,

"Bee, is he dead?"

"No, no, no," cried she, as if she could frighten away her own fears; "he is only stunned. He is—he must be alive. He will come to himself! Help me to lift him up—here—that is it—his head on my lap—"

"O, the blood!" said Willy, recoiling in increased fear, as he saw it streaming from one or two deep cuts and bruises on the side of the face.

"That is not the worst," said Beatrice. "There—hold him towards the wind." She raised his head, untied his handkerchief, and hung over him; but there was not a sound, not a breath; his head sank a dead weight on her knee. She locked her hands together, and gazed round wildly for help; but no one all over the wide lonely common could be seen, except Willy, who stood helplessly looking at her.

"Aunt Mary! O, Aunt Mary!" cried she, in a tone of the bitterest anguish of mind. "Fred—dear, dear Freddy, open your eyes, answer me! Oh, only speak to me! O what shall I do?"

"Pray to God," whispered Willy.

"You—you—Willy; I can't—it was my doing. O, Aunt Mary!" A few moments passed in silence, then she exclaimed, "What are we doing here? Willy, you must go and call them. The Hall is nearest; go through the plantation as fast as you can. Go to papa in the study; if he is not there, find grandpapa—any one but Aunt Mary. Mind, Willy, don't let her hear it, it would kill her. Go, fly! You understand—any one but Aunt Mary."

Greatly relieved at being sent out of the sight of that senseless form, Willy required no second bidding, but rushed off at a pace which bade fair to bring him to the Hall in very brief space. Infinite were the ramifications of thought that now began to chase each other over the surface of her mind, as she sat supporting her cousin's head, all clear and distinct, yet all overshadowed by that agony of suspense which made her sit as if she was all eye and ear, watching for the slightest motion, the faintest sound, that hope might seize as a sign of life. She wiped away the blood which was streaming from the cuts in the face, and softly laid her trembling hand to seek for some trace of a blow amid the fair shining hair; she felt the pulse, but she could not satisfy herself whether it beat or not; she rubbed the cold hand between both her own, and again and again started with the hope that the long black eyelashes were being lifted from the white cheek, or that she saw a quivering of lip or nostril. All this while her thoughts were straying miles away, and yet so wondrously and painfully present. As she thought of her Uncle Frederick, and, as it were, realized his death, which had happened so nearly in this same manner, she experienced a sort of heart-sinking which would almost make her believe in a fate on the family. And that Fred should be cut off in the midst of an act of disobedience, and she the cause! O thought beyond endurance! She tried to pray for him, for herself, for her aunt, but no prayer would come;

and suddenly she found her mind pursuing Willy, following him through all the gates and gaps, entering the garden, opening the study door, seeing her father's sudden start, hearing poor Henrietta's cry, devising how it would be broken to her aunt; and again, the misery of recollecting *her* overpowered her, and she gave a groan, the very sound of which thrilled her with the hope that Fred was reviving, and made her, if possible, watch with double intenseness, and then utter a desponding sigh. She wished it was she who lay there, unconscious of such exceeding wretchedness, and, strange to say, her imagination began to devise all that would be said were it really so; what all her acquaintance would say of the little Queen Bee, how soon Matilda St. Leger would forget her, how long Henrietta would cherish the thought of her, how deeply and silently Alex would grieve. "He would be a son to papa," she thought; but then came a picture of her home, her father and mother without their only one, and tears came into her eyes, which she brushed away, almost smiling at the absurdity of crying for her own imagined death, instead of weeping over this but too positive and present distress.

There was nothing to interrupt her; Fred lay as lifeless as before, and not a creature passed along the lonely road. The frosty air was perfectly still, and through it sounded the barking of dogs, the tinkle of the sheep-bell, the woodman's axe in the plantations, and now and then the rattle of Dumple's harness, as he shook his head or shifted his feet at the gate where he had been left standing. The rooks wheeled above her head in a clear blue sky, the little birds answering each other from the high furze-bushes, and the pee-wits came careering near her with their broad wings, floating movement, and long melancholy note like lamentation.

At length, far away, there sounded on the hard turnpike road a horse's tread, coming nearer and nearer. Help was at hand! Be it who it might, some human sympathy would be with her, and that most oppressive solitude, which seemed to have lasted for years instead of minutes, would be relieved. In almost an agony of nervousness lest the new-comer might pass by, she gently laid her cousin's head on the grass, and flew rather than ran towards the opening of the lane. She was too late, the horseman had passed, but she recognised the shining hat, the form of the shoulders, and with a scream almost wild in its energy, called " Philip! O, Philip Carey !"

Joy, joy! he looked back, he turned his horse, and came up in amazement at finding her there, and asking questions which she could only answer by leading the way down the lane.

In another moment he was off his horse, and she could almost have adored him when she heard him pronounce that Frederick lived.

A few moments passed whilst he was handling his patient, and asking questions, when Beatrice beheld some figures advancing from the plantation. She dashed through the heath and furze to meet them, sending her voice before her with the good news, " He is alive! Philip Carey says he is alive !" and with these words she stood before her father and her Aunt Mary.

Her aunt seemed neither to see nor hear her; but with a face as white and still as a marble figure, hastened on. Mr. Geoffrey Langford stopped for an instant and looked at her with an expression such as she never could forget. " Beatrice, my child !" he exclaimed, " you are hurt !"

" No, no, papa," she cried. " It is Fred's blood—I am quite, quite safe !"

He held her in his arms, pressed her close to him, and kissed her brow, with a whispered exclamation of fervent thankfulness. Beatrice could never remember that moment

without tears; the tone, the look, the embrace,—all had revealed to her the fervour of her father's affection, beyond—
far beyond all that she had ever imagined. It was but
for one instant that he thus gave way; the next, he was
hastening on, and stood beside Frederick as soon as his
sister-in-law.

CHAPTER XIII.

THE drawing-room at Knight Sutton Hall was in that state of bustle incidental to the expectation of company, which was sure to prevail wherever Mrs. Langford reigned. She walked about, removing the covers from chairs and ottomans, shaking out curtains, adjusting china, and appealing to Mrs. Frederick Langford in various matters of taste, though never allowing her to move to assist her. Henrietta, however, often came to her help, and was certainly acting in a way to incur the severe displeasure of the absent queen, by laying aside Midas's robes to assist in the arrangements. "That picture is crooked, I am sure!" said Mrs. Langford; and of course she was not satisfied till she had summoned Geoffrey from the study to give his opinion, and had made him mount upon a chair to settle its position. In the midst of the operation, in walked Uncle Roger. "Hollo! Geoffrey, what are you up to now? So, ma'am, you are making yourself smart to-day. Where is my father?"

"He has ridden over to see the South farm," said Mrs. Langford.

"Oho! got out of the way of the beautifying,—I understand."

"Have you seen anything of Fred and Busy Bee?" asked Mrs. Frederick Langford. "They went out directly after breakfast to walk to Sutton Leigh, and I have not seen them since."

"O yes," said Mr. Roger Langford, "I can tell you what has become of them; they are gone to Allonfield. I have just seen them off in the gig, and Will with them, after some of their acting affairs."

Good, easy man; he little thought what a thunder-clap was this intelligence. Uncle Geoffrey turned round on his elevation to look him full in the face; every shade of colour left the countenance of Mrs. Frederick Langford; Henrietta let her work fall, and looked up in dismay.

"You don't mean that Fred was driving?" said her mother.

"Yes, I do! Why my boys can drive long before they are that age,—sure he knows how!"

"O, Roger, what have you done!" said she faintly, as if the exclamation would break from her in spite of herself.

"Indeed, mamma," said Henrietta, alarmed at her paleness, "I assure you Fred has often told me how he has driven our own horses when he was sitting up by Dawson."

"Ay, ay, Mary," said Uncle Roger, "never fear. Depend upon it, boys do many and many a thing that mammas never guess at, and come out with whole bones after all."

Henrietta, meantime, was attentively watching Uncle Geoffrey's face, in hopes of discovering what he thought of the danger; but she could learn nothing, for he kept his features as composed as possible.

"I do believe those children are gone crazy about their acting," said Mrs. Langford; "and how Mr. Langford can encourage them in it I cannot think. So silly of Bee to go off in this way, when she might just as well have sent by Martin!" And her head being pretty much engrossed with her present occupation, she went out to obey a summons from the kitchen, without much perception of the consternation that prevailed in the drawing-room.

"Did you know they were going, Henrietta?" asked Uncle Geoffrey, rather sternly.

"No! I thought they meant to send Alex. But O! uncle, do you think there is any danger?" exclaimed she, losing self-control in the infection of fear caught from the mute terror which she saw her mother struggling to overcome. Her mother's inquiring, imploring glance followed her question.

"Foolish children!" said Uncle Geoffrey, "I am very much vexed with the Bee for her wilfulness about this scheme, but as for the rest, there is hardly a steadier animal than old Dumple, and he is pretty well used to young hands."

Henrietta thought him quite satisfied, and even her mother was in some degree tranquillized, and would have been more so, had not Mr. Roger Langford begun to reason with her in the following style :—"Come, Mary, you need not be in the least alarmed. It is quite nonsense in you. You know a boy of any spirit will always be doing things that sound imprudent. I would not give a farthing for Fred if he was always to be the mamma's boy you would make him. He is come to an age now when you cannot keep him up in that way, and he must get knocked about some time or other."

"O yes, I know I am very foolish," said she, trying to smile.

"I shall send up Elizabeth to talk to you," said Uncle Roger. "She would have a pretty life of it if she went into such a state as you do on all such occasions."

"Enough to break the heart of ten horses, as they say in Ireland," said Uncle Geoffrey, seeing that the best chance for her was to appear at his ease, and divert his brother's attention. "And by-the-bye, Roger, you never told me if you heard any more of your poor Irish haymakers."

"Why, Geoffrey, you have an absent fit now for once in your life," said his brother. "Are you the man to ask if I

N

heard any more of them, when you yourself gave me a sovereign to send them in the famine?"

Uncle Geoffrey, however, persevered, and finally succeeded in starting Uncle Roger upon his favourite and inexhaustible subject of the doings at the Allonfield Union. During this time Mrs. Frederick Langford put a few stitches into her work, found it would not do, and paused, stood up, seemed to be observing the new arrangements in the room, —then took a long look out at the window, and at last left the room. Henrietta ran after her to assure her that she was convinced that Uncle Geoffrey was not alarmed, and to beg her to set her mind at rest. "Thank you, my dear," said she. "I—no, I really—you know how foolish I am, my dear, and I think I had rather be alone. Don't stay here and frighten yourself too; this is only my usual fright, and it will be better if I am left alone. Go down, my dear, think about something else, and let me know when they come home."

With considerable reluctance Henrietta was obliged to obey, and descended to the drawing-room, where the first words that met her ears were from Uncle Roger. "Well, I wish, with all my heart, they were safe at home again. But do you mean to say, Geoffrey, that I ought not to have let them go?"

"I shall certainly come upon you for damages, if he breaks the neck of little Bee," said Uncle Geoffrey.

"If I had guessed it," said Uncle Roger; "but then, you know, any of my boys would think nothing of driving Dumple,—even Dick I have trusted,—and they came up—you should have seen them—as confidently as if he had been driving four-in-hand every day of his life. Upon my word your daughter has a tolerable spirit of her own, if she knew that he could not drive."

"A tolerable spirit of self-will," said Uncle Geoffrey, with a sigh. "But did you see them off, how did they manage?"

"Ah! why there, I must confess, I was to blame," said his brother. "They did clear out of the yard after a strange fashion, certainly, and I might have questioned a little closer. But never mind, 'tis all straight road. I would lay any wager they will all come back safe,—boys always do."

Uncle Geoffrey smiled, but Henrietta thought it a very bad sign that he, too, looked out at the window; and the confidence founded on his tranquillity deserted her.

Uncle Roger forthwith returned to the fighting o'er again of his battles at the Board of Guardians, and Henrietta was able to get to the window, where for some ten minutes she sat, and at length exclaimed with a start, "Here is Willy running across the paddock!"

"All right!" said Uncle Roger, "they must have stopped at Sutton Leigh."

"It is the opposite way!" said Mr. Geoffrey Langford, who at the same moment stepped up to the window. Henrietta's heart throbbed fearfully as she saw how wearied was the boy's running, and yet how rapid. She could hardly stand as she followed her uncles to the hall; her mother at the same moment came down stairs, and all together met the little boy, as, breathless, exhausted, unable to speak, he rushed into the hall, and threw himself upon his father, leaning his head against him and clinging as if he could not stand.

"Why Will, how now, my boy? Have you been racing?" said his father, kneeling on one knee, and supporting the poor little wearied fellow, as he almost lay upon his breast and shoulder. "What is the matter now?"

There was a deep silence only interrupted by the deep pantings of the boy. Henrietta leant on the banisters, giddy with suspense. Uncle Geoffrey stepped into the dining-room, and brought back a glass of wine and some water. Aunt Mary parted the damp hair that hung over his forehead, laid her cold hand on it, and said, "Poor little fellow."

At her voice Willy looked up, clung faster to his father, and whispered something unintelligible.

"What? Has anything happened? What is the matter?" were questions anxiously asked, while Uncle Geoffrey in silence succeeded in administering the wine; after which Willy managed to say, pointing to his aunt, "Don't—tell—her."

It was with a sort of ghastly composure that she leant over him saying, "Don't be afraid, my dear, I am ready to hear it."

He raised himself, and gazed at her in perplexity and wonder. Henrietta's violently throbbing heart took from her almost the perception of what was passing.

"Take breath, Willy," said his father; "don't keep us all anxious."

"Bee said I was to tell Uncle Geoffrey," said the boy.

"Is *she* safe?" asked Aunt Mary earnestly.

"Yes."

"Thanks to God," said she, holding out her hand to Uncle Geoffrey, with a look of relief and congratulation, and yet of inexpressible mournfulness which went to his heart.

"And Fred?" said Uncle Roger.

"Do not ask, Roger," said she, still as calmly as before; "I always knew how it would be."

Henrietta tried to exclaim, to inquire, but her lips would not frame one word, her tongue would not leave the roof of her mouth. She heard a few confused sounds, and then a mist came over her eyes, a rushing of waters in her ears, and she sank on the ground in a fainting fit. When she came to herself she was lying on the sofa in the drawing-room, and all was still.

"Mamma!" said she.

"Here, dear child,"—but it was Mrs. Langford's voice.

"Mamma!" again said she. "Where is mamma? Where are they all? Why does the room turn round?"

"You have not been well, my dear," said her grandmother; "but drink this, and lie still, you will soon be better."

"Where is mamma?" repeated Henrietta, gazing round and seeing no one but Mrs. Langford and Bennet. "Was she frightened at my being ill? Tell her I am better."

"She knows it, my dear: lie still, and try to go to sleep."

"But weren't there a great many people?" said Henrietta. "Were we not in the hall? Did not Willy come? O! grandmamma, grandmamma, do tell me, where are mamma and Fred?"

"They will soon be here, I hope."

"But, grandmamma," cried she vehemently, turning herself round as clearer recollection returned, "something has happened—O! what has happened to Fred?"

"Nothing very serious, we hope, my dear," said Mrs. Langford. "It was Willy who frightened you. Fred has had a fall, and your mamma and uncles are gone to see about him."

"A fall! O, tell me, tell me! I am sure it is something dreadful! O, tell me, tell me all about it, grandmamma, is he much hurt? O, Freddy, Freddy!"

With more quietness than could have been anticipated from so active and bustling a nature, Mrs. Langford gradually told her granddaughter all that she knew, which was but little, as she had been in attendance on her, and had only heard the main fact of Willy's story. Henrietta clasped her hands wildly together in an agony of grief. "He is killed— he is, I'm sure of it!" said she. "Why do you not tell me so?"

"My dear, I trust and believe that he is only stunned."

"No, no, no! papa was killed in that way, and I am sure

he is! O, Fred, Fred, my own dear, dear brother, my only one! O, I cannot bear it! O, Fred!"

She rose up from the sofa, and walked up and down the room in an ecstasy of sorrow. "And it was I that helped to bring him here! It was my doing! O, my own, my dearest, my twin brother, I cannot live without him!"

"Henrietta," said Mrs. Langford, "you do not know what you are saying; you must bear the will of GOD, be it what it may."

"I can't, I can *not*," repeated Henrietta; "if I am to lose him, I can't live; I don't care for anything without Fred!"

"Your mother, Henrietta."

"Mamma! O don't speak of her: she would die, I am sure she would, without him; and then I should too, for I should have nothing."

Henrietta's grief was the more ungovernable that it was chiefly selfish: there was little thought of her mother,—little indeed, for anything but the personal loss to herself. She hid her face in her hands and sobbed violently, though without a tear, while Mrs. Langford vainly tried to make her hear of patience and resignation, turning away, and saying, "I can't be patient—no, I can't!" and then again repeating her brother's name with all the fondest terms of endearment.

Then came a sudden change: it was possible that he yet lived—and she became certain that he had been only stunned for a moment, and required her grandmamma to be so too. Mrs. Langford at the risk of a cruel disappointment, was willing to encourage her hope; but Henrietta, fancying herself treated like a petted child, chose to insist on being told, really and exactly, what was her view of the case. Then she was urgent to go out and meet the others, and learn the truth; but this Mrs. Langford would not permit. It was in kindness, to spare her some fearful sight, which might shock and startle her, but Henrietta was far from taking it so; her habitual want of submission made itself felt in spite of her usual gentleness, now that she had been thrown off her balance, and she burst into a passionate fit of weeping.

In such a dreadful interval of suspense, her conduct was, perhaps, scarcely under her own control; and it is scarcely just to mention it as a subject of blame. But, be it remembered, that it was the effect of a long previous selfishness and self-will: quiet, amiable selfishness: gentle, caressing self-will; but no less real, and more perilous and deceitful. But for this, Henrietta would have thought more of her mother, prepared for her comfort, and braced herself in order to be a support for her; she would have remembered how terrible must be the shock to her grandmother in her old age, and how painful must be the remembrances thus excited of the former bereavement; and in the attempt to console her, the sense of her own sorrow would have been in some degree relieved; whereas she now seemed to forget that Frederick was anything to any one but herself. She prayed, but it was one wild repetition of " O, give him back to me!—save his life!—let him be safe and well!" She had no room for any other entreaty; she did not call for strength and resignation on the part of herself and her mother, for whatever might be appointed; she did not pray that his life might be granted only if it was for his good; she could ask nothing but that *her* own beloved brother might be spared to *herself,* and she ended her prayer as unsubdued, and therefore as miserable, as when she began it.

The first intelligence that arrived was brought by Uncle Roger and Beatrice, who, rather to their surprise, came back in the gig, and greatly relieved their minds with the intelligence of Frederick's life, and of Philip Carey's arrival.

Henrietta had sprung eagerly up on their first entrance, with parted lips and earnest eyes, and listened to their narration with trembling throbbing hope, but with scarcely a word; and when she heard that Fred still lay senseless and motionless, she again turned away, and hid her face on the arm of the sofa, without one look at Beatrice, reckless of the pang that shot through the heart of one fresh from that trying watch over her brother.   Beatrice longed for one word, one kiss, and looked wistfully at the long veil of half-uncurled ringlets that floated over the crossed arms on which her forehead rested, and meantime submitted with a kind of patient indifference to her grandmother's cares, drank hot wine and water, sat by the fire, and finally was sent up stairs to change her dress.   Too restless, too anxious, too wretched to stay there alone, longing for some interchange of sympathy,—but her mind too turbid with agitation to seek it where it would most surely have been found,—she hastened down again.   Grandmamma was busied in giving directions for the room which was being prepared for Fred; Uncle Roger had walked out to meet those who were conveying him home : and Henrietta was sitting in the window, her forehead resting against the glass, watching intently for their arrival.

"Are they coming?" asked Beatrice anxiously.

"No !" was all the answer, hardly uttered, and without looking round, as if her cousin's entrance was perfectly indifferent to her.   Beatrice went up and stood by her, looking out for a few minutes; then taking the hand that lay in her lap, she said in an imploring whisper, "Henrietta, you forgive me?"

The hand lay limp and listless in hers, and Henrietta scarcely raised her face as she answered, in a low, languid, dejected voice, "Of course, Bee ; only I am so wretched. Don't talk to me."

Her head sank again, and Beatrice stepped hastily back to the fire, with a more bitter feeling than she had ever known. This was no forgiveness; it was worse than anger or reproach; it was a repulse, and that when her whole heart was yearning to relieve the pent-up oppression that almost choked her, by weeping with her. She leant her burning forehead on the cool marble chimney-piece, and longed for her mother,—longed for her almost as much for her papa's, her Aunt Mary's, and her grandmother's sake, as for her own. But O! what an infinite relief would one talk with her have been! She turned towards the table, and thought of writing to her, but her hand was trembling—every pulse throbbing; she could not even sit still enough to make the attempt.

At last she saw Henrietta spring to her feet, and hastening to the window beheld the melancholy procession; Fred carried on a mattress by Uncle Geoffrey and three of the labourers; Philip Carey walking at one side, and on the other Mrs. Frederick Langford leaning on Uncle Roger's arm.

Both girls hurried out to meet them, but all attention was at that moment for the patient, as he was carried in on his mattress, and deposited for a few minutes on the large hall table. Henrietta pushed between her uncles, and made her way up to him, unconscious of the presence of any one else—even of her mother—while she clasped his hand, and hanging over him looked with an agonized intensity at his motionless features. The next moment she felt her mother's hand on her shoulder, and was forced to turn round and look into her face, the sweet mournful meekness of which came for a moment like a soft cooling breeze upon the dry burning desert of her grief.

" My poor child," said the gentle voice.

" O, mamma, is—is— ?" She could not speak; her face

was violently agitated, and the very muscles of her throat quivered.

"They hope for the best, my dear," was the reply; but both Mr. Geoffrey Langford and Beatrice distinguished her own hopelessness in the intonation, and the very form of the expression: whereas Henrietta only took in and eagerly seized the idea of comfort which it was intended to convey to her. She would have inquired more, but Mrs. Langford was telling her mother of the arrangements she had made, and entreating her to take some rest.

"Thank you, ma'am—thank you very much indeed—you are very kind: I am very sorry to give so much trouble," were her answers; and simple as were the words, there was a whole world of truth and reality in them.

Preparations were now made for carrying Fred up stairs, but even at that moment Aunt Mary was not without thought for Beatrice, who was retreating, as if she feared to be as much in her way as she had been in Henrietta's.

"I did not see you before, Queenie," she said, holding out her hand and kissing her, "you have gone through more than any one."

A thrill of fond grateful affection brought the tears into Queen Bee's eyes. How much there was even in the pronunciation of that pet playful name to touch her heart, and fill it to overflowing with love and contrition. She longed to pour out her whole confession, but there was no one to attend to her—the patient occupied the whole attention of all. He was carried to his mother's room, placed in bed, and again examined by young Mr. Carey, who pronounced with increased confidence that there was no fracture, and gave considerable hopes of improvement. While this was passing, Henrietta sat on the upper step of the stairs, her head on her hands, scarcely moving or answering when addressed. As evening twilight began to close in, the surgeon left the room, and went down to make his report to those who were anxiously waiting it in the drawing-room ; and she took advantage of his exit to come to the door, and beg to be let in.

Uncle Geoffrey admitted her ; and her mother, who was sitting by the bedside, held out her hand. Henrietta came up to her, and at first stood by her, intently watching her brother ; then after a time sat down on a footstool, and, with her head resting on her mother's lap, gave herself up to a sort of quiet heavy dream, which might be called the very luxury of grief. Uncle Geoffrey sat by the fire, watching his sister-in-law even more anxiously than the patient, and thus a considerable interval passed in complete silence, only broken by the crackling of the fire, the ticking of the watches, or some slight change of posture of one or other of the three nurses. At last the stillness was interrupted by a little movement among the bedclothes, and with a feeling like transport, Henrietta saw the hand, which had hitherto lain so still and helpless, stretched somewhat out, and the head turned upon the pillow. Uncle Geoffrey stood up, and Mrs. Frederick Langford pressed her daughter's hand with a sort of convulsive tremor. A faint voice murmured "Mamma!" and while a flush of trembling joy illumined her pale face, she bent over him, answering him eagerly and fondly, but he did not seem to know her, and again repeating "mamma," opened his eyes with a vacant gaze, and tried in vain to express some complaint.

In a short time, however, he regained a partial degree of consciousness. He knew his mother, and was continually calling to her, as if for the sake of feeling her presence, but without recognising any other person, not even his sister or his uncle. Henrietta stood gazing sadly upon him, while his mother hung over him soothing his restlessness, and answering his half-uttered complaints, and Uncle Geoffrey was ever ready with assistance and comfort to each in turn, as it was needed, and especially supporting his sister-in-law with that sense of protection and reliance so precious to a sinking heart.

Aunt Roger came up to announce that dinner was ready, and to beg that she might stay with Fred while the rest went down. Mrs. Frederick Langford only shook her head, and thanked her, saying with a painful smile that it was impossible, but begging Uncle Geoffrey and Henrietta to go. The former complied, knowing how much alarm his absence would create downstairs; but Henrietta declared that she could not bear the thoughts of going down, and it was only by a positive order that he succeeded in making her come with him. Grandpapa kissed her, and made her sit by him, and grandmamma loaded her plate with all that was best on the table, but she looked at it with disgust, and leaning back in her chair, faintly begged not to be asked to eat.

Uncle Geoffrey poured out a glass of wine, and said, in a tone which startled her by its unwonted severity, " This will not do, Henrietta; I cannot allow you to add to your mamma's troubles by making yourself ill. I desire you will eat, as you certainly can."

Every one was taken by surprise, and perhaps Mrs. Langford might have interfered, but for a sign from grandpapa. Henrietta, with a feeling of being cruelly treated, silently obeyed; swallowed down the wine, and having done so, found herself capable of making a very tolerable dinner, by which she was greatly revived and refreshed.

Uncle Geoffrey said a few cheering words to his father and mother, and returned to Fred's room as soon as he could, without giving that appearance of hurry and anxiety which would have increased their alarm. Henrietta, without the same thoughtfulness, rushed rather than ran after him, and neither of the two came down again to tea.

Philip Carey was to stay all night, and though Beatrice was of course very glad that he should do so, yet she was much harassed by the conversation kept up with him for civility's sake. She had been leading a forlorn dreary life all the afternoon, busy first in helping grandmamma to write notes to be sent to the intended guests, and afterwards, with a feeling of intense disgust putting out of sight all the preparations for their own self-chosen sport. She desired quiet, and yet when she found it, it was unendurable, and to talk to her father or grandfather would be a great relief, yet the first beginning might well be dreaded. Neither of them was forthcoming, and now in the evening to hear the quiet grave discussion of Allonfield gossip was excessively harassing and irritating. No one spoke for their own pleasure, the thoughts of all were elsewhere, and they only talked thus for the sake of politeness; but she gave them no credit for this, and felt fretted and wearied beyond bearing. Even this, however, was better than when they did return to the engrossing thought, and spoke of the accident, requiring of her a more exact and particular account of it. She hurried over it. Grandmamma praised her, and each word was a sting.

"But, my dear," said Mrs. Roger Langford, "what could have made you so anxious to go to Allonfield?"

"O, Aunt Roger, it was very—" but here Beatrice, whose agitated spirits made her particularly accessible to momentary emotion, was seized with such a sense of the absurdity of undertaking so foolish an expedition, with no other purpose than going to buy a pair of ass's cars, that she was overpowered by a violent fit of laughing. Grandmamma and Aunt Roger, after looking at her in amazement for a moment, both started up, and came towards her with looks of alarm that set her off again still more uncontrollably. She struggled to speak, but that only made it worse, and when she perceived that she was supposed to be hysterical, she laughed the more, though the laughter was positive pain. Once she for a moment succeeded in recovering some degree of composure, but every kind demonstration of solicitude brought on a fresh access of laughter, and a certain whispering threat of calling Philip Carey was worse than all. When, however, Aunt Roger was actually setting off for the purpose, the dread of his coming had a salutary effect, and enabled her to make a violent effort, by which she composed herself, and at length sat quite still, except for the trembling, which she could not control.

Grandmamma and Aunt Roger united in ordering her to bed, but she could not bear to go without seeing her papa, nor would she accept Mrs. Langford's offer of calling him; and at last a compromise was made that she should go up to bed, on condition that her papa should come and visit her when he came out of Fred's room. Her grandmamma came up with her, helped her to undress, gave her the unwonted indulgence of a fire, and summoned Judith to prepare things as quickly and quietly as possible for Henrietta, who was to sleep with her that night. It was with much difficulty that she could avoid making a promise to go to bed immediately, and not to get up to breakfast. At last, with a very affectionate kiss, grandmamma left her to brush her hair, an operation which she resolved to lengthen out until her papa's visit.

It was long before he came, but at last his step was heard along the passage, his knock was at her door. She flew to it, and stood before him, her large black eyes looking larger, brighter, blacker than usual from the contrast with the pale or rather sallow face, and the white nightcap and dressing-gown.

"How is Fred?" asked she as well as her parched tongue would allow her to speak.

" Much the same, only talking a little more. But why are you up still ? Your grandmamma said—"

" Never mind, papa," interrupted she, " only tell me this —is Fred in danger ?"

" You have heard all we can tell, my dear—"

Beatrice interrupted him by an impatient despairing look, and clasped her hands : " I know—I know ; but what do *you* think ?"

" My own impression is," said her father, in a calm, kind, yet almost reproving tone, as if to warn her to repress her agitation, " that there is no reason to give up hope, although it is impossible as yet to ascertain the extent of the injury."

Beatrice retreated a step or two : she stood by the table, one hand upon it, as if for support, yet her figure quite erect, her eyes fixed on his face, and her voice firm, though husky, as she said, slowly and quietly, " Papa, if Fred dies, it is my doing."

His face did not express surprise or horror—nothing but kindness and compassion, while he answered, " My poor girl, I was afraid how it might have been." Then he led her to a chair and sat down by her side, so as to let her perceive that he was ready to listen, and would give her time. He might be in haste, but it was no time to show it.

She now spoke with more hurry and agitation. " Yes, yes, papa, it was the very thing you warned me against—I mean—I mean—the being set on my own way, and liking to tease the boys. O if I could but speak to tell you all, but it seems like a weight here choking me," and she touched her throat. " I can't get it out in words ! O !" Poor Beatrice even groaned aloud with oppression.

" Do not try to express it," said her father : " at least, it is not I who can give you the best comfort. Here"—and he took up a Prayer Book.

" Yes, I feel as if I could turn there now I have told you,

papa," said Beatrice; "but when I could not get at you, everything seemed dried up in me. Not one prayer or confession would come;—but now, O! now you know it, and —and—I feel as if He would not turn away His face. Do you know I did try the 51st Psalm, but it would not do, not even 'deliver me from blood-guiltiness,' it would only make me shudder! O, papa, it was dreadful!"

Her father's answer was to draw her down on her knees by his side, and read a few verses of that very Psalm, and a few clauses of the prayer for persons troubled in mind, and he ended with the LORD's Prayer. Beatrice, when it was over, leant her head against him, and did not speak, nor weep, but she seemed refreshed and relieved. He watched her anxiously and affectionately, doubting whether it was right to bestow so much time on her exclusively, yet unwilling to leave her. When she again spoke, it was in a lower, more subdued, and softer voice, "Aunt Mary will forgive me, I know; you will tell her, papa, and then it will not be quite so bad! Now I can pray that he may be saved—O, papa—disobedient, and I the cause; how could I ever bear the thought?"

"You can only pray," replied her father.

"Now that I can once more," said Beatrice; and again there was a silence, while she stood thinking deeply, but contrary to her usual habit, not speaking, and he knowing well her tendency to lose her repentant feelings by expressing them, was not willing to interrupt her. So they remained for nearly ten minutes, until at last he thought it time to leave her, and made some movement as if to do so. Then she spoke, "Only tell me one thing, papa. Do you think Aunt Mary has any hope? There was something—something death-like in her face. Does she hope?"

Mr. Geoffrey Langford shook his head, "Not yet," said he. "I think it may be better after this first night is over.

She is evidently reckoning the hours, and I think she has a kind of morbid expectation that it will be as it was with his father, who lived twelve hours after his accident."

"But surely, surely," said Beatrice eagerly, "this is a very different case; Fred has spoken so much more than my uncle did; and Philip says he is convinced that there is no fracture—"

"It is a morbid feeling," said Mr. Geoffrey Langford, "and therefore impossible to be reasoned away. I see she dreads to be told to hope, and I shall not even attempt it till these fatal twelve hours are over."

"Poor dear aunt!" sighed Beatrice. "I am glad, if it was to be, that you were here, for nobody else would understand her."

"Understand her!" said he, with something of a smile. "No, Bee, such sorrow as hers has a sacredness in it which is not what can be understood."

Beatrice sighed, and then with a look as if she saw a ray of comfort, said, "I suppose mamma will soon be here?"

"I think not," said her father, "I shall tell her she had better wait to see how things go on, and keep herself in reserve. At present it is needlessly tormenting your aunt to ask her to leave Fred for a moment, and I do not think she has even the power to rest. While this goes on, I am of more use in attending to him than your mamma could be; but if he is a long time recovering, it will be a great advantage to have her coming fresh, and not half knocked up with previous attendance."

"But how she will wish to be here!" exclaimed Beatrice, "and how you will want her!"

"No doubt of that, Queenie," said her father smiling, "but we must reserve our forces, and I think she will be of the same mind. Well, I must go. Where is Henrietta to sleep to-night?"

O

"With me," said Beatrice.

"I will send her to you as soon as I can. You must do what you can with her, Bee, for I can see that the way she hangs on her mamma is quite oppressive. If she had but a little vigour!"

"I don't know what to do about her!" said Beatrice with more dejection than she had yet shown, "I wish I could be of any comfort to her, but I can't—I shall never do good to anybody—only harm."

"Fear the harm, and the good will come," said Mr. Geoffrey Langford. "Good night, my dear."

Beatrice threw herself on her knees as soon as the door had closed on her father, and so remained for a considerable time in one earnest, unexpressed outpouring of confession and prayer, for how long she knew not, all that she was sensible of was a feeling of relief, the repose of such humility and submission, such heartfelt contrition as she had never known before.

So she continued till she heard Henrietta's approaching steps, when she rose and opened the door, ready to welcome her with all the affection and consolation in her power. There stood Henrietta, a heavy weight on her eyes, her hair on one side all uncurled and flattened, the colour on half her face much deepened, and a sort of stupor about her whole person, as if but one idea possessed her. Beatrice went up to meet her, and took her candle, asking what account she brought of the patient. "No better," was all the answer, and she sat down making no more detailed answers to all her cousin's questions. She would have done the same to her grandmamma, or any one else, so wrapped up was she in her own grief, but this conduct gave more pain to Beatrice than it could have done to any one else, since it kept up that most miserable feeling of being unforgiven. Beatrice let her sit still for some minutes, looking at her all the time with an almost piteous glance of entreaty, of which Henrietta was perfectly unconscious, and then began to beg her to undress, seconding the proposal by beginning to unfasten her dress.

Henrietta moved pettishly, as if provoked at being disturbed.

"I beg your pardon, dear Henrietta," said Beatrice; "if you would but let me! You will be ill to-morrow, and that would be worse still."

"No, I shan't," said Henrietta shortly, "never mind me."

"But I must, dear Henrietta. If you would but—"

"I can't go to bed," replied Henrietta, "thank you, Bee, never mind—"

Beatrice stood still, much distressed at her own inability to be of any service, and pained far more by the sight of Henrietta's grief than by the unkind rejection of herself. "Papa thinks there is great hope," said she abruptly.

"Mamma does not," said Henrietta, edging away from her cousin as if to put an end to the subject.

Beatrice almost wrung her hands. O this wilfulness of grief, how hard it was to contend with it! At last there was a knock at the door—it was grandmamma, suspecting that they were still up. Little recked Beatrice of the scolding that fell on herself for not having been in bed hours ago; she was only rejoiced at the determination that swept away all Henrietta's feeble opposition. The bell was rung, Bennet was summoned, grandmamma peremptorily ordered her to be undressed, and in another half hour the cousins were lying side by side, Henrietta's lethargy had become a heavy sleep, Beatrice was broad awake, listening to every sound, forming every possible speculation on the future, and to her own overstretched fancy seeming actually to *feel* the thoughts chasing each other through her throbbing head.

CHAPTER XIV

"HALF-PAST one," said Mr. Geoffrey Langford, as if it was a mere casual observation, though in reality it was the announcement that the fatal twelve hours had passed more than half an hour since.

There was no answer, but he heard a slight movement, and though carefully avoiding any attempt to penetrate the darkness around the sick bed, he knew full well that his sister was on her knees, and when he again heard her voice in reply to some rambling speech of her son, it had a tremulous tone, very unlike its former settled hopelessness.

Again, when Philip Carey paid his morning visit, she studied the expression of his face with anxious, inquiring, almost hopeful eyes, the crushed heart-broken indifference of yesterday had passed away; and when the expediency of obtaining further advice was hinted at, she caught at the suggestion with great eagerness, though the day before her only answer had been, "As you think right." She spoke so as to show the greatest consideration for the feelings of Philip Carey, then with her usual confiding spirit, she left the selection of the person to be called in entirely to him, to her brother and father-in-law, and returned to her station by Frederick, who had already missed and summoned her.

Philip, in spite of the small follies which provoked Beatrice's sarcasm, was by no means deficient in good sense or

ability; his education had owed much to the counsels of
Mr. Geoffrey Langford, whom he regarded with great reverence, and he was so conscious of his own inexperience and
diffident of his own opinion, as to be very anxious for
assistance in this, the first very serious case which had fallen
under his own management. The proposal had come at
first from himself, and this was a cause of great rejoicing to
those who had to reconcile Mrs. Langford to the measure.
In her eyes a doctor was a doctor, member of a privileged
fraternity in which she saw no distinctions, and to send for
advice from London would, she thought, not only hurt the
feelings of Mrs. Roger Langford, and all the Carey connec-
tion, but seriously injure the reputation of young Mr. Carey
in his own neighbourhood.

Grandpapa answered, and Beatrice was glad he did so,
that such considerations were as nothing when weighed in
the scale against Frederick's life; she was silenced, but unconvinced, and unhappy till her son Geoffrey, coming down
late to breakfast, greatly comforted her by letting her make
him some fresh toast with her own hands, and persuading
her that it would be greatly in favour of Philip's practice
that his opinion should be confirmed by an authority of
note.

The electric telegraph and the railroad brought the surgeon even before she had begun seriously to expect him,
and his opinion was completely satisfactory as far as regarded Philip Carey and the measures already taken; Uncle
Geoffrey himself feeling convinced that his approval was
genuine and not merely assumed for courtesy's sake. He
gave them, too, more confident hope of the patient than
Philip, in his diffidence, had ventured to do, saying that
though there certainly was concussion of the brain, he
thought there was great probability that the patient would
do well, provided that they could combat the feverish symp-

toms which had begun to appear. He consulted with Philip Carey, the future treatment was agreed upon, and he left them with cheered and renewed spirits to enter on a long and anxious course of attendance. Roger, who was obliged to go away the next day, cheered up his brother Alex into a certainty that Fred would be about again in a week, and though no one but the boys shared this belief, yet the assurances of any one so sanguine, inspired them all with something like hope.

The attendance at first fell almost entirely on Mrs. Frederick Langford and Uncle Geoffrey, for the patient, who had now recovered a considerable degree of consciousness, would endure no one else. If his mother's voice did not answer him the first moment, he instantly grew restless and uneasy, and the plaintive inquiry, " Is Uncle Geoffrey here?" was many times repeated. He would recognise Henrietta, but his usual answer to her was, " You speak so loud;" though in reality, her tone was almost exactly the same as her mother's; and above all others he disliked the presence of Philip Carey.

" Who is that?" inquired he the first time that he was at all conscious of the visits of other people : and when his mother explained, he asked quickly, " Is he gone?"

The next day, Fred was alive to all that was going on, but suffering considerable pain, and with every sense quickened to the most acute and distressing degree, his eyes dazzled by light which, as he declared, glanced upon the picture-frames in a room where his mother and uncle could scarcely see to find their way, and his ears pierced, as it were, by the slightest sound in the silent house, sleepless with pain, incapable of thought, excessively irritable in temper, and his faculties, as it seemed, restored only to be the means of suffering. Mrs. Langford came to the door to announce that Philip Carey was come. Mr. Geoffrey

Langford went to speak to him, and grandmamma and Henrietta began to arrange the room a little for his reception. Fred, however, soon stopped this. "I can't bear the shaking," said he. "Tell them to leave off, mamma."

Grandmamma, unconscious of the pain she was inflicting, and believing that she made not the slightest noise, continued to put the chairs in order, but Fred gave an impatient, melancholy sort of groan and exclamation, and Mrs. Langford remarked, "Well, if he cannot bear it, it cannot be helped; but it is quite dangerous in this dark room!" And out she went, Fred frowning with pain at every step she took.

"Why do you let people come?" asked he sharply of his mother. "Where is Uncle Geoffrey gone?"

"He is speaking to Mr. Philip Carey, my dear: he will be here with him directly."

"I don't want Philip Carey; don't let him come."

"My dear boy, he must come; he has not seen you to-day; perhaps he may do something for this sad pain."

Fred turned away impatiently, and at the same moment Uncle Geoffrey opened the door, to ask if Fred was ready.

"Yes," said Mrs. Frederick Langford: and Philip entered. But Fred would not turn towards him till desired to do so, nor give his hand readily for his pulse to be felt. Philip thought it necessary to see his face a little more distinctly, and begged his pardon for having the window-shutters partly opened; but Fred contrived completely to frustrate his intention, as with an exclamation which had in it as much of anger as of pain, he turned his face inwards to the pillow, and drew the bed-clothes over it.

"My dear boy," said his mother, pleadingly, "for one moment only!"

"I told you I could not bear the light," was all the reply.

"If you would but oblige me for a few seconds," said Philip.

"Fred!" said his uncle gravely; and Fred made a slight demonstration as if to obey, but at the first glimpse of the dim light, he hid his face again, saying, "I can't;" and Philip gave up the attempt, closed the shutter, unfortunately not quite as noiselessly as Uncle Geoffrey had opened it, and proceeded to ask sundry questions; to which the patient scarcely vouchsafed a short and pettish reply. When at last he quitted the room, and was followed by Mrs. Frederick Langford, a "Don't go, mamma," was immediately heard.

"You must spare me for a very little while, my dear," said she, gently but steadily.

"Don't stay long, then," replied he.

Uncle Geoffrey came up to his bedside, and with a touch soft and light as a woman's, arranged the coverings disturbed by his restlessness, and for a few moments succeeded in tranquillizing him, but almost immediately he renewed his entreaties that his mother would return, and had it been any other than his uncle who had taken her place, would have grumbled at his not going to call her. On her return, she was greeted with a discontented murmur: "What an immense time you have stayed away!"—presently after, "I wish you would not have that Carey!" and then, "I wish we were at Rocksand,—I wish Mr. Clarke was here."

Patience in illness is a quality so frequently described in books, as well as actually found in real life, that we are apt to believe that it comes as a matter of course, and without previous training, particularly in the young, and that peevishness is especially reserved for the old and querulous, who are to try the amiability of the heroine. To a certain degree this is often the case; the complete prostration of strength, and the dim awe of approaching death in the acute illnesses of the young often tame down the stubborn or petulant temper, and their patience and forbearance become the wonder and admiration of those who have seen germs of far other dispositions. And when this is not the case, who would have the heart to complain? Certainly not those who are like the mother and uncle who had most to endure from the exacting humours of Frederick Langford. High spirits, excellent health, a certain degree of gentleness of character, and a home where, though he was not over-indulged, there was little to ruffle him, all had hitherto combined to make him appear one of the most amiable good-tempered boys that ever existed ; but there was no substance in this apparent good quality, it was founded on no real principle of obedience or submission, and when to an habitual spirit of quiet determination to have his own way, was superadded the irritability of nerves which was a part of his illness, when his powers of reflection were too much weakened to endure or comprehend argument ; when, in fact, nothing was left to fall back upon but the simple obedience which would have been required in a child, and when that obedience was wanting, what could result but increased discomfort to himself and all concerned? Yes, even as we should lay up a store of prayers against that time when we shall be unable to pray for ourselves, so surely should we lay up a store of habits against the time when we may be unable to think or reason for ourselves ! How often have lives been saved by the mere instinct of unquestioning instantaneous obedience !

Had Frederick possessed that instinct, how much present suffering and future wretchedness might have been spared him ! His ideas were as yet too disconnected for him to understand or bear in mind that he was subjecting his mother to excessive fatigue, but the habit of submission would have led him to bear her absence patiently, instead

of perpetually interrupting even the short repose which she
would now and then be persuaded to seek on the sofa.
He would have spared her his perpetual harassing complaints,—not so much of the pain he suffered, as of every
thing and every person who approached him, his Uncle
Geoffrey being the only person against whom he never
murmured. Nor would he have rebelled against measures
to which he was obliged to submit in the end, after he had
distressed every one, and exhausted himself, by his fruitless
opposition.

It was marvellous that the only two persons whose attendance he would endure could bear up under the fatigue.
Even Uncle Geoffrey, one of those spare wiry men, who,
without much appearance of strength, are nevertheless capable of such continued exertion, was beginning to look
worn and almost aged; and yet Mrs. Frederick Langford
was still indefatigable, unconscious of weariness, quietly
active, absorbed in the thought of her son, and yet not so
absorbed as not to be full of consideration for all around.
All looked forward with apprehension to the time when the
consequences of such continued exertion must be felt; but
in the mean time it was not in the power of any one except
her brother Geoffrey to be of any assistance to her, and her
relations could only watch and wait with such patience as
they could command, for the period when their services
might be effectual.

Mrs. Langford was the most visibly impatient. The
hasty bustling of her very quietest steps gave such torture
to Frederick, as to excuse the upbraiding eyes which he
turned on his poor perplexed mother, whenever she entered
the room; and her fresh arrangements and orders always
created a disturbance, which did him such positive injury,
that it was the aim of the whole family to prevent her visits
there. This was, as may be supposed, no easy task. Grand-

papa's "You had better not, my dear," checked her for a little while, but was far from satisfying her : Uncle Geoffrey, who might have had the best chance, had not time to spare for her; and no one could persuade her how impossible, nay, how dangerous it was to attempt to reason with the patient : so she blamed the whole household for indulging his fancies, and half a dozen times a day pronounced that he would be the death of his mother. Beatrice did the best she could to tranquillize her; but two spirits so apt to clash did not accord particularly well even now, though Busy Bee was too much depressed to queen it as usual. To feel herself completely useless in the midst of the suffering she had occasioned was a severe trial; and above all, poor child, she longed for her mother, and the repose of confession and parental sympathy. She saw her father only at meal times ; she was anxious and uneasy at his worn looks, and even he could not be all that her mother was. Grandpapa was kind as ever, but the fault that sat so heavy on her mind was not one for discussion with any one but a mother, and this consciousness was the cause of a little reserve with him, such as had never before existed between them.

Alexander was more of a comfort to her than any one else, and that chiefly because he wanted her to be a comfort to him. All the strong affection and esteem which he really entertained for Frederick was now manifested, and the remembrance of old rivalries and petty contentions served but to make the reaction stronger. He kept aloof from his brothers, and spent every moment he could at the Hall, either reading in the library, or walking up and down the garden paths with Queen Bee. One of the many conversations which they held will serve as a specimen of the rest.

"So they do not think he is much better to-day?" said

Alex, walking into the library, where Beatrice was sealing some letters.

Beatrice shook her head. "Every day that he is not worse is so much gained," said she.

"It is very odd," meditated Alex : "I suppose the more heads have in them, the easier it is to knock them !"

Beatrice smiled. "Thick skulls are proverbial, you know, Alex."

"Well, I really believe it is right. Look, Bee," and he examined his own face in the glass over the chimney; "there, do you see a little bit of a scar under my eye-brow?—there ! Well, that was where I was knocked over by a cricket-ball last half, pretty much harder than poor Fred could have come against the ground, but what harm did it do me? Why everything spun round with me for five minutes or so, and I had a black eye enough to have scared you, but I was not a bit the worse otherwise. Poor Fred, he was quite frightened for me I believe : for the first thing I saw was him, looking all green and yellow, standing over me, and so I got up and laughed at him for thinking I could care about it. That was the worst of it ! I wish I had not been always set against him. I would give any-thing now."

"Well, but Alex, I don't understand. You were very good friends at the bottom, after all; you can't have any-thing really to repent of towards him."

"Oh, haven't I though?" was the reply. "It was more the other fellows' doing than my own, to be sure, and yet, after all, it was worse, knowing all about him as I did : but somehow, every one, grandmamma and all of you, had been preaching up to me all my life that Cousin Fred was to be *such* a friend of mine. And then when he came to school, there he was—a fellow with a pink and white face, like a girl's, and that did not even know how to shy a stone, and cried for his mamma! Well, I wish I could begin it all over again."

"But do you mean that he was really a—a—what you call a Miss Molly?"

"Who said so? No, not a bit of it!" said Alex. "No one thought so in reality, though it was a good joke to put him in a rage, and pretend to think he could not do anything. Why, it took a dozen times more spirit for him to be first in everything than for me, who had been knocked about all my life. And he was up to anything, Bee, to anything. The matches at foot-ball will be good for nothing now; I am sure I shan't care if we do win."

"And the prize," said Beatrice, "the scholarship!"

"I have no heart to try for it now! I would not, if Uncle Geoffrey had not a right to expect it of me. Let me see: if Fred is well by the summer, why then—hurrah! Really, Queenie, he might get it all up in no time, clever fellow as he is, and be first after all. Don't you think so?"

Queen Bee shook her head. "They say he must not read or study for a very long time," said she.

"Yes, but six months—a whole year is an immense time," said Alex. "O yes, he must, Bee! Reading does not cost him half the trouble it does other people; and his verses, they never fail—never except when he is careless; and the sure way to prevent that is to run him up for time. That is right. Why there!" exclaimed Alex joyfully, "I do believe this is the very best thing for his success!"

Beatrice could not help laughing, and Alex immediately sobered down as the remembrance crossed him, that if Fred were living a week hence, they would have great reason to be thankful.

"Ah! they will all of them be sorry enough to hear of this," proceeded he. "There was no one so much thought of by the fellows, or the masters either."

"The masters, perhaps," said Beatrice; "but I thought you said there was a party against him among the boys?"

"Oh, nonsense! It was only a set of stupid louts who, just because they had pudding-heads themselves, chose to say that I did better without all his reading and Italian, and music, and stuff; and I was foolish enough to let them go on, though I knew all the time it was nothing but chaff. I shall let them all know what fools they were for their pains, as soon as I go back. Why, Queenie, you, who only know Fred at home, you have not the slightest notion what a fellow he is. I'll just tell you one story of him."

Alexander forthwith proceeded to tell not one story alone, but many, to illustrate the numerous excellencies which he ascribed to Fred, and again and again blaming himself for the species of division which had existed between them, although the fact was that he had always been the most conciliatory of the two. Little did he guess, good, simple-hearted fellow, that each word was quite as much, or more, to his credit, as to Frederick's; but Beatrice well appreciated them, and felt proud of him.

These talks were her chief comfort, and always served to refresh her, if only by giving her the feeling that some one wanted her, and not that the only thing she could do for anybody was the sealing of the letters which her father, whose eyes were supposed to be acquiring the power of those of cats, contrived to write in the darkness of Fred's room. She thought she could have borne everything excepting Henrietta's coldness, which still continued, not from intentional unkindness or unwillingness to forgive, but simply because Henrietta was too much absorbed in her own troubles to realise to herself the feelings which she wounded. Her Uncle Geoffrey had succeeded in awakening her consideration for her mother; but with her and Fred it began and ended, and when outside the sick-room, she seemed not to have a thought beyond a speedy return to it. She seldom or never left it, except at meal-times, or when her grandfather insisted on her taking a walk with him, as he did almost daily. Then he walked between her and Beatrice, trying in vain to arouse her to talk, and she, replying as shortly as possible when obliged to speak, left her cousin to sustain the conversation.

The two girls went to church with grandpapa on the feast of the Epiphany, and strange it was to them to see again the wreaths which their own hands had woven, looking as bright and festal as ever, the glistening leaves unfaded, and the coral berries looking fresh and gay. A tear began to gather in Beatrice's eye, and Henrietta hung her head, as if she could not bear the sight of those branches, so lately gathered by her brother. As they were leaving the church, both looked towards the altar at the wreath which Henrietta had once started to see, bearing a deeper and more awful meaning than she had designed. Their eyes met, and they saw that they had the same thought in their minds.

When they were taking off their bonnets in their own room, Queen Bee stretched out a detaining hand, not in her usual commanding manner, but with a gesture that was almost timid, saying,

" Look, Henrietta, one moment, and tell me if you were not thinking of this."

And hastily opening the Lyra Innocentium, she pointed out the verse—

" Such garland grave and fair,
    His Church to-day adorns,
    And—mark it well—e'en there
    He wears His Crown of Thorns.

" Should aught profane draw near,
    Full many a guardian spear
    Is set around, of power to go
Deep in the reckless hand, and stay the grasping foe."

" They go very deep," sighed Henrietta, raising her eyes, with a mournful complaining glance.

Beatrice would have said more, but when she recollected her own conduct on Christmas Eve, it might well strike her that she was the " thing profane" that had then dared to draw near ; and it pained her that she had even appeared for one moment to accuse her cousin. She was beginning to speak, but Henrietta cut her short by saying, " Yes, yes, but I can't stay," and was flying along the passage the next moment.

Beatrice sighed heavily, and spent the next quarter of an hour in recalling, with all the reality of self-reproach, the circumstances of her recklessness, vanity and self-will on that day. She knelt and poured out her confession, her prayer for forgiveness, and grace to avoid the very germs of these sins for the future, before Him Who seeth in secret : and a calm energetic spirit of hope, in the midst of true repentance, began to dawn upon her.

It was good for her, but was it not selfish in Henrietta thus to leave her alone to bear her burthen ? Yes, selfish it was ; for Henrietta had heard the last report of Frederick since their return, and knew that her presence in his room was quite useless ; and it was only for the gratification of her own feelings that she hurried thither without even stopping to recollect that her cousin might also be unhappy, and be comforted by talking to her.

Her thought was only the repining one : " the thorns go deep !" Poor child, had they yet gone deep enough ? The patient may cry out, but the skilful surgeon will nevertheless probe on, till he has reached the hidden source of the malady.

CHAPTER XV.

ON a soft hazy day in the beginning of February the Knight Sutton carriage was on the road to Allonfield, and in it sat the Busy Bee and her father, both of them speaking far less than was their wont when alone together.

Mr. Geoffrey Langford took off his hat, so as to let the moist spring breeze play round his temples and in the thin locks where the silvery threads had lately grown more perceptible, and gazed upon the dewy grass, the tiny wood-bine leaf, the silver "pussycats" on the withy, and the tasselled catkin of the hazel, with the eyes of a man to whom such sights were a refreshment—a sort of holiday—after the many springs spent in close courts of law and London smoke; and now after his long attendance in a warm dark sick-room. His daughter sat by him, thinking deeply, and her heart full of a longing earnestness which seemed as if it would not let her speak. She was going to meet her mother, whom she had not seen for so long a time; but it was only to be for one evening! Her father, finding that his presence was absolutely required in London, and no longer actually indispensable at Knight Sutton, had resolved on changing places with his wife, and she was to go with him and take her mother's place in attending on Lady Susan St. Leger. They were now going to fetch Mrs. Geoffrey Langford home from the Allonfield station, and they would have

P

one evening at Knight Sutton with her, returning themselves the next morning to Westminster.

They arrived at Allonfield, executed various commissions with which Mrs. Langford had been delighted to entrust Geoffrey; they ordered some new books for Frederick, and called at Philip Carey's for some medicines; and then driving up to the station watched eagerly for the train.

Soon it was there, and there at length she was; her own dear self,—the dark aquiline face, with its sweetest and brightest of all expressions; the small youthful figure, so active, yet so quiet and elegant; the dress so plain and simple, and yet with that distinguished air. How happy Beatrice was that first moment of feeling herself at her side!

"My dear! my own dear child!" Then anxiously following her husband with her eye, as he went to look for her luggage, she said, "How thin he looks, Queenie!"

"O, he has been doing *so* much," said Busy Bee. "It is only for this last week he has gone to bed at all, and then only on the sofa in Fred's room. This is the first time he has been out, except last Sunday to church, and a turn or two round the garden with grandmamma."

He came back before Queen Bee had done speaking. "Come, Beatrice," said he to his wife, "I am in great haste to have you at home; that fresh face of yours will do us all so much good."

"One thing is certain," said she; "I shall send home orders that you shall be allowed no strong coffee at night, and that Busy Bee shall hide half the mountain of letters in the study. But tell me honestly, Geoffrey, are you really well?"

"Perfectly, except for a growing disposition to yawn," said her husband laughing.

"Well, what are the last accounts of the patient?"

"He is doing very well; the last thing I did before coming away, was to lay him down on the sofa, with Retzsch's outlines to look at : so you may guess that he is getting on quickly. I suppose you have brought down the books and prints ?"

" Such a pile, that I almost expected my goods would be overweight."

" It is very fortunate that he has a taste for this kind of things : only take care, they must not be at Henrietta's discretion, or his own, or he will be overwhelmed with them,— a very little oversets him, and might do great mischief."

" You don't think the danger of inflammation over yet, then ?"

" O, no ! his pulse is so very easily raised, that we are obliged to keep him very quiet, and nearly to starve him, poor fellow; and his appetite is returning so fast, that it makes it very difficult to manage him."

" I should be afraid that now would be the time to see the effects of poor Mary's over-gentleness."

" Yes ; but what greatly increases the difficulty is that Fred has some strange prejudice against Philip Carey."

Busy Bee, who had heard nothing of this, felt her cheeks flush, while her father proceeded :

" I do not understand it at all : Philip's manners in a sick-room are particularly good—much better than I should have expected, and he has been very attentive and gentle-handed ; but, from the first, Fred has shown a dislike to him, questioned all his measures, and made the most of it whenever he was obliged to give him any pain. The last time the London doctor was here, I am sure he hurt Fred a great deal more than Philip has ever done, yet the boy bore it manfully, though he shrinks and exclaims the moment Philip touches him. Then he is always talking of wishing for old Clarke at Rocksand, and I give Mary infinite [credit for never having proposed to send for him. I used to think she had great faith in the old man, but I believe it was only her mother."

"Of course it was. It is only when Mary has to act alone that you really are obliged to perceive all her excellent sense and firmness; and I am very glad that you should be convinced now and then, that in nothing but her fears, poor thing, has she anything of the spoiling mamma about her."

"As if I did not know that," said he, smiling.

"And so she would not yield to this fancy? Very wise indeed. But I should like to know the reason of this dislike on Fred's part. Have you ever asked him?"

"No: he is not in a fit state for argument; and besides, I think the prejudice would only be strengthened. We have praised Philip again and again, before him, and said all we could think of to give him confidence in him, but nothing will do; in fact, I suspect Mr. Fred was sharp enough to discover that we were talking for a purpose. It has been the great trouble this whole time, though neither Mary nor I have mentioned it, for fear of annoying my mother."

"Papa," said Busy Bee, "I am afraid I know the reason but too well. It was my foolish way of talking about the Careys: I used to tease poor Fred about Roger's having taken him for Philip, and say all sorts of things that I did not really mean."

"Hem!" said her father. "Well, I should think it might be so: it always struck me that the prejudice must be grounded upon some absurd notion, the memory of which had passed away, while the impression remained."

"And do you think I could do anything towards removing it? You know I am to go and wish Fred 'good-bye' this afternoon."

"Why, yes; you might as well try to say something cheerful, which might do away with the impression. Not that I think it will be of any use ; only do not let him think it has been under discussion."

Beatrice assented, and was silent again while they went on talking.

" And Mary has held out wonderfully?" said her mother.

" Too wonderfully," said Mr. Geoffrey Langford, "in a way which I fear will cost her dearly. I have been positively longing to see her give way as she ought to have done under the fatigue : and now I am afraid of the old complaint. She puts her hand to her side now and then, and I am persuaded that she had some of those spasms a night or two ago."

" Ah !" said his wife, with great concern, "that is just what I have been dreading the whole time. When she consulted Dr. ——, how strongly he forbade her to use any kind of exertion. Why would you not let me come? I assure you it was all I could do to keep myself from setting off."

" It was very well behaved in you, indeed, Beatrice," said he, smiling ; " a sacrifice which very few husbands would have had resolution either to make themselves, or to ask of their wives. I thanked you greatly when I did not see you."

" But why would you not have me ? Do you not repent it now ?"

" Not in the least. Fred would let no one come near but his mother and me : you could not have saved either of us an hour's nursing then, whereas now you can keep Fred in order, and take care of Mary, if she will suffer it, and that she will do better from you than from any one else."

They were now reaching the entrance of Sutton Leigh Lane, and Queen Bee was called upon for the full history of the accident, which, often as it had been told by letter, must again be narrated in all its branches. Even her father had

never had time to hear it completely: and there was so
much to ask and to answer on the merely external circumstances, that they had not begun to enter upon feelings and
thoughts when they arrived at the gate of the paddock,
which was held open by Dick and Willy, excessively delighted to see Aunt Geoffrey.

In a few moments more she was affectionately welcomed
by old Mrs. Langford, whose sentiments with regard to the
two Beatrices were of a curiously varying and always opposite description. When her daughter-in-law was at a distance, she secretly regarded with a kind of respectful aver-
sion, both her talents, her learning, and the fashionable life
to which she had been accustomed ; but in her presence
the winning, lively simplicity of her manners completely
dispelled all these prejudices in an instant, and she loved
her most cordially for her own sake, as well as because she
was Geoffrey's wife. On the contrary, the younger Beatrice
while absent, was the dear little granddaughter,—the Queen
of Bees, the cleverest of creatures ; and while present, it
has already been shown how constantly the two tempers
fretted each other, or had once done so, though now, so care-
ful had Busy Bee lately been, that there had been only one
collision between them for the last ten days, and that was
caused by her strenuous attempts to convince grandmamma
that Fred was not yet fit for boiled chicken and calves' foot
jelly.

Mrs. Langford's greetings were not half over when Henrietta and her mamma hastened down stairs to embrace dear
Aunt Geoffrey.

"My dear Mary, I am so glad to be come to you at
last."

"Thank you, O ! thank you, Beatrice. How Fred will
enjoy having you now !"

"Is he tired ?" asked Uncle Geoffrey.

"No, not at all; he seems to be very comfortable. He has been talking of Queen Bee's promised visit. Do you like to go up now, my dear?"

Queen Bee consented eagerly, though with some trepidation, for she had not seen her cousin since his accident, and besides, she did not know how to begin about Philip Carey. She ran to take off her bonnet, while Henrietta went to announce her coming. She knocked at the door, Henrietta opened it, and coming in, she saw Fred lying on the sofa by the fire, in his dressing-gown, stretched out in that languid listless manner that betokens great feebleness. There were the purple marks of leeches on his temples; his hair had been cropped close to his head; his face was long and thin, without a shade of colour, but his eyes looked large and bright; and he smiled and held out his hand: "Ah, Queenie, how d'ye do?"

"How d'ye do, Fred? I am glad you are better."

"You see I have the ass's ears after all," said he, pointing to his own, which were very prominent in his shorn and shaven condition.

Beatrice could not very easily call up a smile, but she made an effort, and succeeded, while she said, "I should have complimented you on the increased wisdom of your looks. I did not know the shape of your head was so like papa's."

"Is Aunt Geoffrey come?" asked Fred.

"Yes," said his sister: "but mamma thinks you had better not see her till to-morrow."

"I wish Uncle Geoffrey was not going," said Fred. "Nobody else has the least notion of making one tolerably comfortable."

"O, your mamma, Fred!" said Queen Bee.

"O yes, mamma, of course! But then she is getting fagged."

" Mamma says she is quite unhappy to have kept him so long from his work in London," said Henrietta; "but I do not know what we should have done without him."

" I do not know what we shall do now," said Fred, in a languid and doleful tone.

The Queen Bee, thinking this a capital opportunity, spoke with almost alarmed eagerness, " O yes, Fred, you will get on famously; you will enjoy having *my* mamma so much, and you are so much better already, and Philip Carey manages you so well—"

" Manages !" said Fred; "ay, and I'll tell you how, Queenie; just as the man managed his mare when he fed her on a straw a day. I believe he thinks I am a ghool, and can live on a grain of rice. I only wish he knew himself what starvation is. Look here ! you can almost see the fire through my hand, and if I do but lift up my head, the whole room is in a merry-go-round. And that is nothing but weakness; there is nothing else on earth the matter with me, except that I am starved down to the strength of a midge !"

" Well, but of course he knows," said Busy Bee, " papa says he has had an excellent education, and he must know."

" To be sure he does, perfectly well : he is a sharp fellow, and knows how to keep a patient when he has got one."

" How can you talk such nonsense, Fred ? One comfort is, that it is a sign you are getting well, or you would not have spirits to do it."

" I am talking no nonsense," said Fred, sharply; " I am as serious as possible."

" But you can't really think that if Philip was capable of acting in such an atrocious way, that papa would not find it out, and the other doctor too ?"

" What ! when that man gets I don't know how many

guineas from mamma every time he comes, do you think that it is for his interest that I should get well?"

"My dear Fred," interposed his sister, "you are exciting yourself, and that is so very bad for you."

"I do assure you, Henrietta, you would find it very little exciting to be shut up in this room with half a teaspoonful of wishy-washy pudding twice a day, and all just to fill Mr. Philip Carey's pockets! Now, there was old Clarke at Rocksand, he had some feeling for one, poor old fellow; but this man, not the slightest compunction has he; and I am ready to kick him out of the room when I hear that silky voice of his trying to be gen-tee-eel, and condoling: and those boots—O! Busy Bee! those boots! whenever he makes a step I always hear them say, ' O what a pretty fellow I am.' "

"You seem to be very merry here, my dears," said Aunt Mary, coming in; "but I am afraid you will tire yourself, Freddy; I heard your voice even before I opened the door."

Fred was silent, a little ashamed, for he had sense enough not absolutely to believe all that he had been saying, and his mother, sitting down, began to talk to the visitor: "Well, my little Queen, we have seen very little of you of late, but we shall be very sorry to lose you. I suppose your mamma will have all your letters, and Henrietta must not expect any, but we shall want very much to know how you get on with Aunt Susan and her little dog."

"O very well, I dare say," said Beatrice, rather absently, for she was looking at her aunt's delicate fragile form, and thinking of what her father had been saying.

"And, Queenie," continued her aunt, earnestly, "you must take great care of your papa—make him rest, and listen to your music, and read story-books instead of going back to his work all the evening."

"To be sure I shall, Aunt Mary, as much as I possibly can."

"But, Bee," said Fred, "you don't mean that you are going to be shut up with that horrid old Lady Susan all this time? Why don't you stay here, and let her take care of herself?"

"Mamma would not like that; and besides, to do her justice, she is really ill, Fred," said Beatrice.

"It is too bad, now I am just getting better—if they would let me, I mean," said Fred: "just when I could enjoy having you, and now there you go off to that old woman. It's a downright shame."

"So it is, Fred," said Queen Bee gaily, but not coquettishly, as once she would have answered him, "a great shame in you not to have learned to feel for other people, now you know what it is to be ill yourself."

"That is right, Bee," said Aunt Mary, smiling; "tell him he ought to be ashamed of having monopolized you all so long, and spoilt all the comfort of your household. I am sure I am," added she, her eyes filling with tears, as she affectionately patted Beatrice's hand.

Queen Bee's heart was very full, but she knew that to give way to the expression of her feelings would be hurtful to Fred, and she only pressed her aunt's long thin fingers very earnestly, and turned her face to the fire, while she struggled down the rising emotion. There was a little silence, and when they began to talk again, it was of the engravings at which Fred had just been looking. The visit lasted till the dressing-bell rang, when Beatrice was obliged to go, and she shook hands with Fred, saying cheerfully, "Well, good-bye, I hope you will be better friends with the doctors next time I see you."

"Never will I like one inch of a doctor, never!" repeated Fred, as she left the room, and ran to snatch what mo-

ments she could with her mamma in the space allowed for
dressing.

Grandmamma was happy that evening, for, except poor
Frederick's own place, there were no melancholy gaps at
the dinner-table. He had Bennet to sit with him, and besides, there was within call the confidential old man-servant,
who had lived so many years at Rocksand, and in whom
both Fred and his mother placed considerable dependence.

Everything looked like recovery; Mrs. Frederick Langford came down and talked and smiled like her own sweet
self; Mrs. Geoffrey Langford was ready to hear all the
news, old Mr. Langford was quite in spirits again, Henrietta
was bright and lively. The thought of long days in London
with Lady Susan, and of long evenings with no mamma,
and with papa either writing or at his chambers, began from
force of contrast to seem doubly like banishment to poor
little Queen Bee, but whatever faults she had, she was no
repiner. "I deserve it," said she to herself, "and surely I
ought to bear my share of the trouble my wilfulness has
occasioned. Besides, with even one little bit of papa's company I am only too well off."

So she smiled, and answered grandpapa in his favourite
style, so that no one would have guessed from her demea-
nour that a task had been imposed upon her which she so
much disliked, and in truth her thoughts were much more
on others than on herself. She saw all hopeful and happy
about Fred, and as to her aunt, when she saw her as usual
with all her playful gentleness, she could not think that there
was anything seriously amiss with her, or if there was,
mamma would find it out and set it all to rights. Then
how soothing and comforting, now that the first acute pain
of remorse was over, was that affectionate kindness, which
in every little gesture and word, Aunt Mary had redoubled
to her ever since the accident.

Fred was all this time lying on his sofa, very glad to rest after so much talking : weak, dizzy, and languid, and throwing all the blame of his uncomfortable sensations on Philip Carey and the starvation system, but still, perhaps, not without thoughts of a less discontented nature, for when Mr. Geoffrey Langford came to help him to bed, he said, as he watched the various arrangements his uncle was for the last time sedulously making for his comfort, " Uncle Geoffrey, I ought to thank you very much ; I am afraid I have been a great plague to you."

Perhaps Fred did not say this in all sincerity, for any one but Uncle Geoffrey would have completely disowned the plaguing, and he fully expected him to do so ; but his uncle had a stern regard for truth, coupled with a courtesy which left it no more harshness than was salutary.

" Anything for your good, my dear sir," said he, with a smile. " You are welcome to plague me as much as you like, only remember that your mamma is not quite so tough."

" Well, I do try to be considerate about her," said Fred. " I mean to make her rest as much as possible ; Henrietta and I have been settling how to save her."

" You could save her more than all, Fred, if you would spare her discussions."

Fred held his tongue, for though his memory was rather cloudy about the early part of his illness, he did remember having seen her look greatly harassed one day lately when he had been arguing against Philip Carey.

Uncle Geoffrey proceeded to gather up some of the outlines which Henrietta had left on the sofa. " I like those very much," said Fred, " especially the Fight with the Dragon."

" You know Schiller's poem on it ?" said Uncle Geoffrey.

" Yes, Henrietta has it in German."

"Well, it is what I should especially recommend to your consideration."

"I am afraid it will be long enough before I am able to go out on a dragon-killing expedition," said Fred, with a weary helpless sigh.

"Fight the dragon at home, then, Freddy. Now is the time for—

> ' The duty hardest to fulfil,
>   To learn to yield our own self-will.' "

"There is very little hasty pudding in the case," said Fred, rather disconsolately, and at the same time rather drolly, and with a sort of resolution of this kind, "I will try then, I will not bother mamma, let that Carey serve me as he may. I will not make a fuss, if I can help it, unless he is very unreasonable indeed, and when I get well I will submit to be coddled in an exemplary manner; I only wonder when I shall feel up to anything again ! O ! what a nuisance it is to have this swimming head and aching knees, all by the fault of that Carey !"

Uncle Geoffrey said no more, for he thought a hint often was more useful than a lecture, even if Fred had been in a state for the latter, and besides he was in greater request than ever on this last evening, so much so that it seemed as if no one was going to spare him even to have half an hour's talk with his wife. He did find the time for this at last, however, and his first question was, "What do you think of the little Bee ?"

"I think with great hope, much more satisfactorily than I have been able to do for some time past," was the answer.

"Poor child, she has felt it very deeply," said he, "I have been grieved to have so little time to bestow on her."

"I am disposed to think," said Mrs. Geoffrey Langford, thoughtfully, "that it was the best thing for her to be thrown on herself. Too much talk has always been the mischief with her, as with many another only child, and it struck me to-day as a very good sign that she said so little. There was something very touching in the complete absence of moralizing to-day."

"None of her sensible sayings," said her father, with a gratified though a grave smile. "It was perfectly open confession, and yet with no self in it. Ever since the accident there has been a staidness and sedateness about her manner which seemed like great improvement, as far as I have seen. And when it was proposed for her to go to Lady Susan, I was much pleased with her, she was so simple : 'Very well,' she said, 'I hope I shall be able to make her comfortable ;' no begging off, no heroism. And really, Beatrice, don't you think we could make some other arrangement? It is too great a penance for her, poor child. Lady Susan will do very well, and I can have an eye to her ; I am much inclined to leave the poor little Queen here with you."

"No, no, Geoffrey," said his wife, "that would never do : I do not mean on my aunt's account, but on the Busy Bee's ; I am sure, wish it as we may," and the tears were in her eyes, "this is no time for even the semblance of neglecting a duty for her sake."

"Not so much hers as yours," said Mr. Geoffrey Langford, "you have more on your hands than I like to leave you alone to encounter, and she is a valuable little assistant. Besides you have been without her so long, it is your turn to keep her now."

"No, no, no," she repeated, though not without an effort, "it is best as it is settled for all, and decidedly so for me, for with her to write to me about you every day, and to look after you, I shall be a hundred times more at ease than if I thought you were working yourself to death with no one to remonstrate."

So it remained as before decided, and the pain that the decision cost both mother and daughter was only to be inferred by the way in which they kept close together, as if determined not to lose unnecessarily one fragment of each other's company ; but they had very few moments alone together, and those were chiefly employed in practical matters, in minute directions as to the little things that conduced to keep Lady Susan in good humour, and above all, the arrangements for papa's comfort. There was thus not much time for Beatrice to spend with Henrietta, nor indeed would much have resulted if there had been more. As she grew more at ease about her brother, Henrietta had gradually resumed her usual manner, and was now as affectionate to Beatrice as ever, but she was quite unconscious of her previous unkindness, and therefore made no attempt to atone for it. Queen Bee had ceased to think of it, and if a reserve had grown up between the two girls, they neither of them perceived it.

Mr. Geoffrey Langford and his daughter set out on their return to London so early the next morning that hardly any of the family were up ; but their hurried breakfast in the grey of morning was enlivened by Alex, who came in just in time to exchange some last words with Uncle Geoffrey about his school work, and to wish Queen Bee good-bye, with hopes of a merrier meeting next summer.

CHAPTER XVI

M RS. Geoffrey Langford had from the first felt considerable anxiety for her sister-in-law, who, though cheerful as ever, began at length to allow that she felt worn out,
and consented to spare herself more than she had hitherto
done. The mischief was, however, not to be averted, and
after a few days of increasing languor, she was attacked by
a severe fit of the spasms, to which she had for several years
been subject at intervals, and was obliged to confine herself
entirely to her own room, relying with complete confidence
on her sister for the attendance on her son.

It was to her however, that Mrs. Geoffrey Langford wished
most to devote herself; viewing her case with more uneasiness than that of Frederick, who was decidedly on the fair
road to convalescence ; and she only gave him as much time
as was necessary to satisfy his mother, and to superintend
the regulation of his room. He had all the society he
wanted in his sister, who was always with him, and in grandpapa and grandmamma, whose short and frequent visits he
began greatly to enjoy. He had also been more amenable
to authority of late, partly in consequence of his uncle's
warning, partly because it was not quite so easy to torment
an aunt as a mother, and partly too because, excepting always the starving system, he had nothing in particular of

which to complain. His mother's illness might also have its effect in subduing him; but it did not dwell much on his spirits, or Henrietta's, as they were too much accustomed to her ill health to be easily alarmed on her account.

It was the last day of the holidays, and Alexander was to come late in the afternoon—Fred's best time in the day—to take his leave. All the morning Fred was rather out of spirits, and talked to Henrietta a great deal about his school life. It might have been a melancholy day if he had been going back to school, but it was more sad to be obliged to stay away from the world where he had hitherto been measuring his powers, and finding his most exciting interests. It was very mortifying to be thus laid helplessly aside; a mere nobody, instead of an important and leading member of a community; at such an age too that it was probable that he would never return there again.

He began to describe to Henrietta all the scenes where he would be missing, but not missed; the old cathedral town, with its nest of trees, and the chalky hills; the quiet river creeping through the meadows: the "beech-crowned steep," girdled in with the "hollow trench that the Danish pirate made;" the old collegiate courts, the painted windows of the chapel, the surpliced scholars,—even the very shops in the street had their part in his description: and then falling into silence he sighed at the thought that there he would be known no more,—all would go on as usual, and after a few passing inquiries and expressions of compassion, he would be forgotten; his rivals would pass him in the race of distinction; his school-boy career be at an end.

His reflections were interrupted by Mrs. Langford's entrance with Aunt Geoffrey, bringing a message of invitation from grandpapa to Henrietta, to walk with him to Sutton Leigh. She went; and Aunt Geoffrey, after putting a book within Fred's reach, and seeing that he and grandmamma were quite willing to be companionable, again returned to his mother.

Mrs. Langford thought him low and depressed, and began talking about his health, and the present mode of treatment, —a subject on which they were perfectly agreed : one being as much inclined to bestow a good diet as the other could be to receive it.

If his head was still often painfully dizzy and confused; if his eyes dazzled when he attempted to read for a long time together; if he could not stand or walk across the room without excessive giddiness—what was that but the effect of want of nourishment? "If there was a craving, that was a sure sign that the thing was wholesome." So she said, and her grandson assented with his whole heart.

In a few minutes she left the room, and presently returned with the most tempting-looking glass of clear amber-coloured jelly.

"O, grandmamma!" said Fred, doubtfully, though his eyes positively lighted up at the sight.

"Yes, my dear, I had it made for your mamma, and she says it is very good. It is as clear as possible, and quite innocent; I am sure it must do you good."

"Thank you! O, thank you! It does look very nice," said Fred, gazing on it with wistful eyes, "but really I do not think I ought."

"If it was to do you any harm, I am sure I would not think of such a thing," said Mrs. Langford. "But I have lived a good many more years in the world than these young people, and I never saw any good come of all this keeping low. There was old Mr. Hilton, now, that attended all the neighbourhood when I was a girl; he kept you low enough while the fever was on you, but as soon as it was gone, why then re-invigorate the system,—that was what he used to say."

"Just like old Clarke, of Rocksand!" sighed Fred. "I know my system would like nothing better than to be re-invigorated with that splendid stuff; but you know it would put them all in a dreadful state if they knew it."

"Never mind," said grandmamma; "'tis all my doing, you know. Come, to oblige me, taste it, my dear."

"One spoonful," said Fred—"to oblige grandmamma," added he to himself: and he let grandmamma lift him up on the cushions as far as he could bear to have his head raised. He took the spoonful, then started a little,—"There is wine in it!" said he.

"A very little—just enough to give it a flavour; it cannot make any difference. Do you like it, my dear?" as the spoon scooped out another transparent rock. "Ay, that is right! I had the receipt from my old Aunt Kitty, and no-body ever could make it like Judith."

"I am in for it now," thought Fred. "Well, 'tis excellent," said he; "capital stuff! I feel it all down to my fingers' ends," added he with a smile, as he returned the glass, after fishing in vain for the particles remaining in the small end.

"That is right; I am so glad to see you enjoy it!" said grandmamma, hurrying off with the empty glass with speed at which Fred smiled, as it implied some fears of meeting Aunt Geoffrey. He knew the nature of his own case suffi-ciently to be aware that he had acted very imprudently,— that is to say, his better sense was aware—but his spirit of self-will made him consider all these precautions as nonsense, and was greatly confirmed by his feeling himself much more fresh and lively. Grandmamma returned to announce Alex-ander and Willy, who soon followed her, and after shaking hands, stood silent, much shocked at the alteration in Fred's appearance.

This impression, however, soon passed off, as Fred began to talk over school affairs in a very animated manner; send-

ing messages to his friends, discussing the interests of the
coming half-year, the games, the studies, the employments;
Alex lamenting Fred's absence, engaging to write, undertaking numerous commissions, and even prognosticating his
speedy recovery, and attainment of that cynosure,—the
prize. Never had the two cousins met so cordially, or so
enjoyed their meeting. There was no competition; each
could afford to do the other justice, and both felt great
satisfaction in doing so; and so high and even so loud became their glee, that Alex could scarcely believe that Fred
was not in perfect health. At last Aunt Geoffrey came to
put an end to it; and finding Fred so much excited, she
made Alex bring his blunt honest farewells and good wishes
to a speedy conclusion, desired Fred to lie quiet and rest,
and sat down herself to see that he did so.

Fred could not easily be brought to repose; he went on
talking fast and eagerly in praise of Alex, and in spite of
her complete assent, he went on more and more vehemently, just as if he was defending Alex from some one who
wanted to detract from his merits. She tried reading to
him, but he grew too eager about the book; and at last she
rather advanced the time for dressing for dinner, both for
herself and Henrietta, and sent Bennet to sit with him,
hoping thus perforce to reduce him to a quiescent state.
He was by this means a little calmed for the rest of the
evening; but so wakeful and restless a night ensued, that he
began to be alarmed, and fully came to the conclusion that
Philip Carey was in the right after all. Towards morning,
however, a short sleep visited him, and he awoke at length
quite sufficiently refreshed to be self-willed as ever; and,
contrary to advice, insisted on leaving his bed at his usual
hour.

Philip Carey came at about twelve o'clock, and was disappointed as well as surprised to find him so much more

languid and uncomfortable, as he could not help allowing that he felt. His pulse, too, was unsatisfactory; but Philip thought the excitement of the interview with Alex well accounted for the sleepless night, as well as for the exhaustion of the present day : and Fred persuaded himself to believe so too.

Henrietta did not like to leave him to-day, but she was engaged to take a ride with grandpapa, who felt as if the little Mary of years long gone by was restored to him, when he had acquired a riding companion in his granddaughter. Mrs. Langford undertook to sit with Fred, and Mrs. Geoffrey Langford, who had been at first afraid that she would be too bustling a nurse for him just now, seeing that he was evidently impatient to be left alone with her, returned to Mrs. Frederick Langford, resolving, however, not to be long absent.

In that interval Mrs. Langford brought in the inviting glass, and Fred, in spite of his good sense, could not resist it. Perhaps the recent irritation of Philip's last visit made him more willing to act in opposition to his orders. At any rate, he thought of little save of swallowing it before Aunt Geoffrey should catch him in the fact, in which he succeeded ; so that grandmamma had time to get the tell-tale glass safely into the store-closet just as Mrs. Frederick Langford's door was opened at the other end of the passage.

Fred's sofa cushions were all too soft or too hard that afternoon,—too high or too low; there was a great mountain in the middle of the sofa, too, so that he could not lie on it comfortably. The room was chilly, though the fire was hot, and how grandmamma did poke it ! Fred thought she did nothing else the whole afternoon ; and there was a certain concluding shovel that she gave to the cinders, that very nearly put him in a passion. Nothing would make him comfortable till Henrietta came in, and it seemed very long before he heard the paddock gate, and the horses' feet upon the gravel. Then he grew very much provoked because his sister went first to her mamma's room; and it was grandpapa who came to him full of a story of Henrietta's good management of her horse when they suddenly met the hounds in a narrow lane. In she came, at last, in her habit, her hair hanging loosely round her face, her cheeks and eyes lighted up by the exercise, and some early primroses in her hand, begging his pardon, for having kept him waiting, but saying she thought he did not want her directly, as he had grandpapa.

Nevertheless he scolded her, ordered her specimens of the promise of spring out of the room on an accusation of their possessing a strong scent, made her make a complete revolution on his sofa, and then insisted on her going on with Nicolo de Lapi, which she was translating to him from the Italian. Warm as the room felt to her in her habit, she sat down directly, without going to take it off; but he was not to be thus satisfied. He found fault with her for hesitating in her translation, and desired her to read the Italian instead; then she read first so fast that he could not follow, and then so slowly that it was quite unbearable, and she must go on translating. With the greatest patience and sweetest temper she obeyed; only when next he interrupted her to find fault, she stopped, and said gently, " Dear Fred, I am afraid you are not feeling so well."

"Nonsense! What should make you think so? You think I am cross, I suppose. Well, never mind, I will go on for myself," said he, snatching the book.

Henrietta turned away to hide her tears, for she was too wise to vindicate herself.

"Are you crying? I am sure I said nothing to cry about; I wish you would not be so silly."

"If you would only let me go on, dear Fred," said she, thinking that occupying him would be better than arguing. "It is so dark where you are, and I will try to get on better. There is an easier piece coming."

Fred agreed, and she went on without interruption for some little time, till at last he grew so excited by the story as to be very angry when the failing light obliged her to pause. She tried to extract some light from the fire, but this was a worse offence than any; it was too bad of her, when she knew how he hated both the sound of poking, and that horrible red flickering light which always hurt his eyes. This dislike, which had been one of the symptoms of the early part of his illness, so alarmed her that she had thoughts of going to call Aunt Geoffrey, and was heartily glad to see her enter the room.

"Well, how are you going on?" she said cheerfully. "Why, my dear, how hot you must be in that habit!"

"Rather," said poor Henrietta, whose face between the heat and her perplexity, was almost crimson. "We have been reading 'Nicolo,' and I am very much afraid it is as bad as Alex's visit, and has excited Fred again."

"I am quite sick of hearing that word excitement!" said Fred, impatiently.

"Almost as tired as of having your pulse felt," said Aunt Geoffrey. "But yet I must ask you to submit to that disagreeable necessity."

Fred moved pettishly, but as he could not refuse, he only told Henrietta that he could not bear any one to look at him while his pulse was felt.

"Will you fetch me a candle, my dear?" said Aunt Geoffrey, amazed as well as terrified by the fearful rapidity of the throbs, and trying to acquire sufficient composure to count them calmly. The light came, and still she held his wrist, beginning her reckoning again and again, in the hope that it was only some momentary agitation that had so quickened them.

"What! 'tis faster?" asked Fred, speaking in a hasty alarmed tone, when she released him at last.

"You are flushed, Fred," she answered very quietly, though she felt full of consternation, "Yes, faster than it ought to be; I think you had better not sit up any longer this evening, or you will sleep no better than last night."

"Very well," said Fred.

"Then I will ring for Stephens," said she.

The first thing she did on leaving his room was to go to her own, and there write a note to young Mr. Carey, giving an account of the symptoms that had caused her so much alarm. As she wrote them down without exaggeration, and trying to give each its just weight, going back to recollect the first unfavourable sign, she suddenly remembered that as she left her sister's room, she had seen Mrs. Langford, whom she had left with Fred, at the door of the store-closet. Could she have been giving him any of her favourite nourishing things? Mrs. Geoffrey Langford could hardly believe that either party could have acted so foolishly, yet when she remembered a few words that had passed about the jelly that morning at breakfast, she could no longer doubt, and bitterly reproached herself for not having kept up a stricter surveillance. Of her suspicion she however said nothing, but sealing her note, she went down to the drawing-room, told Mr. Langford that she did not think Fred quite so well that evening, and asked him if he did not think it might be better to let Philip Carey know. He agreed instantly, and rang the bell to order a servant to ride to Allonfield ; but Mrs. Langford, who could not bear any one but Geoffrey to act without consulting her, pitied man and horse for being sent out so late, and opined that Beatrice forgot that she was not in London, where the medical man could be called in so easily.

It was fortunate that it was the elder Beatrice instead of the younger, for provoked as she already had been before with the old lady, it was not easy even for her to make a cheerful answer. "Well, it is very kind in you to attend to my London fancies," said she; "I think if we can do anything to spare him such a night as the last, it should be tried."

"Certainly, certainly," said Mr. Langford. "It is very disappointing when he was going on so well. He must surely have been doing something imprudent."

It was very tempting to interrogate Mrs. Langford, but her daughter-in-law had long since come to a resolution never to convey to her anything like reproach, let her do what she might in her mistaken kindness of heart, or her respectable prejudices; so, without entering on what many in her place might have made a scene of polite recrimination, she left the room, and on her way up, heard Frederick's door gently opened. Stephens came quickly and softly to the end of the passage to meet her. "He is asking for you, ma'am," said he; "I am afraid he is not so well; I did not like to ring, for fear of alarming my mistress, but——"

Mrs. Geoffrey Langford entered the room, and found that the bustle and exertion of being carried to his bed had brought on excessive confusion and violent pain. He put his hand to his forehead, opened his eyes, and looked wildly about. "Oh, Aunt Geoffrey," he exclaimed, "what shall I do? It is as bad—worse than ever!"

"You have been doing something imprudent, I fear," said Aunt Geoffrey, determined to come to the truth at once.

"Only that glass of jelly—if I had guessed!"

"Only one?"

"One to-day, one yesterday. It was grandmamma's do-ing. Don't let her know that I told. I wish mamma was here !"

Aunt Geoffrey tried to relieve the pain by cold applica-tions, but could not succeed, and Fred grew more and more alarmed.

"The inflammation is coming back !" he cried, in an agony of apprehension that almost overcame the sense of pain. "I shall be in danger—I shall lose my senses—I shall die ! Mamma ! O ! where is mamma ?"

"Lie still, my dear Fred," said Mrs. Geoffrey Langford, laying her hand on him so as to restrain his struggling move-ments to turn round or to sit 'up. "Resistance and agita-tion will hurt you more than anything else. You must con-trol yourself, and trust to me, and you may be sure I will do the best in my power for you. The rest is in the hands of GOD."

"Then you think me very ill ?" said Fred, trying to speak more composedly.

"I think you will certainly make yourself very ill, unless you will keep yourself quiet, both mind and body. There" —she settled him as comfortably as she could : "Now I am going away for a few minutes. Make a resolution not to stir till I come back. Stephens is here, and I shall soon come back."

This was very unlike the way in which his mother used to beseech him as a favour to spare her, and yet his aunt's tone was so affectionate as well as so authoritative, that he could not feel it unkind. She left the room, and as soon as she found herself alone in the passage, leant against the wall and trembled, for she felt herself for a moment quite over-whelmed, and longed earnestly for her husband to think for her, or even for one short interval in which to reflect. For this, however, there was no time, and with one earnest mental supplication, summoning up her energies, she walked on to the person whom she at that moment most dreaded to see, her sister-in-law. She found her sitting in her arm-chair, Henrietta with her, both looking very anxious, and she was glad to find her prepared.

" What is it ?" was the first eager question.

" He has been attempting rather too much of late," was the answer, "and has knocked himself up. I came to tell you, because I think I had better stay with him, and perhaps you might miss me."

" O no, no, pray go to him. Nothing satisfies me so well about him as that you should be there, except that I cannot bear to give you so much trouble. Don't stay here answering questions. He will be so restless if he misses you—"

" Don't you sit *imagining*, Mary ; let Henrietta read to you."

This proposal made Henrietta look so piteous and wistful, that her mother said, " No, no, let her go to Freddy, poor child : I dare say he wants her."

" By no means," said Aunt Geoffrey, opening the door ; " he will be quieter without her."

Henrietta was annoyed, and walked about the room, instead of sitting down to read. She was too fond of her own will to like being thus checked, and she thought she had quite as good a right to be with her brother as her aunt could have. Every temper has one side or other on which it is susceptible ; and this was hers. She thought it affection for her brother, whereas it was impatience of being ordered.

Her mother forced herself to speak cheerfully. " Aunt Geoffrey is a capital nurse," said she ; " there is something so decided about her, that it always does one good. It saves all the trouble and perplexity of thinking for oneself."

" I had rather judge for myself," said Henrietta.

"That is all very well to talk of," said her mother, smiling sadly, "but it is a very different thing when you are obliged to do it."

"Well, what do you like to hear?" said Henrietta, who found herself too cross for conversation : "The Old Man's Home?"

" Do not read unless you like it, my dear ; I think you must be tired. You want 'lungs of brass' to go on all day to both of us. You had better not. I should like to talk."

Henrietta being in a wilful fit, chose nevertheless to read, because it gave her the satisfaction of feeling that Aunt Geoffrey was inflicting a hardship upon her ; although her mother would decidedly have preferred conversation. So she took up a book, and began, without any perception of the sense of what she was reading, but her thoughts dwelling partly on her brother, and partly on her aunt's provoking ways. She read on through a whole chapter, then closing the book hastily, exclaimed, "I must go and see what Aunt Geoffrey is doing with Fred."

" She is not such a very dangerous person," said Mrs. Frederick Langford, almost laughing at the form of the expression.

" Well, but you surely want to know how he is, mamma?"

" To be sure I do, but I am so afraid of his being disturbed. If he was just going to sleep now."

" Yes, but you know how softly I can open the door."

" Your aunt would let us know if there was anything to hear. Pray take care, my dear."

" I must go, I can't bear it any longer ; I will only just listen," said Henrietta ; "I will not be a moment."

" Let me have the book, my dear," said her mother, who knew but too well the length of Henrietta's moments, and who had just, by means of a great effort, succeeded in making herself take interest in the book.

Henrietta gave it to her, and darted off. The door of Fred's room was ajar, and she entered. Aunt Geoffrey, Bennet, and Judith were standing round the bed, her aunt sponging away the blood that was flowing from Frederick's temples. His eyes were closed, and he now and then gave long gasping sighs of oppression and faintness. " Leeches !" thought Henrietta, as she started with consternation and displeasure. " This is pretty strong ! Without telling me or mamma ! Well, this is what I call doing something with him indeed."

She advanced to the table, but no one saw her for more than a minute, till at last Aunt Geoffrey stepped quickly up to it in search of some bottle.

" Let me do something," said Henrietta, catching up the bottle that she thought likely to be the right one.

Her aunt looked vexed, and answered in a low quick tone, " You had better stay with your mamma."

" But why are you doing this? Is he worse? Is Mr. Philip Carey here? Has he ordered it?"

" He is not come yet. My dear, I cannot talk to you : I should be much obliged if you would go back to your mamma."

Aunt Geoffrey went back to Fred, but a few minutes after she looked up and still saw Henrietta standing by the table. She came up to her : " Henrietta, you are of no use here ; every additional person oppresses him ; your mamma must be kept tranquil. Why will you stay ?"

" I was just going," said Henrietta, taking this hurrying as an additional offence, and walking off in a dignified way.

It was hard to say what had affronted her most, the proceeding itself, the neglect, or the commands which Aunt Geoffrey had presumed to lay upon her, and away she went to her mamma, a great deal too much displeased, and too distrustful to pay the smallest attention to any precautions which her aunt might have tried to impress upon her.

" Well !" asked her mother anxiously.

" She would not let me stay," answered Henrietta. " She has been putting on leeches."

" Leeches !" exclaimed her mother. " He must be much worse. Poor fellow ! Is Mr. Carey here ?"

" No, that is the odd thing."

" Has he not been sent for ?"

" I am sure I don't know. Aunt Geoffrey seems to like to do things in her own way."

" It must be very bad indeed if she cannot venture to wait for him !" said Mrs. Frederick Langford, much alarmed.

" And never to tell you !" said Henrietta.

" O, that was her consideration. She knew how foolishly anxious I should be. I have no doubt that she is doing right. How did he seem to be ?"

" Very faint, I thought," said Henrietta, " there seemed to be a great deal of bleeding, but Aunt Geoffrey would not let me come near."

" She knows exactly what to do," said Mrs. Frederick Langford. " How well it was that she should be here."

Henrietta began to be so fretted at her mother's complete confidence in her aunt, that without thinking of the consequences she tried to argue it away. " Aunt Geoffrey is so quick—she does things without half the consideration other people do. And she likes to settle everything."

But happily the confiding friendship of a lifetime was too strong to be even harassed for a moment by the petulant suspicions of an angry girl.

" My dear, if you were not vexed and anxious, I should tell you that you were speaking very improperly of your aunt. I am perfectly satisfied that she is doing what is right by dear Fred, as well as by me ; and if I am satisfied, no one else has any right to object."

There was nothing left for Henrietta in her present state of spirits but to have a hearty cry, one of the best possible ways she could find of distressing her mother, who all the time was suffering infinitely more than she could imagine from her fears, her efforts to silence them, and the restraint which she was exercising upon herself, longing as she did to fly to her son's room, to see with her own eyes, and only detained by the fear that her sudden appearance there might agitate him. The tears, whatever might be their effect upon her, did Henrietta good, and restored her to something more like her proper senses. She grew rather alarmed, too, when she saw her mamma's pale looks, as she leant back almost exhausted with anxiety and repressed agitation.

Mrs. Langford came up to bring them some tea, and she, having little idea of the real state of things, took so encouraging a view as to cheer them both, and her visit did much service at least to Henrietta. Then they heard sounds announcing Philip Carey's arrival, and presently after in came Bennet with a message from Mr. Frederick that he was better, and his mother was not to be frightened. At last came Aunt Geoffrey, saying, "Well, Mary, he is better. I have been very sorry to leave you so long, and I believe Henrietta," looking at her with a smile, "thinks I have used you very ill."

" I believe she did," said her mother, "but I was sure you would do right ; you say he is better? Let me hear."

" Much better; only—. But, Mary, you look quite worn out, you should go to bed."

" Let me hear about him first."

Aunt Geoffrey accordingly told the whole history, as, perhaps, every one would not have told it, for one portion of it in some degree justified Henrietta's opinion that she had been doing a great deal on her own responsibility. It had been very difficult to stop the bleeding, and Fred, already very weak, had been so faint and exhausted that she had felt considerable alarm, and was much rejoiced by the arrival of Philip Carey, who had not been at home when the messenger reached his house. Now, however, all was well; he had fully approved all that she had done, and, although she did not repeat this to Mrs. Frederick Langford, had pronounced that her promptitude and energy had probably saved the patient's life. Fred, greatly relieved, had fallen asleep, and she had now come, with almost an equal sense of relief, to tell his mother all that had passed, and ask her pardon.

"Nay, Beatrice, what do you mean by that? Is it not what you and Geoffrey have always done to treat him as your own son instead of mine? and is it not almost my chief happiness to feel assured that you always will do so? You know that is the reason I never thank you."

Henrietta hung her head, and felt that she had been very unjust and ungrateful, more especially when her aunt said, "You thought it very hard to have your mouth stopped, Henrietta, my dear, and I was sorry for it, but I had not much time to be polite."

"I am sorry I was in the way," said she, an acknowledgment such as she had seldom made.

Fred awoke the next morning much better, though greatly fallen back in his progress towards recovery, but his mother had during the night the worst fit of spasms from which she had ever suffered.

But Henrietta thought it so well accounted for by all the agitations of the evening before, that there was no reason for further anxiety.

It was a comfort to Aunt Geoffrey, who took it rather

more seriously, that she received that morning a letter from her husband, concluding,

"As to the Queen Bee, I have no doubt that you can judge of her frame better from the tone of her letters than from anything I have to tell. I think her essentially improved and improving, and you will think I do not speak without warrant, when I tell you that Lady Susan expressed herself quite warmly respecting her this morning. She continues to imagine that she has the charge of Queen Bee, and not Queen Bee of her, and I think it much that she has been allowed to continue in the belief. Lady Amelia comes tomorrow, and then I hope the poor little woman's penance may be over, for though she makes no complaints, there is no doubt that it is a heavy one, as her thorough enjoyment of a book, and an hour's freedom from that little gossiping flow of plaintive talk sufficiently testify."

CHAPTER XVII

FREDERICK had lost much ground, and yet on the whole his relapse was of no slight service to him. In the earlier part of his illness he had been so stupefied by the accident, that he had neither been conscious of his danger, nor was able to preserve any distinct remembrance of what he had suffered. But this return to his former state, with all his senses perfect, made him realise the rest, and begin to perceive how near to the grave he had been brought. A deep shuddering sense of awe came over him, as he thought what it would have been to die then, without a minute of clear recollection, and his last act one of wilful disobedience. And how had he requited the mercy which had spared him? He had shown as much of that same spirit of self-will as his feebleness would permit; he had been exacting, discontented, rebellious, and well indeed had he deserved to be cut off in the midst of the sin in which he had persisted.

He was too weak to talk, but his mind was wide awake; and many an earnest thanksgiving, and resolution strengthened by prayer, were made in silence during the two or three days that passed, partly in such thoughts as these, and for many hours more in sleep; while sometimes his aunt, sometimes his sister, and sometimes even Bennet, sat by his bed-side unchidden for not being " mamma."

" Above all," said he to himself, " he would for the future

devote himself, to make up to her for all that he had caused her to suffer for his sake. Even if he were never to mount a horse or fire a gun for the rest of his life, what would such a sacrifice be for such a mother?" It was very disappointing that, at present, all he could even attempt to do for her was to send her messages—and affection does not travel well by message,—and at the same time to show submission to her known wishes. And after all, it would have been difficult not to have shown submission, for Aunt Geoffrey, as he had already felt, was not a person to be argued with, but to be obeyed; and for very shame he could not have indulged himself in his Philippics after the proof he had experienced of their futility.

So, partly on principle, and partly from necessity, he ceased to grumble, and from that time forth it was wonderful how much less unpleasant even external things appeared, and how much his health benefited by the tranquillity of spirits thus produced. He was willing to be pleased with all that was done with that intent; and as he grew better, it certainly was a strange variety with which he had to be amused throughout the day. Very good-naturedly he received all such civilities, especially when Willy brought him a bottle of the first live sticklebacks of the season, accompanied by a message from Arthur that he hoped soon to send him a bason of tame tadpoles,—and when John rushed up with a basket of blind young black satin puppies, their mother following in a state of agitation only equalled by that of Mrs. Langford and Judith.

Willy, a nice intelligent little fellow, grew very fond of him, and spent much time with him, taking delight in his books and prints, beyond what could have been thought possible in one of the Sutton Leigh party.

When he was strong enough to guide a pencil or pen, a very enjoyable correspondence commenced between him and his mother, who was still unable to leave her apartment; and hardly any one ever passed between the two rooms without being the bearer of some playful greeting, or droll description of the present scene and occupation, chronicles of the fashionable arrivals of the white clouds before the window, of a bunch of violets, or a new book: the fashionable departure of the headache, the fire, or a robin; notices that tom-tits were whetting their saws on the next tree, or of the domestic proceedings of the rooks who were building their house opposite to Mrs. Frederick Langford's window, and whom she watched so much that she was said to be in a fair way of solving the problem of how many sticks go to a crow's nest; criticisms of the books read by each party, and very often a reference to that celebrated billet, unfortunately delivered overnight to Prince Talleyrand, informing him that his devoted friend had scarce closed her eyes all night, and then only to dream of him!

Henrietta grew very happy. She had her brother again, as wholly hers as in their younger days,—depending upon her, participating in all her pleasures, or rather giving her favourite occupations double zest, by their being for him, for his amusement. She rode and walked in the beautiful open spring country with grandpapa, to whom she was a most valuable companion; and on her return she had two to visit, both of whom looked forward with keen interest and delight to hearing her histories of down and wood, of field and valley, of farmhouse, cottage, or school; had a laugh for the least amusing circumstance, admiration for the spring flower or leaf, and power to follow her descriptions of budding woods, soft rising hills, and gorgeous sunsets. How her mamma enjoyed comparing notes with her about those same woods and dells, and would describe the adventures of her own youth! And now it might be noticed that she did not avoid speaking of those in which Henrietta's father had been engaged; nay, she dwelt on them by preference, and without the suppressed sigh which had formerly followed anything like a reference to him. Sometimes she would smile to identify the bold open down with the same where she had run races with him, and even laugh to think of the droll adventures. Sometimes the shady woodland walk would make her describe their nutting parties, or it would bring her thoughts to some fit of childish mischief and concealment, and to the confession to which his bolder and more upright counsel had at length led her. Or she would tell of the long walks they had taken together when older grown, when each had become prime counsellor and confidante to the other; and the interests and troubles of home and of school were poured out to willing ears, and sympathy and advice exchanged. She told how Fred and Mary had been companions from the very first, how their love had grown up unconsciously, in the sports in the sunny fields, shady coombs, and green woods of their home; how it had strengthened and ripened with advancing years, and how bright and unclouded their sunshine had been : to dwell on this was her delight, while the sadness which once spoke of crushed hopes, and lost happiness, had gone from her smile. It was as if she still felt herself walking in the light of his love, and at the same time, as if she wished to show him to his daughter as he was, and to tell Henrietta of those words and those ways of his which were most characteristic, and which used to be laid up so fast in her heart, that she could never have borne to speak of them. The bitterness of his death, as it regarded herself, seemed to have passed, the brightness of his memory alone remaining. Henrietta loved to listen, but scarcely so much as her mother loved to tell; and instead of agitating her, these recollections always seemed to soothe and make her happy.

Henrietta knew that Aunt Geoffrey and grandpapa were both of them anxious about her mother's health, but for her own part she did not think her worse than she had often been before; and whilst she continued in nearly the same state, rose every day, sat in her arm-chair, and was so cheerful, and even lively, there could not be very much amiss, even though there was no visible progress in amendment. Serious complaint there was, as she knew of old, to cause the spasms; but it had existed so long, that after the first shock of being told of it two years ago, she had almost ceased to think about it. She satisfied herself to her own mind that it could not, should not be progressing, and that this was only a very slow recovery from the last attack.

Time went on, and a shade began to come over Fred. He was bright and merry when anything occurred to amuse him, did not like reading less, or take less interest in his occupations; but in the intervals of quiet he grew grave and almost melancholy, and his inquiries after his mother grew minute and anxious.

"Henrietta," said he, one day when they were alone together, "I was trying to reckon how long it is since I have seen mamma."

"O, I think she will come and see you in a few days more," said Henrietta.

"You have told me that so many times," said Fred. "I think I must try to get to her. That passage, if it was not so *very* long! If Uncle Geoffrey comes on Saturday, I am sure he can manage to take me there."

"It will be a festival day indeed when you do meet!" said Henrietta.

"Yes," said he thoughtfully. Then returning to the former subject, "But how long is it, Henrietta? This is the twenty-seventh of March, is it not?"

"Yes; a whole quarter of a year you have been laid up here."

"It was somewhere about the beginning of February that Uncle Geoffrey went."

"The fourth," said Henrietta.

"And it was three days after he went away that mamma had those first spasms. Henrietta, she has been six weeks ill!"

"Well," said Henrietta, "you know she was five weeks without stirring out of the room, that last time she was ill at Rocksand,—and she is getting better."

"I don't think it is getting better," said Fred. "You always say so, but I don't think you have anything to show for it."

"You might say the same for yourself," said Henrietta, laughing. "You have been getting better these three months, poor man, and you need not boast."

"Well, at least I can show something for it," said Fred; "they allow me a lark's diet instead of a wren's, I can hold up my head like other people now, and I actually made my own legs and the table's carry me to the window yesterday, which is what I call getting on. But I do not think it is so with mamma. A fortnight ago she used to be up by ten or eleven o'clock; now I don't believe she ever is till one."

"It has been close damp weather," said Henrietta, surprised at the accurate remembrance which she could not confute. "She misses the cold bracing wind."

"I don't like it," said Fred, growing silent, and after a short interval beginning again more earnestly, "Henrietta, neither you nor any one else are keeping anything from me, I trust?"

"O no, no!" said Henrietta, eagerly.

"You are quite sure?"

"Quite," responded she, "you know all I know, every

bit; and I know all Aunt Geoffrey does, I am sure I do, for she always tells me what Mr. Philip Carey says. I have heard Uncle and Aunt Geoffrey both say strong things about keeping people in the dark, and I am convinced they would not do so."

"I don't think they would," said Fred; "but I am not satisfied. Recollect and tell me clearly, are they convinced that this is only recovering slowly—I do not mean that; I know too well that this is not a thing to be got rid of; but do they think that she is going to be as well as usual?"

"I do," said Henrietta, "and you know I am more used to her illness than any of them. Bennet and I were agreeing to-day that, considering how bad the spasms were, and how much fatigue she had been going through, we could not expect her to get on faster."

"You do? But that is not Aunt Geoffrey."

"O! Aunt Geoffrey is anxious, and expected her to get on faster, just like Busy Bee expecting everything to be so quick; but I am sure you could not get any more information from her than from me, and impressions—I am sure you may trust mine, used as I am to watch mamma."

Fred asked no more; but it was observable that from that day he never lost one of his mother's little notes, placing them as soon as read in his pocket-book, and treasuring them carefully. He also begged Henrietta to lend him a miniature of her mother, taken at the time of her marriage. It represented her in all her youthful loveliness, with the long ringlets and plaits of dark brown hair hanging on her neck, the arch suppressed smile on her lips, and the laughing light in her deep blue eye. He looked at it for a little while, and then asked Henrietta if she thought that she could find, among the things sent from Rocksand which had not yet been unpacked, another portrait, taken in the earlier months of her widowhood, when she had in some partial degree recovered from her illness, but her life seemed still to hang on a thread. Mrs. Vivian, at whose especial desire it had been taken, had been very fond of it, and had always kept it in her room, and Fred was very anxious to see it again. After a long search, with Bennet's help, Henrietta found it, and brought it to him. Thin, wan, and in the deep black garments, there was much more general resemblance to her present appearance in this than in the portrait of the beautiful smiling bride. "And yet," said Fred, as he compared them, "do not you think, Henrietta, that there is more of mamma in the first?"

"I see what you mean," said Henrietta. "You know it is by a much better artist."

"Yes," said he, "the other is like enough in feature,— more so certainly to anything we have ever seen : but what a difference ! And yet what is it? Look ! Her eyes generally have something melancholy in their look, and yet I am sure those bright happy ones put me much more in mind of hers than these, looking so weighed down with sorrow. And the sweet smile, that is quite her own !"

"If you could but see her now, Fred," said Henrietta, " I think you would indeed say so. She has now and then a beautiful little pink flush, that lights up her eyes as well as her cheeks ; and when she smiles and talks about those old times with papa, she does really look just like the miniature, all but her thinness."

"I do not half like to hear of all that talking about my father," murmured Fred to himself as he leant back. Henrietta at first opened her eyes ; then a sudden perception of his meaning flashed over her, and she began to talk of something else as fast as she could.

Uncle Geoffrey came on Saturday afternoon, and after paying a minute's visit to Fred, had a conference of more than an hour with his sister-in-law. Fred did not seem

pleased with his sister's information that "it was on business," and only was in a slight degree reassured by being
put in mind that there was always something to settle at
Lady-day.   Henrietta thought her uncle looked grave ; and
as she was especially anxious to prevent either herself or Fred
from being frightened, she would not leave him alone in
Fred's room, knowing full well that no questions would be
asked except in private—none at least of the description
which she dreaded.

All Fred attempted was the making his long meditated
request that he might visit his mother, and Uncle Geoffrey
undertook to see whether it was possible.   Numerous messages passed, and at length it was arranged that on Sunday,
just before afternoon service, when the house was quiet, his
uncle should help him to her room, where his aunt would
read to them both.

Frederick made quite a preparation for what was to him
a great undertaking.   He sat counting the hours all the
morning ; and when at length the time arrived, his heart
beat so violently, that it seemed to take away all the little
strength he had.   His uncle came in, but waited a few
moments ; then said, with some hesitation, " Fred, you must
be prepared to see her a good deal altered."

" Yes," said Fred, impatiently.

" And take the greatest care not to agitate her.   Can you
be trusted ?   I do not ask it for your own sake."

" Yes," said Fred, resolutely.

" Then come."

And in process of time Fred was at her door.   There he
quitted his uncle's arm, and came forward alone to the large
easy chair where she sat by the fireside.   She started joyfully forward, and soon he was on one knee before her, her
arms round his neck, her tears dropping on his face, and a
quiet sense of excessive happiness felt by both.   Then ris-

ing, he sank back into another great chair, which his sister had arranged for him close to hers, and too much out of breath to speak, he passively let Henrietta make him comfortable there ; while holding his mother's hand, he kept his eyes fixed upon her, and she, anxious only for him, patted his cushions, offered her own, and pushed her footstool towards him.

A few words passed between Mr. and Mrs. Geoffrey Langford outside the door.

" I still think it a great risk," said she.

" But I should not feel justified in preventing it," was his answer, " only do not leave them long alone." Then opening the door, he called, " Henrietta, there is the last bell." And Henrietta, much against her will, was obliged to go with him to church.

" Good-bye, my dear," said her mother. " Think of us prisoners in the right way at church, and not in the wrong one."

Strangely came the sound of the church-bell to their ears through the window, half open to admit the breezy breath of spring; the cawing of the rooks and the song of the blackbird came with it ; the sky was clear and blue, the buds were bursting into life.

" How very lovely it is !" added she.

Fred made a brief reply, but without turning his head to the window. His eyes, his thoughts, his whole soul, were full of the contemplation of what was to him a thousand times more lovely,—that frail wasted form, namely, whose hand he held. The delicate pink colour which Henrietta had described was on her cheek, contrasting with the ivory whiteness of the rest of her face ; the blue eyes shone with a sweet subdued brightness under their long black lashes : the lips smiled, though languidly yet as sunnily as ever; the dark hair lay in wavy lines along the sides of her face ; and but for the helplessness with which the figure rested in the chair, there was less outward token of suffering than he had often seen about her,—more appearance almost of youth and beauty. But it was not an earthly beauty; there was something about it which filled him with a kind of undescribable undefined awe, together with dread of a sorrow towards which he shrank from looking. She thought him fatigued with the exertion he had made, and allowed him to rest, while she contemplated with pleasure even the slight advances which he had already made in shaking off the traces of illness.

The silence was not broken till Aunt Geoffrey came in, just as the last stroke of the church-bell died away, bringing in her hand a fragrant spray of the budding sweet-briar.

"The bees are coming out with you, Freddy," said she. "I have just been round the garden watching them revelling in the crocuses."

"How delicious!" said Mrs. Frederick Langford, to whom she had offered the sweet-briar. "Give it to him, poor fellow; he is quite knocked up with his journey."

"O no, not in the least, mamma, thank you," said Fred, sitting up vigorously; "you do not know how strong I am growing." And then turning to the window, he made an effort, and began observing on her rook's nest, as she called it, and her lilac buds. Then came a few more cheerful questions and comments on the late notes, and then Mrs. Frederick Langford proposed that the reading of the service should begin.

Aunt Geoffrey, kneeling at the table, read the prayers, and Fred took the alternate verses of the Psalms. It was the last day of the month, and as he now and then raised his eyes to his mother's face, he saw her lips follow the glorious responses in those psalms of praise, and a glistening in her lifted eyes such as he could never forget.

"He healeth those that are broken in heart, and giveth medicine to heal their sickness.

"He telleth the number of the stars, and calleth them all by their names."

He read this verse as he had done many a time before, without thinking of the exceeding beauty of the manner in which it is connected with the former one; but in after years he never read it again without that whole room rising before his eyes, and above all his mother's face. It was a sweet soft light, and not a gloom, that rested round that scene in his memory; springtide sights and sounds, the beams of the declining sun, with its quiet spring radiance; the fresh mild air : even the bright fire, and the general look of calm cheerfulness which pervaded all around, all conduced to that impression which never left him.

The service ended, Aunt Geoffrey read the hymn for the day in the "Christian Year," and then left them for a few minutes; but strange as it may seem, those likewise were spent in silence, and though there was some conversation when she returned, Fred took little share in it. Silent as he was, he could hardly believe that he had been there more than ten minutes, when sounds were heard of the rest of the family returning from church, and Mrs. Geoffrey Langford went down to meet them.

In another instant Henrietta came up, very bright and joyous, with many kind messages from Aunt Roger. Next came Uncle Geoffrey, who, after a few cheerful observations on the beauty of the day, to which his sister responded with pleasure, said, "Now, Freddy, I must be hard-hearted; I am coming back almost directly to carry you off."

"So soon !" exclaimed Henrietta. "Am I to be cheated of all the pleasure of seeing you together ?"

No one seemed to attend to her; but as soon as the door had closed behind his uncle, Fred moved as if to speak, paused, hesitated, then bent forward, and, shading his face with his hand, said in a low voice, " Mamma, say you forgive me."

She held out her arm, and again he sank on his knee, resting his head against her.

" My own dear boy," said she, " I will not say I have nothing to forgive, for that I know is not what you want; but well do you know how freely forgiven and forgotten is all that you may ever feel to have been against my wish. GOD bless you, my own dear Frederick !" she added, pressing her hand upon his head. " His choicest blessings be with you for ever."

Uncle Geoffrey's knock was heard ; Frederick hastily rose to his feet, was folded in one more long embrace, then, without another word, suffered his uncle to lead him out of the room, and support him back to his own. He stretched himself on the sofa, turned his face inwards, and gave two or three long gasping sighs, as if completely overpowered, though his uncle could scarcely determine whether by grief or by physical exhaustion.

Henrietta looked frightened, but her uncle made her a sign to say nothing : and after watching him anxiously for some minutes, during which he remained perfectly still, her uncle left the room, and she sat down to watch him, taking up a book, for she dreaded the reveries in which she had once been so prone to indulge. Fred remained for a long time tranquil, if not asleep ; and when at length he was disturbed, complained that his head ached, and seemed chiefly anxious to be left in quiet. It might be that, in addition to his great weariness, he felt a charm upon him which he could not bear to break. At any rate, he scarcely looked up or spoke all the rest of the evening, excepting that, when he went to bed, he sent a message that he hoped Uncle Geoffrey would come to his room the next morning before setting off, as he was obliged to do at a very early hour.

He came, and found Fred awake, looking white and heavy-eyed, as if he had slept little, and allowing that his head still ached.

"Uncle Geoffrey," said he raising himself on his elbow, and looking at him earnestly, "would it be of no use to have further advice?"

His uncle understood him, and answered, "I hope that Dr. —— will come this evening or to-morrow morning. But," added he, slowly and kindly, "you must not build your hopes upon that, Fred. It is more from the feeling that nothing should be untried, than from the expectation that he can be of use."

"Then there is no hope?" said Fred, with a strange quietness.

"Man can do nothing," answered his uncle. "You know how the case stands; the complaint cannot be reached, and there is scarcely a probability of its becoming inactive. It may be an affair of days or weeks, or she may yet rally, and be spared to us for some time longer."

"If I could but think so!" said Fred. "But I cannot. Her face will not let me hope."

"If ever a ray from heaven shone out upon a departing saint," said Uncle Geoffrey,—but he could not finish the sentence, and turning away, walked to the window.

"And you must go?" said Fred, when he came back to his side again.

"I must," said Uncle Geoffrey. "Nothing but the most absolute necessity could make me leave you now. I scarcely could feel myself an honest man if I was not in my place to-morrow. I shall be here again on Thursday, at latest, and bring Beatrice. Your mother thinks she may be a comfort to Henrietta."

"Henrietta knows all this?" asked Fred.

"As far as she will bear to believe it," said his uncle. "We cannot grudge her her unconsciousness, but I am afraid it will be worse for her in the end. You must nerve yourself, Fred, to support her. Now, good-bye, and may God bless and strengthen you in your trial!"

Fred was left alone again to the agony of the bitterest thoughts he had ever known. All his designs of devoting himself to her at an end! Her whom he loved with such an intensity of enthusiastic admiration and reverence,—the gentlest, the most affectionate, the most beautiful being he knew! Who would ever care for him as she did? To whom would it matter now whether he was in danger or in safety? whether he distinguished himself or not? And how thoughtlessly had he trifled with her comfort, for the mere pleasure of a moment, and even fancied himself justified in doing so! Even her present illness, had it not probably been brought on by her anxiety and attendance on him? and it was his own wilful disobedience to which all might be traced. It was no wonder that, passing from one such miserable thought to another, his bodily weakness was considerably increased, and he remained very languid and unwell; so much so that had Philip Carey ever presumed to question anything Mr. Geoffrey Langford thought fit to do, he would have pronounced yesterday's visit a most imprudent measure. In the afternoon, as Fred was lying on his sofa, he heard a foot on the stairs, and going along the passage.

"Who is that?" said he; "the new doctor already? It is a strange step."

"O! Fred, don't be the fairy Fine Ear, as you used to be when you were at the worst," said Henrietta.

"But do you know who it is?" said he.

"It is Mr. Franklin," said Henrietta. "You know mamma

has only been once at church since your accident, and then there was no Holy Communion. So you must not fancy she is worse, Fred."

"I wish we were confirmed," said Fred, sighing, and presently adding, "My Prayer Book, if you please, Henrietta."

"You will only make your head worse, with trying to read the small print," said she; "I will read anything you want to you."

He chose nevertheless to have it himself, and when he next spoke, it was to say, "I wish, when Mr. Franklin leaves her, you would ask him to come to me."

Henrietta did not like the proposal at all, and said all she could against it; but Fred persisted, and made her at last undertake to ask Aunt Geoffrey's consent. Even then she would have done her best to miss the opportunity; but Fred heard the first sounds, and she was obliged to fetch Mr. Franklin. The conference was not long, and she found no reason to regret that it had taken place; for Fred did not seem so much oppressed and weighed down when she again returned to him.

The physician who had been sent for arrived. He had seen Mrs. Frederick Langford some years before, and well understood her case, and his opinion was now exactly what Fred had been prepared by his uncle to expect. It was impossible to conjecture how long she might yet survive: another attack might come at any moment, and be the last. It might be deferred for weeks or months, or even now it was possible that she might rally, and return to her usual state of health.

It was on this possibility, or as she chose to hear the word, probability, that Henrietta fixed her whole mind. The rest was to her as if unsaid; she would not hear nor believe it, and shunned anything that brought the least impression of the kind. The only occasion when she would avow her fears even to herself, was when she knelt in prayer; and then how wild and unsubmissive were her petitions! How embittered and wretched she would feel at her own power-lessness! Then the next minute she would drive off her fears as by force; call up a vision of a brightly smiling future; think, speak, and act as if hiding her eyes would prevent the approach of the enemy she dreaded.

Her grandmamma was as determined as herself to hope; and her grandpapa, though fully alive to the real state of the case, could not bear to sadden her before the time, and let her talk on and build schemes for the future, till he him-self almost caught a glance of her hopes, and his deep sigh was the only warning she received from him. Fred, too weak for much argument, and not unwilling to rejoice now and then in an illusion, was easily silenced, and Aunt Geoffrey had no time for any one but the patient. Her whole thought, almost her whole being, was devoted to " Mary," the friend, the sister of her childhood, whom she now attended upon with something of the reverent devotedness with which an angel might be watched and served, were it to make a brief sojourn upon earth; feeling it a privilege each day that she was still permitted to attend her, and watching for each passing word and expression as a treasure to be dwelt on in many a subsequent year.

It could not be thus with Henrietta, bent on seeing no illness, on marking no traces of danger; shutting her eyes to all the tokens that her mother was not to be bound down to earth for ever. She found her always cheerful, ready to take interest in all that pleased her, and still with the play-fulness which never failed to light up all that approached her. A flower,—what pleasure it gave her! and how sweet her smile would be!

It was on the evening of the day after the physician's

visit, that Henrietta came in talking, with the purpose of, as she fancied, cheering her mother's spirits, of some double lilac primroses which Mrs. Langford had promised her for the garden at the Pleasance. Her mamma smelt the flowers, admired them, and smiled as she said, " Your papa planted a root of those in my little garden the first summer I was here."

" Then I am sure you will like to have them at the Pleasance, mamma."

" My dear child,"—she paused, while Henrietta started, and gazed upon her, frightened at the manner—"you must not build upon our favourite old plan ; you must prepare—"

" O but, mamma, you are better ! You are much better than two days ago ; and these clear days do you so much good ; and it is all so bright."

" Thanks to Him Who has made it bright !" said her mother, taking her hand. " But I fear, my own dearest, that it will seem far otherwise to you. I want you to make up your mind—"

Henrietta broke vehemently upon the feeble accents. " Mamma ! mamma ! you must not speak so ! It is the worst thing people can possibly do to think despondingly of themselves. Aunt Geoffrey, do tell her so !"

" Despondingly ! my child ; you little know what the thought is to me !"

The words were almost whispered, and Henrietta scarcely marked them.

" No, no, you must not ! It is too cruel to me,—I can't bear it !" she cried : the tears in her eyes, and a violence of agitation about her, which her mother, feeble as she was, could not attempt to contend with. She rested her head on her cushions, and silently and mournfully followed with her eyes the hasty trembling movements of her daughter, who continued to arrange the things on the table, and make desperate attempts to regain her composure ; but completely failing, caught up her bonnet, and hurried out of the room.

" Poor dear child," said Mrs. Frederick Langford, " I wish she was more prepared. Beatrice, the comforting her is the dearest and saddest task I leave you. Fred, poor fellow, is prepared, and will bear up like a man; but it will come fearfully upon her. And Henrietta and I have been more like sisters than mother and daughter. If she would only bear to hear me—but no, if I were to be overcome while speaking to her, it might give her pain in the recollection. Beatrice, you must tell her all I would say."

" If I could !"

" You must tell her, Beatrice, that I was as undisciplined as she is now. Tell her how I have come to rejoice in the great affliction of my life : how little I knew how to bear it when Frederick was taken from me and his children, in the prime of his health and strength. You remember how crushed to the ground I was, and how it was said that my life was saved chiefly by the calmness that came with the full belief that I was dying. And O ! how my spirit rebelled when I found myself recovering ! Do you remember the first day I went to church to return thanks ?"

" It was after we were gone home."

" Ah ! yes. I had put it off longer than I ought, because I felt so utterly unable to join in the service. The sickness of heart that came with those verses of thanksgiving ! All I could do was to pray to be forgiven for not being able to follow them. Now I can own with all my heart the mercy that would not grant my blind wish for death. My treasure was indeed in heaven, but O ! it was not the treasure that was meant. I was forgetting my mother, and so selfish and untamed was I, that I was almost forgetting my poor babies ! Yes, tell her this, Beatrice, and tell her that, if duties and happiness sprang up all around me, forlorn and desolate as I thought myself, so much the more will they for her; and 'at evening time there shall be light.' Tell her that I look to her for guiding and influencing Fred. She must never let a week pass without writing to him, and she must have the honoured office of waiting on the old age of her grandfather and grandmother. I think she will be a comfort to them, do not you? They are fond of her, and she seems to suit them."

" Yes, I have little doubt that she will be everything to them. I have especially noticed her ways with Mrs. Langford, they are so exactly what I have tried to teach Beatrice."

" Dear little Busy Bee! I am glad she is coming; but in case I should not see her, give her her godmother's love, and tell her that she and Henrietta must be what their mammas have been to each other; and that I trust that after thirty-five years' friendship, they will still have as much comfort in one another as I have in you, my own dear Beatrice. I have written her name in one of these books," she added after a short interval, touching some which were always close to her. "And, Beatrice, one thing more I had to say," she proceeded, taking up a Bible, and finding out a place in it. " Geoffrey has always been a happy, prosperous man, as he well deserves; but if ever trouble should come to him in his turn, then show him this." She pointed out the verse, " Be as a father to the fatherless, and instead of a husband unto their mother; so shalt thou be as the son of the Most High, and He shall love thee more than thy mother doth." " Show him that, and tell him it is his sister Mary's last blessing."

CHAPTER XVIII

O N Thursday morning, Henrietta began to awake from her sound night's rest. Was it a dream that she saw a head between her and the window? She thought it was, and turned to sleep again; but at her movement the head turned, the figure advanced, and Mrs. Geoffrey Langford stood over her.

Henrietta opened her eyes, and gazed upon her without saying a word for some moments; then, as her senses awakened, she half sprang up: "How is mamma? Does she want me? Why?" Her aunt made an effort to speak, but it seemed beyond her power.

"O, aunt, aunt!" cried she, "what is the matter? What has happened? Speak to me!"

"Henrietta," said her aunt, in a low, calm, but hoarse tone, "she bade you bear up for your brother's sake."

"But—but—" said Henrietta, breathlessly; "and she—"

"My dear child, she is at rest."

Henrietta laid her head back, as if completely stunned, and unable to realise what she had heard.

"Tell me," she said, after a few moments.

Her aunt knelt by her and steadily, without a tear, began to speak. "It was at half-past twelve; she had been asleep some little time very quietly. I was just going to lie down on the sofa, when I thought her face looked different, and stood watching. She woke, said she felt oppressed, and asked me to raise her pillows. While she was leaning against my arm, there was a spasm, a shiver, and she was gone! Yes, we must only think of her as in perfect peace!"

Henrietta lay motionless for some moments, then at last broke out with a sort of anger, "O why did you not call me?"

"There was not one instant, my dear, and I could not ring, for fear of disturbing Fred. I could not call any one till it was too late."

"O, why was I not there? I would—I would—she must have heard me. I would not have let her go. O, mamma!" cried Henrietta, almost unconscious of what she said, and bursting into a transport of ungovernable grief; sobbing violently and uttering wild, incoherent exclamations. Her aunt tried in vain to soothe her by kind words, but all she said seemed only to add impulse to the torrent; and at last she found herself obliged to wait till the violence of the passion had in some degree exhausted itself; and young, strong, and undisciplined as poor Henrietta was, this was not quickly. At last, however, the sobs grew less loud, and the exclamations less vehement. Aunt Geoffrey thought she could be heard, leant down over her, kissed her, and said, "Now we must pray that we may fulfil her last desire; bear it patiently, and try to help your brother."

"Fred, O, poor Fred!" and she seemed on the point of another burst of lamentation, but her aunt went on speaking —"I must go to him; he has yet to hear it, and you had better come to him as soon as you are dressed."

"O, aunt, I could not bear to see him. It will kill him, I know it will! O no, no, I cannot, cannot see Fred! O, mamma, mamma!" A fresh fit of weeping succeeded, and Mrs. Geoffrey Langford herself feeling most deeply, was in great doubt and perplexity; she did not like to leave Henrietta in this condition, and yet there was an absolute necessity that she should go to poor Fred, before any chance accident or mistake should reveal the truth.

"I must leave you, my dear," said she, at last. "Think how your dear mother bowed her head to His will. Pray to your FATHER in Heaven, Who alone can comfort you. I must go to your brother, and when I return, I hope you will be more composed."

The pain of witnessing the passionate sorrow of Henrietta was no good preparation for carrying the same tidings to one, whose bodily weakness made it to be feared that he might suffer even more; but Mrs. Geoffrey Langford feared to lose her composure by stopping to reflect, and hastened down from Henrietta's room, with a hurried step.

She knocked at Fred's door, and was answered by his voice. As she entered he looked at her with anxious eyes, and before she could speak, said, "I know what you are come to tell me."

"Yes, Fred," said she; "but how?"

"I was sure of it," said Fred. "I knew I should never see her again; and there were sounds this morning. Did not I hear poor Henrietta crying?"

"She has been crying very much," said his aunt.

"Ah! she would never believe it," said Fred. "But after last Sunday—O, no one could look at that face, and think she was to stay here any longer!"

"We could not wish it for her sake," said his aunt, for the first time feeling almost overcome.

"Let me hear how it was," said Frederick, after a pause.

His aunt repeated what she had before told Henrietta, and then he asked quickly, "What did you do? I did not hear you ring."

"No, that was what I was afraid of. I was going to call

some one, when I met grandpapa, who was just going up. He came with me, and—and was very kind—then he sent me to lie down; but I could not sleep, and went to wait for Henrietta's waking."

Frederick gave a long, deep, heavy sigh, and said, "Poor Henrietta! Is she very much overcome?"

"So much, that I hardly know how to leave her."

"Don't stay with me, then, Aunt Geoffrey. It is very kind in you, but I don't think anything is much good to me." He hid his face as he spoke thus, in a tone of the deepest dejection.

"Nothing but prayer, my dear Fred," said she, gently. "Then I will go to your sister again."

"Thank you." And she had reached the door when he asked, "When does Uncle Geoffrey come?"

"By the four o'clock train," she answered, and moved on.

Frederick hid his head under the clothes, and gave way to a burst of agony, which, silent as it was, was even more intense than his sister's. O! the blank that life seemed without her look, her voice, her tone! the frightful certainty that he should never see her more! Then it would for a moment seem utterly incredible that she should thus have passed away; but then returned the conviction, and he felt as if he could not even exist under it. But this excessive oppression and consciousness of misery seemed chiefly to come upon him when alone. In the presence of another person he could talk in the same quiet matter-of-fact way in which he had already done to his aunt; and the blow itself, sudden as it was, did not affect his health as the first anticipation of it had done. With Henrietta things were quite otherwise. When alone she was quiet, in a sort of stupor, in which she scarcely even thought: but the entrance of any person into her room threw her into a fresh paroxysm of grief, ever increasing in vehemence; then she was quieted a

little, and was left to herself, but she could not, or would
not, turn where alone comfort could be found, and repelled
almost as if it was an insult to her affection, any entreaty
that she would even try to be comforted.   Above all, in the
perverseness of her undisciplined affliction, she persisted in
refusing to see her brother.   She should "do him harm,"
she said.   "No, it was utterly impossible for her to control
herself so as not to do him harm."   And thereupon her sobs
and tears redoubled.   She would not touch a morsel of
food; she would not consent to leave her bed when asked
to do so, though ten minutes after, in the restlessness of her
misery, she was found walking up and down her room in her
dressing-gown.

   Never had Mrs. Geoffrey Langford known a more trying
day.   Old Mr. Langford, who had loved "Mary" like his
own child, did indeed bear up under the affliction with all
his own noble spirit of Christian submission; but, excepting
by his sympathy, he could be of little assistance to her in the
many painful offices which fell to her share.   Mrs. Langford
walked about the house, active as ever; now sitting down in
her chair, and bursting into a flood of tears for "poor Mary,"
or "dear Frederick," all the sorrow for whose loss seemed
renewed; then rising vigorously, saying, "Well, it is His
will : it is all for the best!" and hastening away to see how
Henrietta and Fred were, to make some arrangement about
mourning, or to get Geoffrey's room ready for him.   And in
all these occupations she wanted Beatrice to consult, or to
sympathise, or to promise that Geoffrey would like and
approve what she did.   In the course of the morning Mr.
and Mrs. Roger Langford came from Sutton Leigh, and the
latter, by taking the charge of, talking to, and assisting Mrs.
Langford, greatly relieved her sister-in-law.   Still there were
the two young mourners.   Henrietta was completely unman-
ageable, only resting now and then to break forth with more

violence; and her sorrow far too selfish and unsubmissive to
be soothed either by the thought of Him Who sent it, or of
the peace and rest to which that beloved one was gone; and
as once the anxiety for her brother had swallowed up all
care for her mother, so now grief for her mother absorbed
every consideration for Frederick; so that it was useless to
attempt to persuade her to make any exertion for his sake.
Nothing seemed in any degree to tranquillise her except
Aunt Geoffrey's reading to her; and then it was only that
she was lulled by the sound of the voice, not that the sense
reached her mind. But then, how go on reading to her all
day, when poor Fred was left in his lonely room, to bear his
own share of sorrow in solitude? For though Mr. and Mrs.
Langford, and Uncle and Aunt Roger, made him many
brief kind visits, they all of them had either too much on
their hands, or were unfitted by disposition to be the companions he wanted. It was only Aunt Geoffrey who could
come and sit by him, and tell him all those precious sayings
of his mother in her last days, which in her subdued low
voice renewed that idea of perfect peace and repose which
came with the image of his mother, and seemed to still the
otherwise overpowering thought that she was gone. But in
the midst the door would open, and grandmamma would
come in, looking much distressed, with some such request
as this—" Beatrice, if Fred can spare you, would you just go
up to poor Henrietta? I thought she was better, and that
it was as well to do it at once; so I went to ask her for
one of her dresses, to send for a pattern for her mourning,
and that has set her off crying to such a degree, that Elizabeth and I can do nothing with her. I wish Geoffrey was
come!"

Nothing was expressed so often through the day as this
wish, and no one wished more earnestly than his wife,
though, perhaps, she was the only person who did not say

so a dozen times. There was something cheering in hearing that his brother had actually set off to meet him at Allonfield; and at length Fred's sharpened ears caught the sound of the carriage wheels, and he was come. It seemed as if he was considered by all as their own exclusive property. His mother had one of her quick, sudden bursts of lamentation as soon as she saw him; his brother, as usual, wanted to talk to him; Fred was above all eager for him; and it was only his father who seemed even to recollect that his wife might want him more than all. And so she did. Her feelings were very strong and impetuous by nature, and the loss was one of the greatest she could have sustained. Nothing save her husband and child was so near to her heart as her sister; and worn out as she was by long attendance, sleepless nights, and this trying day, when all seemed to rest upon her, she now completely gave way, and was no sooner alone with her husband and daughter, than her long repressed feelings relieved themselves in a flood of tears, which, though silent, were completely beyond her own control. Now that he was come, she could, and indeed must, give way; and the more she attempted to tell him of the peacefulness of her own dear Mary, the more her tears would stream forth. He saw how it was, and would not let her either reproach herself for her weakness, or attempt any longer to exert herself; but made her lie down on her bed, and told her that he and Queen Bee could manage very well.

Queen Bee stood there pale, still, and bewildered-looking. She had scarcely spoken since she heard of her aunt's death; and new as affliction was to her sunny life, scarce knew where she was, or whether this was her own dear Knight Sutton; and even her mother's grief seemed to her almost more like a dream.

"Ah, yes," said Mrs. Geoffrey Langford, as soon as her

daughter had been named, " I ought to have sent you to
Henrietta before."

" Very well," said Beatrice, though her heart sank within
her as she thought of her last attempt at consoling Henrietta.

" Go straight up to her," continued her mother ; " don't
wait to let her think whether she will see you or not. I
only wish poor Fred could do the same."

" If I could but do her any good," sighed Beatrice, as
she opened the door and hastened up stairs. She knocked,
and entered without waiting for an answer : Henrietta lifted
up her head, came forward with a little cry, threw herself
into her arms and wept bitterly. Mournful as all around
was, there was a bright ray of comfort in Queen Bee's heart
when she was thus hailed as a friend and comforter. She
only wished and longed to know what might best serve to
console her poor Henrietta ; but all that occurred to her
was to embrace and fondle her very affectionately, and call
her by the most caressing names. This was all that Henrietta was as yet fit to bear ; and after a time, growing
quieter, she poured out to her cousin all her grief, without
fear of blame for its violence. Beatrice was sometimes
indeed startled by the want of all idea of resignation, but
she could not believe that any one could feel otherwise,
—least of all Henrietta, who had lost her only parent,
and that parent Aunt Mary. Neither did she feel herself
good enough to talk seriously to Henrietta ; she considered
herself as only sent to sit with her, so she did not make
any attempt to preach the resignation which was so much
wanted ; and Henrietta, who had all day been hearing of it,
and rebelling against it, was almost grateful to her. So
Henrietta talked and talked, the same repeated lamentation, the same dreary views of the future coming over and
over again ; and Beatrice's only answer was to agree with

all her heart to all that was said of her own dear Aunt Mary, and to assure Henrietta of the fervent love that was still left for her in so many hearts on earth.

The hours passed on; Beatrice was called away, and Henrietta was inclined to be fretful at her leaving her; but she presently returned, and the same discourse was renewed, until at last Beatrice began to read to her, and thus did much to soothe her spirits, persuaded her to make a tolerable meal at tea-time, bathed her eyelids that were blistered with tears, put her to bed, and finally read her to sleep. Then, as she crept quietly down, to inquire after her mamma, and wish the others in the drawing-room good night, she reflected whether she had done what she ought for her cousin.

"I have not put a single right or really consoling thought into her head," said she to herself; "for as to the reading, she did not attend to that. But after all I could not have done it. I must be better myself before I try to improve other people; and it is not what I deserve to be allowed to be of any comfort at all."

Thanks partly to Beatrice's possessing no rightful authority over Henrietta, partly to the old habit of relying on her, she contrived to make her get up and dress herself at the usual time next morning. But nothing would prevail on her to go down stairs. She said she could not endure to pass "that door," where ever before the fondest welcome awaited her; and as to seeing her brother, that having been deferred yesterday, seemed to-day doubly dreadful. The worst of this piece of perverseness—for it really deserved no better name—was that it began to vex Fred. "But that I know how to depend upon you, Uncle Geoffrey," said he, "I should really think she must be ill. I never knew anything so strange."

Uncle Geoffrey resolved to put an end to it, if possible;

and soon after leaving Fred's room he knocked at his niece's door. She was sitting by the fire with a book in her hand, but not reading.

"Good morning, my dear," said he, taking her languid hand. "I bring you a message from Fred, that he hopes you are soon coming down to him."

She turned away her head. "Poor dear Fred!" said she; "but it is quite impossible. I cannot bear it as he does; I should only overset him and do him harm."

"And why cannot you bear it as he does?" asked her uncle gravely. "You do not think his affection for her was less than yours? and you have all the advantages of health and strength."

"Oh, no one can feel as I do!" cried Henrietta, with one of her passionate outbreaks. "O how I loved her!"

"Fred did not love her less," proceeded her uncle. "And why will you leave him in sorrow and in weakness to doubt the sister's love that should be his chief stay?"

"He does not doubt it," sobbed Henrietta. "He knows me better."

"Nay, Henrietta, what reason has he to trust to that affection which is not strong enough to overcome the dread of a few moments' painful emotion?"

"Oh, but it is not that only! I shall feel it all so much more out of this room, where she has never been; but to see the rest of the house—to go past her door! O, uncle, I have not the strength for it."

"No, your affection for him is not strong enough."

Henrietta's pale cheeks flushed, and her tears were angry. "You do not know me, Uncle Geoffrey," said she proudly, and then she almost choked with weeping at unkindness where she most expected kindness.

"I know thus much of you, Henrietta. You have been nursing up your grief and encouraging yourself in murmuring and repining, in a manner which you will one day see to have been sinful : you are obstinate in making yourself useless."

Henrietta, little used to blame, was roused to defend herself with the first weapon she could. "Aunt Geoffrey is just as much knocked up as I am," said she.

If ever Uncle Geoffrey was made positively angry, he was so now, though if he had not thought it good that Henrietta should be roused, he would have repressed even such demonstrations as he made. "Henrietta, this is too bad ! Has she been weakly yielding ?—has she been shutting herself up in her room, and keeping aloof from those who most needed her, lest she should pain her own feelings ? Have not you rather been perplexing, and distressing, and harassing her with your wilful selfishness, refusing to do the least thing to assist her in the care of your own brother, after she has been wearing herself out in watching over your mother ? And now, when her strength and spirits are exhausted by the exertions she has made for you and yours, and I have been obliged to insist on her resting, you fancy her example an excuse for you ! Is this the way your mother would have acted ? I see arguing with you does you no good : I have no more to say."

He got up, opened the door, and went out : Henrietta, dismayed at the accusation, but too well founded on her words, had but one thought, that he should not deem her regardless of his kindness. "Uncle Geoffrey !" she cried, "O, uncle—" but he was gone ; and forgetting everything else, she flew after him down the stairs, and before she recollected anything else, she found herself standing in the hall, saying, "O, uncle, do not think I meant that !"

At that moment her grandpapa came out of the drawing-room. "Henrietta !" said he, "I am glad to see you downstairs."

Henrietta hastily returned his kiss, and looked somewhat confused; then laying her hand entreatingly on her uncle's arm, said, " Only say you are not angry with me."

" No, no, Henrietta, not if you will act like a rational person," said he with something of a smile, which she could not help returning in her surprise at finding herself downstairs after all.

" And you do not imagine me ungrateful ?"

" Not when you are in your right senses."

" Ungrateful !" exclaimed Mr. Langford. " What is he accusing you of, Henrietta? What is the meaning of all this ?"

" Nothing," said Uncle Geoffrey, " but that Henrietta and I have both been somewhat angry with each other; but we have made it up now, have we not, Henrietta?"

It was wonderful how much good the very air of the hall was doing Henrietta, and how fast it was restoring her energy and power of turning her mind to other things. She answered a few remarks of grandpapa's with very tolerable cheerfulness, and even when the hall-door opened, and admitted Uncle and Aunt Roger, she did not run away, but stayed to receive their greetings before turning to ascend the stairs.

" You are not going to shut yourself up in your own room again ?" said grandpapa.

" No, I was only going to Fred," said she, growing as desirous of seeing him as she had before been averse to it.

" Suppose," said Uncle Geoffrey, " that you were to take a turn or two round the garden first. There is Queen Bee, she will go out with you, and you will bring Fred in a fresher face."

" I will fetch your bonnet," said Queen Bee, who was standing at the top of the stairs, wisely refraining from expressing her astonishment at seeing her cousin in the hall.

And before Henrietta had time to object, the bonnet was on her head, a shawl thrown round her, Beatrice had drawn her arm within hers, and had opened the sashed door into the garden.

It was a regular April day, with all the brilliancy and clearness of the sunshine that comes between showers, the white clouds hung in huge soft masses on the blue sky, the leaves of the evergreens were glistening with drops of rain, the birds sang sweetly in the shrubs around. Henrietta's burning eyes felt refreshed, and though she sighed heavily, she could not help admiring, but Beatrice was surprised that the first thing she began to say was an earnest inquiry after Aunt Geoffrey, and a warm expression of gratitude towards her.

Then the conversation died away again, and they completed their two turns in silence ; but Henrietta's heart began to fail her when she thought of going in without having her to greet. She lingered and could hardly resolve to go, but at length she entered, walked up the stairs, gave her shawl and bonnet to Beatrice, and tapped at Fred's door.

" Is that you ?" was his eager answer, and as she entered he came forward to meet her. " Poor Henrietta !" was all he said, as she put her arm round his neck and kissed him, and then leaning on her he returned to his sofa, made her sit by him, and showed all sorts of kind solicitude for her comfort. She had cried so much that she felt as if she could cry no longer, but she reproached herself excessively for having left him to himself so long, when all he wanted was to comfort her ; and she tried to make some apology.

" I am sorry I did not come sooner, Fred."

" O, it is of no use to talk about it," said Fred, playing with her long curls as she sat on a footstool close to him,

just as she used to do in times long gone by. " You are
come now, and that is all I want. Have you been out? I
thought I heard the garden door just before you came in."

" Yes, I took two turns with Queen Bee. How bright
and sunny it is. And how are you this morning, Freddy?"

" O, pretty well, I think," said he, sighing, as if he cared
little about the matter. "I wanted to show you this, Henrietta." And he took up a book where he had marked a
passage for her. She saw several paper marks in some other
books, and perceived with shame that he had been reading
yesterday, and choosing out what might comfort her, his
selfish sister, as she could not help feeling herself.

And here was the first great point gained, though there
was still much for Henrietta to learn. It was the first time
she had ever been conscious of her own selfishness, or perhaps more justly, of her proneness to make all give way to
her own feeling of the moment.

CHAPTER XIX

THERE was some question as to who should attend the
funeral. Henrietta shuddered and trembled all over
as if it were a cruelty to mention it before her ; but Frederick was very desirous that she should be there, partly
from a sort of feeling that she would represent himself, and
partly from a strong conviction that it would be good for
her. She was willing to do anything or everything for him,
to make up for her day's neglect : and she consented, though
with many tears, and was glad that at least Fred seemed
satisfied, and her uncle looked pleased with her.

Aunt Geoffrey undertook to stay with Fred, and Henrietta,
who clung much to Beatrice, felt relieved by the thought of
her support in such an hour of trial. She remembered the
day when, with a kind of agreeable emotion, she had figured
to herself her father's funeral, little thinking of the reality
that so soon awaited her, so much worse, as she thought,
than what any of them could even then have felt ; and it
seemed to her perfectly impossible that she should ever have
power to go through with it.

It was much, however, that she should have agreed to
what in the prospect gave her so much pain ; and perhaps,
for that very reason, she found the reality less overwhelming
than she had dreaded. Seeing nothing, observing nothing,
hardly conscious of anything, she walked along, wrapped in

one absorbing sense of wretchedness : and the first words
that " broke the stillness of that hour," healing as they were,
seemed but to add certainty to that one thought that " she
was gone." But while the Psalms and the Lessons were
read, the first heavy oppression of grief seemed in some
degree to grow lighter. She could listen, and the words
reached her mind ; a degree of thankfulness arose to Him
Who had wiped away the tears from her mother's eyes, and
by Whom the sting of death had been taken away. Yes ;
she had waited in faith, in patience, in meek submission,
until now her long widowhood was over ; and what better
for her could those who most loved her desire, than that she
should safely sleep in the chancel of the church of her childhood, close to him whom she had so loved and so mourned,
until the time when both should once more awaken—
the corruptible should put on incorruption, the mortal
should put on immortality, and death be swallowed up in
victory ?

Something of this was what Henrietta began to feel ; and
though the tears flowed fast, they were not the bitter drops
of personal sorrow. She was enabled to bear, without the
agony she had expected, the standing round the grave in the
chancel ; nor did her heart swell rebelliously against the
expression that it was " in great mercy that the soul of this
our dear sister" was taken, even though she shrank and
shivered at the sound of the earth cast in, which would seem
to close up from her for ever the most loved and loving
creature that she would ever know. No, not for ever,—
might she too but keep her part in Him Who is the Resur-
rection and the Life—might she be found acceptable in His
sight, and receive the blessing to be pronounced to all that
love and fear Him.

It was over : they all stood round for a few minutes. At
last Mr. Langford moved ; Henrietta was also obliged to

turn away, but before doing so, she raised her eyes to her
father's name, to take leave of him as it were, as she always
did before going out of church. She met her Uncle Geoffrey's eye as she did so, and took his arm ; and as soon as
she was out of the church, she said almost in a whisper,
" Uncle, I don't wish for him now."

He pressed her arm, and looked most kindly at her, but
he did not speak, for he could hardly command his voice ;
and he saw, too, that she might safely be trusted to the in-
fluences of that only true consolation which was coming
upon her.

They came home—to the home that looked as if it would
fain be once more cheerful, with the front window blinds
drawn up again, and the solemn stillness no longer observed.
Henrietta hastened up to her own room, for she could not
bear to show herself to her brother in her long crape veil.
She threw her bonnet off, knelt down for a few minutes, but
rose on hearing the approach of Beatrice, who still shared
the same room. Beatrice came in, and looked at her for
a few moments, as if doubtful how to address her ; but at
last she put her hand on her shoulder, and looking earnestly
in her face, repeated—

> " Then cheerly to your work again,
> With hearts new braced and set,
> To run untir'd love's blessed race,
> As meet for those who, face to face,
> Over the grave their LORD have met."

" Yes, Queenie," said Henrietta, giving a long sigh, " it
is a very different world to me now ; but I do mean to try.
And first, dear Bee, you must let me thank you for having
been very kind to me this long time past, though I am
afraid I showed little thankfulness." She kissed her affectionately, and the tears almost choked Beatrice.

" Me ! me, of all people," said she. " O, Henrietta !"

" We must talk of it all another time," said Henrietta ; " but now it will not do to stay away from Fred any longer. Don't think this like the days when I used to run away from you in the winter, Bee,—that time when I would not stop and talk about the verses on the holly."

While she spoke, there was something of the " new bracing" visible in every movement, as she set her dress to rights, and arranged her curls, which of late she had been used to allow to hang in a deplorable way, that showed how little vigour or inclination to bear up there was about her whole frame.

" O no, do not stay with me," said Queen Bee, " I am going"—to mamma she would have said, but she hardly knew how to use the word when speaking to Henrietta.

" Yes," said Henrietta, understanding her. " And tell her, Bee—for I am sure I shall never be able to say it to her,—all about our thanks, and how sorry I am that I cared so little about her or her comfort." " If I had only believed, instead of blinding myself so wilfully !" she almost whispered to herself with a deep sigh ; but being now ready, she ran down stairs and entered her brother's room. His countenance bore traces of weeping, but he was still calm ; and as she came in he looked anxiously at her. She spoke quietly as she sat down by him, put her hand into his, and said, " Thank you, dear Fred, for making me go."

" I was quite sure you would be glad when it was over," said Fred. " I have been reading the service with Aunt Geoffrey, but that is a very different thing."

" It will all come to you when you go to church again," said Henrietta.

" How little I thought that New Year's Day—!" said Fred.

" Ah ! and how little we either of us thought last summer

holidays !" said Henrietta. " If it was not for that, I could bear it all better ; but it was my determination to come here that seems to have caused everything, and that is the thought I cannot bear."

" I was talking all that over with Uncle Geoffrey last night," said Fred, "and he especially warned us against reproaching ourselves with consequences. He said it was he who had helped my father to choose the horse that caused his death, and asked me if I thought he ought to blame himself for that. I said no ; and he went on to tell me that he did not think we ought to take unhappiness to ourselves for what has happened now ; that we ought to think of the actions themselves, instead of the results. Now my skating that day was just as bad as my driving, except, to be sure, that I put nobody in danger but myself ; it was just as much disobedience, and I ought to be just as sorry for it, though nothing came of it, except that I grew more wilful."

" Yes," said Henrietta, " but I shall always feel as if everything had been caused by me. I am sure I shall never dare wish anything again."

" It was just as much my wish as yours," said Fred.

" Ah ! but you did not go on always trying to make her do what you pleased, and keeping her to it, and almost thinking it a thing of course, to make her give up her wishes to yours. That was what I was always doing, and now I can never make up for it !"

" O yes," said Fred, " we can never feel otherwise than that. To know how she forgave us both, and how her wishes always turned to be the same as ours, if ours were not actually wrong ; that is little comfort to remember now, but perhaps it will be in time. But don't you see, Henrietta, my dear, what Uncle Geoffrey means ?—that if you did domineer over her, it was very wrong, and you may be sorry for that; but that you must not accuse yourself of doing all the mischief by bringing her here. He says he does not know whether it was not, after all, what was most for her comfort, if—"

" O, Freddy, to have you almost killed !"

" If the thoughts I have had lately will but stay with me when I am well again, I do not think my accident will be a matter of regret, Henrietta. Just consider, when I was so disobedient in these little things, and attending so little to her or to Uncle Geoffrey, how likely it was that I might have gone on to much worse at school and college."

" Never, never !" said Henrietta.

" Not now, I hope," said Fred; " but that was not what I meant to say. No one could say, Uncle Geoffrey told me, that the illness was brought on either by anxiety or over-exertion. The complaint was of long standing, and must have made progress some time or other; and he said that he was convinced that, as she said to Aunt Geoffrey, she had rather have been here than anywhere else. She said she could only be sorry for grandpapa and grandmamma's sake, but that for herself it was great happiness to have been to Knight Sutton Church once more; and she was most thankful that she had come to die in my father's home, after seeing us well settled here, instead of leaving us to come to it as a strange place."

" How little we guessed it was for that," said Henrietta. " O what were we doing? But if it made her happy—"

" Just imagine what to-day would have been if we were at Rocksand," said Fred. " I, obliged to go back to school directly, and you, taking leave of everything there which would seem to you so full of her; and Uncle Geoffrey just bringing you here without any time to stay with you, and the place and people all strange. I am sure she who thought so much for you, must have rejoiced that you are at home here already."

"Home!" said Henrietta, "how determinedly we used to call it so! But O, that my wish should have turned out in such a manner! If it has been all overruled so as to be happiness to her, as I am sure it has, I cannot complain; but I think I shall never wish again, or care for my own way."

"The devices and desires of our own hearts!" said Fred.

"I don't think I shall ever have spirit enough to be wilful for my own sake," proceeded Henrietta. "Nothing will ever be the same pleasure to me, as when she used to be my other self, and enjoy it all over again for me; so that it was all twofold!" Here she hid her face, and her tears streamed fast, but they were soft and calm; and when she saw that Fred also was much overcome, she recalled her energies in a minute.

"But, Fred, I may well be thankful that I have you, which is far more than I deserve; and as long as we do what she wished, we are still obeying her. I think at last I may get something of the right sort of feeling; for I am sure I see much better now what she and grandpapa used to mean when they talked about dear papa. And now do you like for me to read to you?"

Few words more require to be said of Frederick and Henrietta Langford. Knight Sutton Hall was, according to their mother's wish, their home; and there Henrietta had the consolation, during the advancing spring and summer, of watching her brother's recovery, which was very slow, but at the same time steady. Mrs. Geoffrey Langford stayed with her as long as he required much nursing; and Henrietta learnt to look upon her, not as quite a mother, but at any rate as more than an aunt, far more than she had ever been to her before; and when at length she was obliged to return to Westminster, it was a great satisfaction to think how soon the vacation would bring them all back to Knight Sutton.

The holidays arrived, and with them Alexander, who, to his great disappointment, was obliged to give up all his generous hopes that Fred would be one of his competitors for the prize, when he found him able indeed to be with the family, to walk short distances, and to resume many of his former habits; but still very easily tired, and his head in a condition to suffer severely from noise, excitement, or application. Perhaps this was no bad thing for their newly formed alliance, as Alex had numberless opportunities of developing his consideration and kindness, by silencing his brothers, assisting his cousin when tired, and again and again silently giving up some favourite scheme of amusement when Fred proved to be unequal to it. Even Henrietta herself almost learned to trust Fred to Alex's care, which was so much less irritating than her own; and how greatly the Queen Bee was improved is best shown, when it is related, that neither by word nor look did she once interrupt the harmony between them, or attempt to obtain the attention, of which, in fact, she always had as large a share as any reasonable person could desire.

How fond Fred learnt to be of Alex will be easily understood, and the best requital of his kindness that he could devise was an offer—a very adventurous one, as was thought by all who heard of it—to undertake little Willy's Latin, which being now far beyond Aunt Roger's knowledge, had been under Alex's care during the holidays. Willy was a very good pupil on the whole—better, it was said by most, than Alex himself had been—and very fond of Fred; but Latin grammar and Cæsar formed such a test as perhaps their alliance would scarcely have endured, if in an insensible manner Willy and his books had not gradually been made over to Henrietta, whose great usefulness and good-nature in this respect quite made up, in grandmamma's eyes, for her very tolerable amount of acquirements in Latin and Greek.

By the time care for her brother's health had ceased to be Henrietta's grand object, and she was obliged once more to see him depart to pursue his education, a whole circle of pursuits and occupations had sprung up around her, and given her the happiness of feeling herself both useful and valued. Old Mr. Langford saw in her almost the Mary he had parted with when resumed in early girlhood by Mrs. Vivian; Mrs. Langford had a granddaughter, who would either be petted, sent on messages, or be civil to the Careys as occasion served; Aunt Roger was really grateful to her, as well for the Latin and Greek she bestowed upon Willy and Charlie, as for the braided merino frocks or coats on which Bennet used to exercise her taste when Henrietta's wardrobe failed to afford her sufficient occupation. The boys all liked her, made a friend of her, and demonstrated it in various ways more or less uncouth: her manners gradually acquired the influence over them which Queen Bee had only exerted over Alex and Willy, and when, saving Carey and Dick, they grew less awkward and bearish, without losing their honest downright good-humour and good-nature, Uncle Geoffrey only did her justice in attributing the change to her unconscious power. Miss Henrietta was also the friend of the poor women, the teacher and guide of the school children, and in their eyes and imagination second to no one but Mr. Franklin. And withal she did not cease to be all that she had ever been to her brother,—if not still more. His heart and soul were for her, and scarce a joy and sorrow but was shared between them. She was his home, his everything, and she well fulfilled her mother's parting trust, of being his truest friend and best loved counsellor.

Would that her own want of submission and resignation had not prevented her from hearing the dear accents in which that charge was conveyed! This was, perhaps, the most deeply felt sorrow that followed her through life; and even with the fair peaceful image of her beloved mother, there was linked a painful memory of a long course of wilfulness and domineering on her own part. But there was much to be dwelt on that spoke only of blessedness and love, and each day brought her nearer to her whom she had lost, so long as she was humbly striving to walk in the steps of Him Who "came not to do His own will, but the will of Him that sent Him."

J. MASTERS and Co., Printers, Albion Buildings, Bartholomew Close.